Business English Rebuilding Project

職場英文 精準表達

掌握 140 個常用字句，跨國外商溝通零失誤

Grant Sundbye, LookLook English　著　韓蔚笙　譯

作者序 Preface

Hi there, my name is Grant Sundbye. I'm an award-winning American business English coach and my mission is to help adult Korean professionals gain the English skills necessary to improve their work performance and unlock the lives / careers they've always wanted. My goal is to do far more than just 'teach English'. I want to truly change people's lives by creating English instruction programs that are so effective that they push the entire Korean English learning industry forward.

大家好，我是 Grant Sundbye，是一位備受好評的美國商務英文老師。我幫助韓國上班族掌握必備的英文技能，以提高他們的工作效率並實現他們期望的職涯目標。我想建立一個能全面改善韓國英文學習市場的高效英文教育課程來改變大家的生活，而不僅僅是「教英文」而已。

Over the past four years, I've spent thousands of hours helping hundreds of different Korean professionals improve their professional English communication. I've coached Koreans of all English levels: from beginner to nearly fluent, and in every major industry. The more people I work with, the more I've noticed that there are many common speaking and communication mistakes that a vast majority of Korean adults make. These mistakes can make your English sound unnatural, or (even worse) make it impossible for people to understand you accurately. These mistakes are also rarely addressed directly in traditional English classes, but fortunately most of them are fairly simple to explain and correct.

在過去的四年裡,我投入了大量的時間去提升數百名韓國上班族的職場英文溝通能力。我指導過在各大領域工作的韓國人,從初級者到接近母語人士水準的都有。在指導他們的過程中,我發現大多數韓國成年人在溝通時都會犯類似的錯誤。如果你經常犯這樣的錯誤,你的英文會變得不自然又令對方難以理解。在傳統的英文課程中,很少直接提及這些內容,但幸好這些錯誤都很容易說明與糾正。

This book addresses over 140 of the most common English mistakes Koreans make and shows you exactly how to fix them. Rather than just explaining theoretical grammar principles, everything here will be presented in a clear 'problem → solution' format that will allow you to easily apply what you've learned to your real workplace communication.

這本書涵蓋了韓國人最常犯的 140 多種英文錯誤,並告訴你如何糾正這些錯誤的方法。為了讓各位能輕鬆地將所學知識應用在職場的實際溝通上,本書的所有內容皆以清晰的「問題 → 解決方法」的方式呈現,而不僅僅是針對文法來說明理論。

Every single Korean client I've ever worked with makes at least one of the mistakes included in this book (with most people making a lot more than that!). So, I can personally guarantee that by reading and understanding this book, your English communication will improve. Not only will your English be easier to understand, but you'll also be able to:

— deliver better presentations
— write clearer emails
— make a much better impression on everyone you communicate with in English
— feel more comfortable and confident using English in the workplace
— make major progress towards reaching your English and career goals

在這本書列出的錯誤中，我指導過的每一位韓國學生至少都犯過一個以上類似的錯誤（大多數人犯過更多錯誤！）。因此，如果你閱讀並理解本書的內容，我可以向各位保證，你們的英文溝通能力一定會有所提升。不只是讓你的英文變得更容易理解，這本書還能幫大家達成以下的目標：
— 可以在英文簡報中表現得更優秀

— 可以寫出語意更明確的英文電子郵件

— 可以用英文交流並讓對方留下更好的印象

— 可以更輕鬆、更有自信地在工作中使用英文

— 可以在提升英文能力與實現職涯目標上取得重大進展

I'm excited to be on this journey with you and to share so much of what I've learned over the past four years. First, let's review exactly how to use this book so you get the most value out of it, and then we can get started correcting your English and moving you towards your goals!

很高興能跟各位一起踏上這段旅程，並分享我在過去四年中學過的內容。首先，讓我們看看這本書的正確用法，以便能充分運用它，然後我們將藉由改正各種英文錯誤來幫助各位接近自己的目標！

Grant Sundbye

YouTube @GrantSundbyeCareerCoaching

世界變得越來越小，需要用英文溝通的事情也變多了。不僅如此，隨著 Instagram、Facebook、Kakao Talk、Slack 等社群媒體與通訊軟體在職場上的使用日趨普遍，用文字溝通的情況也變得比以往常見。如果你在外商企業工作，經常會出現需要用英文與人在國外的外籍上司對話、用英文發送電子郵件給客戶，或是使用 Messenger、Zoom、Hangout、Teams 等軟體溝通的情形。雖然也有人說，隨著人工智慧的發展，將來會變成即使不會講英文也能輕鬆生活的社會，但如果能在沒有人工智慧的幫助下，也能用英文有效率地表達自我想法，肯定會有很大的幫助。

我在美國就讀大學並從事各種工作，有很多機會與母語人士進行交流。現在我仍然與母語人士一起工作，而且所有的溝通交流都用英文進行。像這樣用英文交流讓我獲得了許多機會，而我能認識 Grant 這位充滿熱情又與我有共同願景的朋友，也是建立在溝通的基礎上。

本書收錄的內容是根據 Grant 在超過四年的時間內，與韓國人進行英文一對一教學的過程中發現的錯誤用法，親自糾正和整理的成果。並且站在母語人士的立場，進一步說明這些錯誤用法會給人什麼樣的觀感、存在著什麼樣細微的語感差異，以及實際上應該要怎麼說等等。此外，本書還涵蓋了一個人在職場中可能面臨的各種實際情況，從找工作到寄電子郵件、協商、簡報、績效評估等。從這一點來看，我認為這本書對各位進一步提升職場英文能力會有很大的幫助。

LookLook English
YouTube @looklookenglish

目錄 Contents

作者序 2

Chapter 1
錯誤的介系詞 Preposition Mistakes 013

1 ask to / for / about 018
2 prepare / prepare for 022
3 share / share with 024
4 contact / call to 026
5 search / search for 028
5 go / go to / go on 030
7 think / think about 033
8 check / check on / check with 036
9 answer / respond / reply 039
10 agree with / to / on / about 041
11 listen / listen to 044
12 access / access to 046
13 invest / invest in 048
14 familiar with / to 050
15 pay / pay for 052
16 grow / grow up 054

Chapter 2
錯誤的冠詞與限定詞 Article and Determiner Mistakes 061

1 most / most of 066
2 on / in / at for time 069
3 for / since 071
4 this / last / next replacing on / in 073
5 a / an 075

6 using 'the' 077

7 on the Internet 080

8 similar with / to, different from / than 082

9 by / until 084

10 still / until 086

11 during / for / while 088

12 another / other / the other 090

13 besides / except 093

Chapter 3
近似表達的誤用1 Word Set Mistakes 1　　　　101

1 take care of / care for / care about 106

2 wish / hope 108

3 similar / same 110

4 price / cost / fee 112

5 revenue / profit 115

6 convenient / comfortable 118

7 economy / finance 121

8 company / office / industry 124

9 believe / believe in / trust 127

Chapter 4
近似表達的誤用2 Word Set Mistakes 2　　　　135

1 fun / funny 141

2 hear / listen / understand 143

3 say / talk / tell / speak / discuss / debate 146

4 toilet / restroom / bathroom 149

5 trip / travel / tour / journey / vacation 151

6 remember / remind / memory / memorize 155

7 lend / loan / borrow 159

8 wage / salary / income / paycheck 161

9 complain / criticize / confront 164

Chapter 5
不自然的表達 Unnatural Mistakes   173

1 I am sorry / I feel sorry for 178
2 answering 'or' questions 181
3 How's your condition? 183
4 I am (name) 185
5 I am okay / That's okay / It's okay 188
6 Do you know ~? 191
7 negative questions 195
8 I don't care 197
9 as soon as possible 200
10 in touch 203
11 take a rest 206
12 I understand well. 208
13 I'm waiting for your response. 210
14 have a good time 212

Chapter 6
文法錯誤PART 1 Grammar Mistakes Part 1   219

1 comparative sentences 224
2 I am difficult / hard / easy / convenient / inconvenient 228
3 seem / seem like 231
4 passive sentences 233
5 using intransitive verbs 235
6 using transitive verbs 237
7 including questions in statements 239
8 first / at first / the first time 241
9 each / every 244
10 all the time / every time 247
11 gerunds and infinitives 250

12 adjectives involving numbers ⋯⋯⋯⋯⋯ 254

13 using size adjectives ⋯⋯⋯⋯⋯⋯⋯⋯ 256

Chapter 7
文法錯誤PART 2 Grammar Mistakes Part 2   263

1 explaining frequency ⋯⋯⋯⋯⋯⋯⋯⋯ 268

2 using 'mean' ⋯⋯⋯⋯⋯⋯⋯⋯⋯⋯⋯ 271

3 your saying ⋯⋯⋯⋯⋯⋯⋯⋯⋯⋯⋯ 273

4 all / every not / not all / every ⋯⋯⋯ 275

5 I am late for 5 minutes. ⋯⋯⋯⋯⋯⋯ 278

6 one of (something) ⋯⋯⋯⋯⋯⋯⋯⋯ 281

7 -ed / -ing for adjectives ⋯⋯⋯⋯⋯⋯ 284

8 ages, quantities, lengths of time. ⋯⋯ 288

9 using two words with the same function ⋯⋯ 291

10 using intensifiers ⋯⋯⋯⋯⋯⋯⋯⋯⋯ 294

11 forgetting determiners ⋯⋯⋯⋯⋯⋯⋯ 297

12 talking 'in general' ⋯⋯⋯⋯⋯⋯⋯⋯ 300

Chapter 8
詞彙選擇錯誤 Word Choice Mistakes   307

1 question ⋯⋯⋯⋯⋯⋯⋯⋯⋯⋯⋯⋯⋯ 312

2 menu ⋯⋯⋯⋯⋯⋯⋯⋯⋯⋯⋯⋯⋯⋯ 315

3 schedule ⋯⋯⋯⋯⋯⋯⋯⋯⋯⋯⋯⋯⋯ 317

4 shocked ⋯⋯⋯⋯⋯⋯⋯⋯⋯⋯⋯⋯⋯ 319

5 cheer up ⋯⋯⋯⋯⋯⋯⋯⋯⋯⋯⋯⋯⋯ 321

6 expect ⋯⋯⋯⋯⋯⋯⋯⋯⋯⋯⋯⋯⋯ 323

7 almost ⋯⋯⋯⋯⋯⋯⋯⋯⋯⋯⋯⋯⋯ 326

8 organize ⋯⋯⋯⋯⋯⋯⋯⋯⋯⋯⋯⋯ 329

9 cheap ⋯⋯⋯⋯⋯⋯⋯⋯⋯⋯⋯⋯⋯ 331

10 appointment ⋯⋯⋯⋯⋯⋯⋯⋯⋯⋯ 333

11　fresh 335

12　satisfied 337

13　matter 339

14　moment 341

15　overwork 343

16　promotion 345

17　retire 348

18　bea 350

19　point out 352

Chapter 9
與數字相關的錯誤 Number Related Mistakes　359

1　large numbers 366

2　decimals and rounding 375

3　percentages 379

4　saying dates 383

5　saying years 385

6　saying fractions 387

Chapter 10
實用的商務英文詞彙 Useful Business English Words　395

1　significantly / significant 401

2　positively / negatively impact 403

3　objective / subjective 405

4　indefinitely 407

5　commute 408

6　innovation 409

7　unfortunately 410

8　pros and cons 411

9　commit 413

10　hesitant 414

11 clarify 415

12 mandatory 416

13 assertive 417

14 proactive 418

15 stand out 419

16 micromanage 420

17 delegate 421

18 maximize / minimize 422

19 elaborate 423

20 opportunity 424

21 scale up 426

22 insight 427

What Now?! 434

Chapter 1

錯誤的介系詞
Preposition Mistakes

1   ask to / for / about

2   prepare / prepare for

3   share / share with

4   contact / call to

5   search / search for

6   go / go to / go on

7   think / think about

8   check / check on / check with

9   answer / respond / reply

10 agree with / to / on / about

11 listen / listen to

12 access / access to

13 invest / invest in

14 familiar with / to

15 pay / pay for

16 grow / grow up

在以下的敘述中包含錯誤的用法。請閱讀一遍，並試著找出不自然的表達方式。在各章節的最後會提供修正後的正確表達。

以下是應徵 Onward Tech B2B 銷售職位的李智媛初次面試的情形。

Interviewer　Jiwon, it's great to finally meet you. We're looking forward to this interview.

Jiwon　Yes, thank you for this opportunity.

Interviewer　First, let's discuss your past work history. Can you tell us a little more about your previous sales job at Nexus AI?

Jiwon　Sure! I worked at Nexus AI from 2017 to 2020. I started as a sales associate, and my main job duties were to contact to new potential customers. I would share product information to them, answer to their questions, and set up a sales meeting with one of our lead salespeople.

This experience helped me learn how to search and find new customers. It also made me much more familiar to the B2B sales process.

I was promoted to a lead sales position in November 2018. As a lead salesperson I would go to many company offices and conduct in-person sales presentations. To be honest, I wasn't totally prepared this position at first, but after a few months I was much more adjusted to giving sales presentations. Once I closed a sale, I was then in charge of continuing to build the relationship with that customer, so I would often check them and respond any questions they ask to me.

I know you're looking for someone with a lot of B2B sales experience and a deep understanding of the tech industry. The B2B sales process and the tech industry are both incredibly familiar with me, and I would love the chance to show you by working here as a lead sales team member.

Interviewer   Great! What would you say is your proudest work accomplishment?

Jiwon   My proudest accomplishment is winning salesperson of the year in 2020 at Nexus AI. During that year, I actually set a new company record for most sales revenue generated in a single year. I think the key to my success was always listening the customers, and adjusting to my sales pitches based on what they really want. Before a sales session, I always think the problems this specific company has and how I can present whatever I'm selling as the best possible solution to those problems. Because my sales pitches were customized for each specific client, many clients agreed with working with us and paid their first order during our initial meeting.

Nexus AI's total revenue grew up 15% YOY in 2020, which is the largest revenue increase they've ever had. Being a huge part of that success makes me very proud.

Interviewer   Excellent! What makes you want to work here at Onward Tech?

Jiwon   I love your company's mission and it seems like the work environment here is fantastic. When I checked with your company's website, I read about your vision of 'making our world more modernized and connected by helping everyone on Earth access to the technology necessary to improve their lives'.
That mission really resonates with me and I would love to be part of it. Also, I know that you provide a lot of benefits and training opportunities for your employees. I think it's awesome that you invest your employees' success. I know I have the skills and experience necessary to do great things here, and the work environment seems like a perfect fit for me.

Interviewer   Great. That's very good to hear because we're really looking for employees that can fit in well with our corporate culture. It's been great talking with you, Jiwon. I'll discuss our interview to the other hiring managers and we'll call to you sometime tomorrow afternoon. Thank you for your time!

Jiwon   Thank you for the opportunity. Have a great rest of your day.

1 ask to / for / about

Alright Jiwon, we just need to ask to you a few more questions.

Are you going to ask a pay raise?

→ 在使用 ask 時，誤用介系詞的情況很常見。

ask 常見的用法有四種，每種用法需要使用不同的介系詞。

1. 直接詢問某人或想獲得正確資訊時，不需要加介系詞。

Did you ask your boss?（直接詢問某人）
你問過老闆了嗎？

I'll ask what time the meeting starts.（正確資訊）
我會去詢問會議何時開始。

雖然在某些情況下會在被詢問者前面加 to，但在 ask 後面必須直接說出詢問的對象，例如 ask me、ask him、ask your boss 等。因此，下面的句子不該用 ask to you，應該改成 ask you 才對。

✗　　　Alright Jiwon, we just need to ~~ask to you~~ a few more
　　　questions.

○　　　Alright Jiwon, we just need to ask you a few more
　　　questions.

　　　好，智媛小姐，我們只要再多問你幾個問題。

2. 詢問主題時，要用 ask about。

　　　Did you ask about the new work policy?
　　　你問過關於新工作方針的事嗎？

　　　Did you ask about the salary in the interview?
　　　你面試時問過關於年薪的事嗎？

3. 提出請求時，要用 ask for。

　　　He's asking for a project extension.
　　　他正在請求一個項目的延長。

　　　The salesman asked for more money.
　　　那個業務員要求更多的錢。

向對方請求幫助時，可以說 Can I ask for some help? 或是 I'm asking
for your help.

讓我們重新檢視下面的這一句話。這裡要表達的是要求 pay raise（加薪），
所以不該用 ask，應該用 ask for 才對。

✗　　　Are you going to ~~ask~~ a pay raise?
○　　　Are you going to ask for a pay raise?
　　　你要要求加薪嗎？

Details

「向～詢問……」可以用 ask [sb] about [sth] 的形式表達，
「向～拜託／請求……」可以用 ask [sb] for [sth] 的形式表達。

**I asked the team leader about the new advertising
campaign.**
我向組長詢問過有關新廣告活動的事。

**If you aren't sure about anything, just ask the team leader
for some help.**
如果你有任何問題，都可以向組長尋求幫助。

上述句子中的 the team leader 可以省略，之所以放進句中是
為了表明拜託的對象。

4. 表示「要求～做……」時，要用 ask [sb] to V。

如果 ask 後面出現人的話，那個人就是行為的主體。

Make sure you ask each salesman to send you his report.
請務必要求各業務員將報告寄給你。

**The HR team asked each employee to fill out the job
satisfaction survey.**
人事部要求各職員填寫工作滿意度調查表。

但如果 ask 後面沒有接人的話，那麼主詞就是行為的主體。

You should ask to leave the meeting early.
你應該要求在會議中提早離席。

（製藥產業 / 公司）

A: Have you asked the Korean MFDS about our newest prescription drug?

B: I did. They're asking for translated versions of our documents.

A: Ah, got it. I'll ask our translators to make Korean versions of each English document and send them to you by the end of the week.

A：你向韓國 MFDS 確認過關於我們公司最新的處方藥的事了嗎？

B：是的，但他們要求我們提供文件的譯本。

A：啊，原來如此。那我去請翻譯組準備英文文件的韓文譯本，我會在這週內寄給你。

2 prepare / prepare for

I am preparing a big accounting exam next week.

許多人不知道 prepare 後面是否需要加介系詞，如果要加介系詞又應該使用什麼介系詞。

prepare v. to make something ready
prepare for to get yourself ready for (situation)

I am <u>preparing</u> my exam. （出考題）
I am <u>preparing</u> for my exam. （唸書並為考試做準備）

當 prepare 後面直接加受詞時，是表示主詞親自製作或設計該受詞，而除了這種情況之外，都應該要用 prepare for。

My company is <u>preparing</u> our new products for the launch next month.
我們公司正在準備下個月要發表的新產品。

下面的這句話也一樣，由於主詞 I 並非會計學測驗的出題者，而是正在準備考試的學生，因此應該要用 prepare for N 或 prepare to V 來表達。

✗   I am **preparing** a big accounting exam next week.

○ I am preparing for **a big accounting exam next week.**

○ I am preparing to **take a big accounting exam next week.**

我正在準備下週重要的會計學考試。

prepare to 也可以用 be prepared to V 來表達，解釋為「做好（自願）做～的準備」。

I'm prepared to do anything to get a deal.

為了贏得這筆交易，我已經做好做任何事的準備。

I'm not prepared to discuss this.

我不準備討論這件事。

應用

We are currently preparing for our Spring product launch, which will officially start next week. We're also preparing all our financial records so our accountants can finalize our quarterly financial statements.

我們目前正在為將從下週正式展開的春季產品發表做準備。為了讓會計師能完成季度財務報表，我們也準備了所有的財務記錄。

3 share / share with

Each team leader will share to the board members their team's results.

在表達「與～分享」的意思時，經常會用錯與 share 一起使用的介系詞。

動詞 share 可以用 share [sth] with [sb] 來表達。另外，在確定分享對象是誰的情況下，可以省略不提。

I will share the survey results (with you) next Friday.
我下週五會（跟你）分享調查結果。

讓我們重新檢視下面的句子。share 後面應該要立刻接受詞 their team's results，然後再用介系詞 with 連接分享對象 the board members 才對。

× Each team leader will share to the board members their team's results.

○ Each team leader will share their team's results with the board members.
各組組長會與各個董事分享各組的成果。

I'm really looking forward to the global leadership conference next weekend. Several really successful entrepreneurs will be sharing their most effective leadership practices with us.

我非常期待下週末舉辦的全球領袖會議。幾位非常成功的企業家將與我們分享他們實踐過最有效的領導方法。

4 contact / call to

I will contact to the customer about the product review.

A member of our team will call to you tomorrow.

當我們想到「聯絡～」、「打電話給～」時,經常在 contact 或 call 後面加介系詞 to 來表達。

contact 後面應該直接接要聯絡的對象,再於 about 後面接著說具體的內容。

Please contact the developer about our website.
網站相關事宜請與開發人員聯絡。

✗ I will contact to the customer about the product review.
○ I will contact the customer about the product review.
我會聯絡顧客並談論關於產品評價的事。

正如前面所說,contact 後面應該立刻接聯絡對象 the customer,再於介系詞 about 後面說出要聯絡的內容 the product review。

call 也一樣不需要加介系詞，可以直接接要聯絡的對象。

> **I will call you soon.** 我會盡快打電話給你。
>
> **I will call you back later.** 我之後再回電話給你。

在下面的句子裡，call 後面也應該直接加聯絡對象，因此要刪掉 to，改成 call you 才對。

✗ **A member of our team will call to you tomorrow.**
○ **A member of our team will call you tomorrow.**
　　我們的組員明天會打電話給你。

Ⓓetails
contact 可以視為 get in touch with 的同義詞。另外，keep / stay in touch with 是「與～保持聯繫」的意思。

> **Get in touch with me once you visit Korea.**
> 如果你來韓國，請與我聯絡。
> **I still keep in touch with my former workmates.**
> 我到現在還跟前同事保持聯繫。

應用

I always contact each B2B customer about once every two weeks. I usually send an email, but occasionally I call them.
我總是每兩週聯絡所有 B2B 客戶一次。通常我會寄電子郵件，但有時也會打電話。

5 search / search for

> We searched a new candidate to join our team for months.

> 很多人會在應該使用 search for 的時候，卻只用了 search。

表示尋找某樣東西或事物時，必須在 search 後面加介系詞 for。另外，表示探索某個位置（location）、場所（place）或區域（area）時，則只需單獨使用 search。

> **My company is currently searching for a new business partner in the finance industry.**
> 我們公司目前正在尋找新的金融事業夥伴。

> **I searched my bedroom, car, and office but I still didn't find my missing ID card.**
> 我找過臥室、車子和辦公室，但都找不到我遺失的身分證。

讓我們套用上述內容，再重新檢視下面的句子。

✗　　　**We searched a new candidate to join our team for months.**
○　　　**We searched for a new candidate to join our team for months.**
　　　　近幾個月來，我們一直在物色加入我們團隊的新人選。

當我們使用 search 或 search for 時，意味著還沒發現想找的事物。如果在想找的東西已找到的情況下，我們會使用 find。

We searched for a new candidate to join our team for months, and finally found the perfect person last week.
近幾個月來，我們一直在物色加入我們團隊的新人選，最後終於在上週找到了完美的人選。

假如要找的對象是可以在電腦或書籍中找到的資訊（information），也可以使用動詞片語 look up 來表達。

Can you look up this customer's order history on our website?
可以請你從我們的網站中找出這位顧客過去的交易明細嗎？

應用

I've been searching for a new job for months. First, I searched online, but lately I've been actually visiting companies who are hiring and delivering my resume in person.
我這幾個月一直在找新工作。一開始我在網路上搜尋，但最近我拜訪了正在徵才的公司，並且直接遞交履歷。

6 go / go to / go on

I'm going to abroad next week for a business trip.

We should go to there more often.

I would like to go to a vacation.

許多人不清楚前後文會如何根據結合的介系詞不同而改變，如 go to、go on 等。

包含 go 的動詞片語（phrasal verbs）有很多，此處我們將重點介紹表示行動（movement）的 go。

1. go to 用於前往場所或目的地時。

I'm going to Busan to visit my business partner.
我將前往釜山見我的生意夥伴。

I usually go to the gym after work.
下班後，我通常會去健身房。

I have to go to my office this weekend so I can't meet you Saturday.
我這個週末必須進公司，所以週六無法與你見面。

作為參考，there、home、abroad、overseas、east、west、north、south、somewhere、outside、upstairs、downstairs 等單字並非表示地點的名詞，而是副詞，因此前面不加 to。

2. go on 會跟 trip、journey、vacation、walk、drive、hike 等與移動（travel）或行動（movement）有關的名詞一起使用。

I'm about to go on a 3 week business trip.
我預計將出差 3 週左右。

I'll go on a hike this weekend.
我這個週末要去爬山。

3. 提到喜歡的休閒活動時，可以用 go V-ing 來表達。

I'm going golfing with my colleagues this weekend.
我這個週末要跟同事一起去打高爾夫球。

I went snowboarding last winter.
我去年冬天去玩滑雪板。

We're going to go camping soon.
我們很快就要去露營了。

讓我們重新檢視下面這些句子。

✗   I'm **going to abroad** next week for a business trip.
○   I'm going abroad next week for a business trip.
我下週要去海外出差。

✗   We should **go to there** more often.

○   We should go there more often.

我們應該更常去那裡。

✗   I would like to **go to a vacation**.

○   I would like to go on a vacation.

我想去渡假。

> 應用

A: I'm going on a business trip next week so unfortunately, I won't be available.

B: No worries. Where are you going?

A: I'm actually going to Osaka. It'll be my first time in Japan.

B: Nice! I went there last year. It's a beautiful city.

A：可惜我下週要出差，時間可能無法配合。

B：沒關係。你要去哪裡？

A：其實我要去大阪。這是我第一次去日本。

B：真好！我去年去過那裡。那是一座美麗的城市。

7 think / think about

I'm thinking quit my job.

Did anyone think any new advertising ideas?

→ think 和 think about 兩者的區別經常令人混淆。

若要單獨使用 think，不加介系詞的話，後面必須接著說出所想的內容。

I think we should reschedule the meeting.
我認為應該重新安排會議時間。

I think this month will be the best month in our company's history.
我想這個月將會是我們公司史上最棒的一個月。

可以像上述例句一樣，在 think 後面說出詳細的看法；也可以像下面的例句一樣，簡短地表達。

I think so.
我認同。

I think not.
我不這麼認為。

I think it's okay.

我認為沒關係。

think about 是「思考關於～」的意思，所以後面要接主題（topic）。

What do you think about our new product?

你對於我們的新產品有什麼看法？

I often think about the future of my career.

我經常思考我將來的職業生涯。

think of 用於腦海中浮現某種想法或創意時。但是在商務英文中，比起 think of，最好使用 think about，比較能傳達針對主題認真思考的感覺。

The accountants thought of a new way to organize our financial statements.

會計師們想出一種用來整理財務報表的新方法。

概括來說，當我們要表達意見（opinion）時，可以不加介系詞，直接使用 think。當我們談論到正在考慮或關注的主題或想法（topic / idea）時，我們會使用 think about。而當我們提到剛剛浮現的新點子（new idea）時，我們會用 think of。

根據上述內容，我們再來重新檢視下面這幾句話。由於說話者正在考慮辭職（quit my job），所以應該在 think about 後面加動名詞 quitting。

✕　　　**I'm thinking quit my job.**

○　　　**I'm thinking about quitting my job.**

我正在考慮辭職。

構思新廣告比較接近腦海中浮現創意的感覺，所以使用 think of 來表達會更自然。

×   Did anyone **think** any new advertising ideas?

○   Did anyone think of any new advertising ideas?

        有人想出什麼新的廣告點子嗎？

應用

Lately I've been thinking about how our team can be more productive. I think we should create a Slack group chat instead of having our daily morning meetings.

最近我一直在思考如何讓我們的團隊更有效率。我認為與其每天早上開會，不如創建一個 Slack 群組會更好。

8 check / check on / check with

Please send me your sales figures for this month. I'll check with them before sending them to the manager.

I'm fine with you leaving the meeting early, but can you check the operations manager to make sure he's okay with it?

許多人無法理解 check on 與 check with 的細微差異。

check v. to review or examine something in order to evaluate or measure its accuracy, quality, or correctness 為了評估 / 測量正確與否而進行檢查或調查

當 check 單獨使用時，表示與品質或正確性有關。

You review the financial data for your company to make sure it's correct and doesn't contain any errors.
→ **(You are checking the data.)**
你查看公司的財務數據，確認是否正確並檢查有無錯誤。
→（你正在 check 數據。）

讓我們重新檢視下面的句子，這裡的意思是要在確認 sales figures（銷售額）之後，將它寄給經理，因此不需要加 with。

✗　　Please send me your sales figures for this month. I'll ~~check with~~ them before sending them to the manager.

○　　Please send me your sales figures for this month. I'll check them before sending them to the manager.

請將這個月的銷售額寄給我。我會先檢查一遍再寄給經理。

check on 不會用於檢查某樣東西的品質或正確性，它是用在確認狀態的時候。

Your friend lost his job and is very upset about it. You message him to offer some support and see if he's okay.
→ (You are checking on your friend.)

你的朋友因為失業而感到非常難過。你傳訊息給予鼓勵並確認他是否安好。
→（你正在 check on 朋友的狀態。）

There was a large hail storm. You go look at your car to make sure the hail didn't damage your car.
→ (You are checking on your car.)

一場很強的雹暴席捲而過。你去檢查車子的狀態，確認冰雹是否有造成車子損壞。→（你正在 check on 車子的狀態。）

check with [sb] 用於請求許可的時候，也就是「（向～）確認是否可以那樣做」的意思。

One of your team members has a good idea for an advertisement. He goes to the team leader and shares his idea so he can get permission to create the advertisement.

→ (He is checking with your team leader.)

你們團隊裡的一位成員想到一個很好的廣告提案。為了獲得廣告製作許可，他去找組長分享自己的想法。→（他正在 check with 組長的意見。）

下面的句子，是要對方向營運經理確認會議中是否可以提早離席，因此必須使用 check with。

×   I'm fine with you leaving the meeting early, but can you **check** the operations manager to make sure he's okay with it?

○   I'm fine with you leaving the meeting early, but can you check with the operations manager to make sure he's okay with it?

我不介意你會議中提早離席，但是你可以再跟營運經理確認一下嗎？

應用

A: Have you checked our advertising budget proposal for next quarter?

B: I did! I think it looks really good. I just need to check with the marketing director to get his approval before finalizing it.

A：你確認過下個季度的廣告預算提案了嗎？

B：是的！我認為看起來很好。我只需要在敲定之前跟行銷總監確認，獲得他的批准就行了。

9 answer / respond / reply

A: Has the client responded you yet?

B: Yes, she replied the email last night.

→ reply、respond、answer 連接的介系詞各自不同。

當 answer 作動詞使用，表示「回答」、「接電話」的意思時，後面不加 to。

Please answer the question.
請回答問題。

Sorry I missed your call, I didn't answer my phone in time.
很抱歉錯過你的電話，我那時候來不及接電話。

但是，當 answer 作名詞使用時，後面就要加 to。

What is the answer to question 2?
第二題的答案是什麼？

Did you get an answer to your email?
你寄出的電子郵件收到回覆了嗎？

reply 和 respond 無論作名詞或動詞使用，都要加介系詞 to。作為參考，在商務往來等需要使用正式表達的情況下，通常會使用 respond，而不是 reply。

I will respond to you within 3 business days.

我將於 3 個工作天之內給您答覆。

Have you responded to those inquiries yet?

你回覆那些要求了嗎?

讓我們重新檢視下面這些句子。由於是給你(you)答覆,所以必須加 to。

✕　　**Has the client responded you yet?**

○　　**Has the client** responded to **you yet?**

那位客戶給你答覆了嗎?

下面的句子,意思是對方回覆了電子郵件,所以必須加 to。

✕　　**Yes, she replied the email last night.**

○　　**Yes, she** replied to **the email last night.**

是的,她昨晚回覆了那封電子郵件。

應用

Sorry I haven't responded to your email yet! I've had an incredibly busy morning. I'll review it and reply later this afternoon.

因為今天早上太忙了,我還沒回覆你的電子郵件,真是抱歉!我會研究一下,
並在今天下午稍晚的時候回覆你。

10 agree with / to / on / about

> I agree to Sanghyeon's opinion about the new sales policy.

> 有時候，我們會對 agree 應該加什麼介系詞感到困惑。

在大部分的情況下，通常會使用 agree with、agree that、agree to。

1. agree with 用於與其他人意見一致時，它的受詞可以是人，也可以是想法。

I agree with Jiwon.
我同意智媛。

表達同意某人的意見時，我們通常會說 I agree with (person's) opinion，但是也可以省略 opinion，只說同意某人（person）。

I agree with Mike's opinion. → I agree with Mike.
我同意 Mike 的想法。

2. agree that 用於同意想法或意見時。

I agree that we're spending too much money on marketing.
我同意行銷費用的支出太多了。

I agree that we should reschedule the meeting.
我贊成應該重新安排會議行程。

3. agree to 意味著「正式接受提議或合約」。此外，執行合約內容時，也可以使用 agree to V。

They agreed to the new terms of the contract.
他們同意了新的合約條件。

Each client agreed to pay $500 per month for the consulting service.
每位客戶都同意每月支付 500 美元的諮詢服務費用。

Under the new work from home policy, each employee must agree to be available from 10 a.m. to 7 p.m.
根據新的居家上班政策，所有員工從早上10點到晚上7點必須保持可聯繫的狀態。

4. agree on / about 用於同意某個主題或計劃時，後面會接名詞或以疑問詞開頭的單字。

We agreed on the date for the meeting.
我們同意開會日期。

We can be friends even if we don't agree about everything.
即使並非每件事都意見一致，我們仍然可以做朋友。

We don't agree on what to eat.
我們對於要吃什麼意見不一。

從下面的句子來看，是表示同意對方的意見，因此應該使用 agree with。

×   I ~~agree to~~ Sanghyeon's opinion about the new sales policy.

○   I agree with Sanghyeon's (opinion) about the new sales policy.

我同意尚賢對於新銷售方針的看法。

應用

A: Initially, we agreed to meet once a week for our business consulting sessions, but I think it might be better to meet every other week from now on.

B: I completely agree with you. Every other week sounds great.

A：起初，我們決定一週見一次面以進行業務諮詢，但我認為往後隔週見面會比較好。

B：我完全贊同。隔週見面很好。

11 listen / listen to

> Make sure you listen the prospect when they explain their problems, and present our product as the solution to those problems during your sales pitch.
>
> 有些人會在應該使用 listen to 的時候，沒有加 to。

在專心聆聽的聲音或人說的話的前面，必須使用 listen to。順帶一提，要叫人集中注意的時候，可以說「Listen!」，也可以在後面加副詞，例如「Listen carefully!」，但是要注意別跟 listen to 搞混了。

> **Please listen to the full presentation and let me know if you have any questions.**
> 聽完所有簡報後，如果有任何問題，請告訴我。
>
> **It's important to listen closely to what your clients want.**
> 仔細傾聽客戶的需求是很重要的。

讓我們重新檢視下面的句子。這裡要表達的意思是仔細傾聽 the prospect（潛在客戶）說的話，因此應該用 listen to the prospect 才對。

✕   Make sure you ~~listen~~ the prospect when they explain their problems, and present our product as the solution to those problems during your sales pitch.

◯   Make sure you listen to the prospect when they explain their problems, and present our product as the solution to those problems during your sales pitch.

當潛在客戶描述他們的問題時,請傾聽他們說的話,然後在推銷時介紹並推薦購買我們的產品來解決他們的問題。

Ⓓetails

listen 指的是專注地聽某個聲音,而 hear 僅僅只是聽見的意思而已。舉例來說,如果在通話中,要確認對方能不能聽清楚我的聲音,我們會說「Can you hear me?」

［應用］

It's really important to listen to everything the prospect says during your initial sales meeting. If you listen closely and take notes, you can mention those details in your follow up email and that usually makes a really good impression.

在初期銷售會議上,傾聽潛在客戶所說的全部內容非常重要。如果你仔細聆聽並做筆記,你可以在後續的電子郵件提及這些細節,這樣做往往能讓人留下好印象。

12 access / access to

Each employee can access to the breakroom by swiping their ID in front of the door scanner.

許多人對於 access 是動詞還是名詞，以及是否要加介系詞感到困惑。

access   n. a means / way to enter or approach something
進入或接近某物的方法

access   v. to approach or enter something 接近或進入某物

當 access 作動詞使用時，不需要加介系詞。但是當 access 作名詞使用時，必須在想接近的對象前面加 to。

I can't access the files you sent me. What's the password?
我無法打開你寄給我的這些檔案。密碼是什麼？

Can you give me access to these files?
你能給我這些檔案的使用權限嗎？

We can have access to a limitless amount of information with a click of a button.
我們只需要按一個鍵，就能連結到無限的資訊。

在下面的句子裡，access 是作動詞使用，因此可以不加 to，直接加要接的對象，或是用 have access to 來表達。

✗　Each employee can **access to** the breakroom by swiping their ID in front of the door scanner.

○　Each employee can access the breakroom by swiping their ID in front of the door scanner.

○　Each employee can have access to the breakroom by swiping their ID in front of the door scanner.

只要在門禁讀卡機前刷識別證，每個員工都可以出入休息室。

> 應用

Here are your ID cards. You can scan these at the front to access our office 24/7. The 10-digit code on the back is your online password. You can use that to gain access to our company files.

這是你們的員工識別證。只要在前面掃描識別證，你就可以 24 小時進出我們的公司。背面的十位數號碼是你的線上密碼。你可以用這個密碼讀取公司的檔案。

13 invest / invest in

> We invested a lot of money to this new product. I
> hope the result will be worth it.

> invest 是否結合介系詞 in 使用，分別表示著不同的情況。

在提及金錢、時間、努力等投資對象時，可以不加介系詞，單獨使用
invest。

I invested $5,000.
我投資了五千美元。

I invested a lot of time and effort.
我投入了許多時間與心血。

如果 invest 後面加了介系詞 in，就會出現股票、房地產、債券、金、
銀等投資對象。

I invested in Bitcoin last year.
我去年投資了比特幣。

I want to start investing in real estate.
我打算開始投資房地產。

我們也經常使用 invest A in B 的句型，意思是「將 A 投資於 B」。

I invested so much time in my company's new project.

我投資許多時間在公司的新計畫上。

I invest $1,000 per month in various pharmaceutical stocks.

我每個月投資一千美元在各個製藥公司的股票上。

讓我們重新檢視下面的句子。這裡要表達的是投資很多錢在新計畫上，因此介系詞應該用 in，而非用 to。

✗ We invested a lot of money to this new product. I hope the result will be worth it.

○ We invested a lot of money in this new product. I hope the result will be worth it.

我們投資了很多錢在這個新計畫上。我希望結果是值得的。

Details

在日常對話中，經常會用 put 取代 invest，以 put A into B 來表達。

I invested so much money in my company's new project.

= I put so much money into my company's new project.

我投資了很多錢在公司的新計畫上。

應用

We've invested a lot of time and energy in this project. Plus, our shareholders invested over $100K. We really need to make this work.

我們在這個項目投入了大量的時間與精力。而且我們的股東已經投資超過 10 萬美元。我們必須讓這個項目成功。

14 familiar with / to

Sales presentations are not familiar with me.

許多人分不清楚 familiar with 和 familiar to 的區別。

I'm familiar with this place.
This place is familiar to me.

familiar 的意思是「熟悉的、親近的」，上述兩個句子都是「我很熟悉
這個地方（I know this place well.）」的意思。

A: Are you familiar with this concept?
你熟悉這個概念嗎？
B: This concept is not familiar to me.
我並不熟悉這個概念。

從上面的對話便可以看出，familiar with 和 familiar to 的結構與意義正
好相反。可以整理如下。

X is familiar with Y
X 熟悉 Y（Y 是內容）
=   X knows about / has experience with Y
X 了解 Y／有與 Y 相關的經驗

X is familiar to Y

Y 熟悉 X（Y 是人）

= Y knows about / has experience with X

Y 了解 X／有與 X 相關的經驗

讓我們來檢視下面的句子。這裡要表達的意思是（由於經驗不足、缺乏知識等原因）產品介紹對我來説並非熟悉的工作，因此應該用 to me。

× **Sales presentations are not ~~familiar with~~ me.**

○ **Sales presentations are not** familiar to **me.**

我並不熟悉銷售簡報。

作為參考，上面這句話也可以簡單地用「I'm not familiar with sales presentation.」或「I don't know sales presentations well.」來表達。

應用

I was promoted to country manager last year mainly because of my sales performance, but also because I'm incredibly familiar with **the Korean market.**

= **I was promoted to country manager last year mainly because of my sales performance, but also because the Korean market is incredibly** familiar to **me.**

我去年晉升為分公司總經理，主要是因為我的銷售表現，但也是因為我非常了解韓國市場。

15 pay / pay for

> My company pays my English lessons.

> 在使用 pay 這個單字時，經常會發生誤用介系詞的情形。

當 pay 不加介系詞單獨使用時，pay 後面要接明確的金額、與費用相關的名詞（如 fee、rent、bill、invoice 等）或支付費用的對象。

He paid $5,000 for the used car.
他付了五千美元買那輛二手車。

He paid the rental fee yesterday.
他昨天付了租金。

We pay our HR consultant at the beginning of each month.
我們在每月月初付款給人力資源顧問。

pay for 的意思是「支付～的代價」，所以 pay for 後面要接購買的對象。

Who's going to pay for this meal?
這一餐的錢要由誰來付？

I paid for the movie tickets online.
電影票的錢我已經線上支付了。

即使沒有明確指出購買對象，也可以使用 pay for，並且可以用 this / that 或 these / those 等指示代名詞來代替。

Did you pay for this?
這個你付錢了嗎？

I paid for those already.
我已經付錢了。

讓我們重新檢視下面的句子，因為是公司替我支付英文課的費用，所以應該用 pay for 表達。

✗　　**My company pays my English lessons.**
○　　**My company pays (the tuition) for my English lessons.**
　　　我的公司替我支付英文課的費用。

> 應用
>
> **Since I have to travel so often, my company usually pays for my hotels and airfare. Sometimes, they even pay a little extra so I can fly business class.**
> 由於我經常出差，公司通常會支付住宿費和機票費。有時候甚至會提供額外費用，讓我能搭商務艙。

16 grow / grow up

> When I studied at the computer academy, my programming skills definitely grew up.
>
> Our startup was founded in 2016, and since then we've grown up from a team of 3 to a company with over 70 employees and three offices.
>
> ➔ 在應該使用 grow 的情況下，使用 grow up 會顯得很尷尬。

grow 意味著規模變大、數量增加或進步發展。

Instagram grew significantly from 2016 to 2020.
Instagram 自 2016 年到 2020 年急速成長。

不同於 grow，grow up 意味著一個人改變並長大成人。

I grew up in the United States, but I live in Korea now.
我在美國長大，但現在住在韓國。

I saw my cousin for the first time in 5 years last weekend. I was amazed by how much he grew up.
上週末是我時隔五年第一次見到表弟。我很驚訝他都長這麼大了。

讓我們重新檢視下面的句子。因為是我的 skills（技巧、能力）進步了，所以不該用 grow up，應該用 grow 才對。

✗　　When I studied at the computer academy, my programming skills definitely grew up.

○　　When I studied at the computer academy, my programming skills definitely grew.
　　　在電腦補習班學習時，我的程式設計實力確實提升了。

下面這個句子也一樣，因為是公司規模變大，員工數增加，所以應該要用 grow 才對。

✗　　Our startup was founded in 2016, and since then we've grown up from a team of 3 to a full company with over 70 employees and three offices.

○　　Our startup was founded in 2016, and since then we've grown from a team of 3 to a full company with over 70 employees and three offices.
　　　我們公司創立於 2016 年，在那之後，我們從 3 人團隊發展成擁有 70 多名員工和三個辦事處的成熟公司。

┌ 應用 ┐

Lately my company has been growing a lot and is about to open an office in America. I'm going to apply there. I would love for my kids to grow up in the United States.
近來我們公司迅速成長，即將在美國設立辦事處。我想申請調派到那裡去。我希望我的孩子們能在美國長大。

55

下面是針對前面介紹過的 with Error 部分，修正錯誤用法後的內容，你可以在劃底線的部分確認正確的表達方式。

面試官

Jiwon, it's great to finally meet you. We're looking forward to this interview.
智媛，很高興終於見到你了。我們很期待這次的面試。

智媛

Yes, thank you for this opportunity.
是，謝謝您給我這次的機會。

面試官

First, let's discuss your past work history. Can you tell us a little more about your previous sales job at Nexus AI?
首先，我們來聊聊你以前的工作經歷。你能告訴我們關於你之前在 Nexus AI 從事銷售工作的事嗎？

智媛

Sure! I worked at Nexus AI from 2017 to 2020. I started as a sales associate, and my main job duties were to <u>contact new</u> potential customers. I would <u>share</u> product information <u>with</u> them, <u>answer their</u> questions, and set up a sales meeting with one of our lead salespeople. This experience helped me learn how to search and find new customers. It also made me much more <u>familiar with</u> the B2B sales process.
當然！我從 2017 年到 2020 年在 Nexus AI 工作。一開始我擔任銷售員，主要業務是聯絡新的潛在顧客。我與他們分享產品資訊，解答他們的問題，並讓他們與我們的首席銷售員開個銷售會議。這段經歷讓我學會如何發掘新顧客，並且更熟悉 B2B 銷售流程。

I was promoted to a lead sales position in November 2018. As a lead salesperson, I would go to many company offices and conduct in-person sales presentations. To be honest, I wasn't totally prepared for this position at first, but after a few months, I was much more adjusted to giving sales presentations. Once I closed a sale, I was then in charge of continuing to build the relationship with that customer, so I would often check on them and respond to any questions they ask me.

我在 2018 年 11 月晉升為首席銷售員。作為首席銷售員，我會拜訪許多公司並當面做銷售簡報。老實說，我認為我一開始並沒有充分做好擔任該職務的準備。但幾個月之後，我越來越適應做銷售簡報的工作。完成交易後，為了維繫與顧客的關係，我會時常聯繫顧客並回覆他們提出的問題。

I know you're looking for someone with a lot of B2B sales experience and a deep understanding of the tech industry. The B2B sales process and the tech industry are both incredibly familiar to me, and I would love the chance to show you by working here as a lead sales team member.

我知道貴公司正在尋找 B2B 銷售經驗豐富，並且對科技產業有深入了解的人。B2B 銷售流程與科技產業都是我相當熟悉的領域，我希望有機會能成為貴公司首席銷售組的一員，向各位展示我的能力。

面試官　Great! What would you say is your proudest work accomplishment?
很好！你認為你最自豪的工作成就是什麼？

智媛　My proudest accomplishment is winning salesperson of the year in 2020 at Nexus AI. During that year, I actually set a new company record for most sales revenue generated in a single year. I think the key to my success was always listening to the customers, and adjusting to my sales pitches based on what they really wanted. Before a sales session, I always think about the problems this specific company has and how I can present whatever I'm selling as the best possible solution to those problems. Because my sales pitches were customized for each specific client, many clients agreed to work with us and paid for their first order during our initial meeting.

我最自豪的成就是在 Nexus AI 獲得 2020 年年度銷售員獎。事實上，我在那一年內貢獻了最多的銷售收入，創下了公司新紀錄。我認為我成功的關鍵在於傾聽顧客的心聲，並根據他們的需求調整我的銷售術語。在進行銷售活動之前，我總是在思考客戶的公司所面臨的問題，以及我該如何將商品包裝成解決該問題的最佳方案。由於我的銷售話術是根據每位客戶量身打造的，所以很多客戶決定與我們合作，並在初次會面時就成交了與我們的第一筆訂單。

Nexus AI's total revenue grew 15% YOY in 2020, which is the largest revenue increase they've ever had. Being a huge part of that success makes me very proud.

Nexus AI 在 2020 年的總收入比前一年增長了 15%，這可以說是公司史上最大的收入增幅。我很自豪能在那次的獲利中扮演重要的角色。

面試官　Excellent! What makes you want to work here at Onward Tech?

了不起！那麼，你為什麼想來 Onward Tech 工作呢？

智媛　I love your company's mission and it seems like the work

environment here is fantastic. When I checked your company's website, I read about your vision of 'making our world more modernized and connected by helping everyone on Earth access the technology necessary to improve their lives'.

我喜歡貴公司的宗旨，而且這裡的工作環境似乎很棒。我查看了 **Onward Tech** 的網站，並看到貴公司的願景是「使全世界變得更現代化並相互連結，讓所有人都能夠獲得改善生活所需的科技」。

That mission really resonates with me and I would love to be part of it. Also, I know that you provide a lot of benefits and training opportunities for your employees. I think it's awesome that you invest in your employees' success. I know I have the skills and experience necessary to do great things here, and the work environment seems like a perfect fit for me.

這個願景引起了我的共鳴，我也想參與其中。此外，我知道 **Onward Tech** 為員工提供了許多福利和進修機會。我認為投資員工未來的成功是很棒的一件事。我擁有能在這裡成就事業所需的技能與經驗，而且我認為這裡的工作環境很適合我。

面試官　　Great. That's very good to hear because we're really looking for employees that can fit in well with our corporate culture. It's been great talking with you, Jiwon. I'll discuss our interview with the other hiring managers and we'll call you sometime tomorrow afternoon. Thank you for your time!

太好了。很高興聽到你這麼說，我們正在尋找能融入我們公司文化的員工。智媛，跟你聊天很愉快。我會跟其他用人主管討論這次的面試，然後在明天下午打電話聯絡你。謝謝你撥空前來！

智媛 Thank you for the opportunity. Have a great rest of your day.

謝謝你給我這次的機會。祝你今天過得愉快。

Chapter **2**

錯誤的冠詞與限定詞
Article and Determiner Mistakes

1 most / most of

2 on / in / at for time

3 for / since

4 this / last / next replacing on / in

5 a / an

6 using 'the'

7 on the Internet

8 similar with / to, different from / than

9 by / until

10 still / until

11 during / for / while

12 another / other / the other

13 besides / except

以下的敘述中包含錯誤的用法。請閱讀一遍,並試著找出不自然的表達方式。在各章節的最後會提供修正後的正確表達。

下面是智媛進入 Onward Tech 之後,前往公司接受培訓的情形。智媛在那裡遇見她的上司 Michelle 和銷售組長尚賢。

Michelle	It's great to meet you, Jiwon. We're very happy to have you on our team.
Jiwon	It's great meeting you too! I'm really excited to join the team. I've been looking forward to this all week until now.
Michelle	Today morning I thought I could introduce you to the team and explain some of our policies around office. Then at the afternoon I wanna get you started contacting some of our customers.
Jiwon	Sounds great!
Michelle	Most of sales team are actually in client meetings right now, but they should be finished in about a hour. I'll show you your desk ... (walks into desk area)
Michelle	Okay, here's where you'll be. You're sharing a cubicle with Sanghyeon Kim. He's really experienced salesman and is head of sales team. He's been working with us since almost three years and will be happy to help you out if you have any questions.

Jiwon	Great! At my previous job I had to share a cubicle with other coworker but it was half this size. I'm glad I'll have more space to work!
Michelle	Yeah, I really like how open and spacious our office is. We remodeled it in last year and this new layout is so much better. It's a lot different with before! Here let's get you logged in and registered on the computer. Do you have your company ID yet?
Jiwon	Yep, got it right here.
Michelle	Okay, enter your employee email and 10-digit employee ID number here to log in to the company portal. The first thing to do at the start of each shift is to check our sales team alerts by clicking here. It usually doesn't take that long, so if you get to the office in 8:00 a.m. you should be able to finish until around 8:10. I usually send a short sales team agenda so whatever you do after that will depend on the agenda for the day. And ... Sanghyeon, you're back already? I thought you would be in meetings by 10:00.
Sanghyeon	Yeah, the purchasing team from the Apex Apparel actually contacted me a few weeks before. They read about us in Internet and were really interested in our AI marketing systems, so it was a really easy sell. They actually placed their first purchase order while the meeting. We signed a one-year contract that will start two weeks after.

Jiwon	Great! I've heard that their culture is pretty similar from ours so they should be really good long-term client. I'm glad we can get that partnership started. By the way, this is Jiwon, your new cubicle mate.
Sanghyeon	Hey Jiwon, I heard really good things about you. Welcome to the team.
Jiwon	Yeah, it's great meeting you, too. I'm excited to be here.
Michelle	Except Sanghyeon there are 3 other members on your sales team. They should be back about 45 minutes later. Sanghyeon, can you explain a little more about the company portal?
Sanghyeon	Yeah, no problem.
Michelle	Perfect, I'll leave you to it then. Jiwon, if you have another questions, feel free to send me a quick Hangouts message. Again, it was great meeting you.
Jiwon	Great meeting you, too. Thank you!

1 most / most of

Most of Korean companies are in the tech industry.

Most of colleagues have more work experience than me.

有時候，我們會對於名詞前面該用 most，還是 most of 感到困惑。

只要套用以下規則，便能輕鬆地區分。most 會與「非限定的」名詞一起使用。它通常會與複數型的可數名詞一起使用。當我們說 Most Koreans 的時候，指的是大多數韓國人，而不是指屬於任何限定群體的韓國人。在某些情況下，most 也會跟不可數名詞一起使用，如下所示。

Most knowledge is gained through experience.
大部分的知識是透過經驗取得的。

相反的，most of 是用來表示限定的事物，所以 most of 後面通常會接（a / an、the、this、that、my、your、his、their 等）限定詞。

Most of the Koreans I know study English.
我認識的大部分韓國人都學習英文。（限定的複數名詞。僅限於我個人認識的韓國人。）

I finished most of this week's report, but still need some
more information.

本週的報告我已經完成了大部分，但我還需要更多資訊。（限定的單數名詞。
僅限於本週的報告。不代表普遍的每週報告。）

Most of my work experience was overseas.

我大部分的工作經驗都在海外。（限定的不可數名詞。僅限於我的工作經驗。
不代表普遍的經驗。）

根據上述內容，讓我們重新檢視下面這幾個句子，這裡指的是普遍的
韓國公司，而不是限定的韓國公司集團，所以可以用下面的方式表達。

✕　　**Most of Korean companies** are in the tech industry.
○　　**Most Korean companies are in the tech industry.**
　　　大部分的韓國公司都從事科技產業。

由於已經明確表明是現在和我一起工作的同事，所以應該改成 Most of
my colleagues。

✕　　**Most of colleagues** have more work experience than me.
○　　Most of my colleagues **have more work experience than me.**
　　　我大部分的同事工作經驗都比我豐富。

(D)etails
當後面接的是代名詞時，必須使用 most of。

Most of us are happy with the result.
我們大部分都對結果感到滿意。

另外，在國名或地區名稱前面也應該使用 most of。

This is the programmers' office. It's kind of empty because most of them are working remotely right now.

這裡是程式設計師的公司，但現在沒人在，因為目前大多數員工採取遠距工作。

We've sold almost all of our inventory, so we need to order more as soon as possible.

我們的庫存幾乎快用完了，必須盡快追加訂購。

Here are some of our suggestions.

以下是我們的一些建議。

應用

Most people have been working from home lately, but my team can only work effectively from our office. So, most of my team members have still been coming to the office for work. We still need to communicate with our remote colleagues, so we started hosting Zoom conferences with all the departments.

雖然最近大多數人都居家上班，但我們這組只有在公司才能有效率地工作。因此，我的組員大部分都還是會來上班。儘管如此，我們還是需要跟遠方的同事們交流，所以我們開始和所有部門開 Zoom 視訊會議。

2 on / in / at for time

> We're going to launch the new product on October.
>
> The meeting will be on February 14th 9:30 a.m. in the morning.
>
> → 在提及時間（tIme）或日期（specific date）的時候，經常會出現錯誤。

1. in 用於提及年份、月份、季節和一天的某個時段時。

in 2020, in February, in (the) winter, in the morning

2. on 用於日期或星期之前。

on Tuesday, on Marth 27th , on Independence Day

有時會出現同時提到日期和星期的情況，此時必須使用介系詞 on，並將星期寫在日期前面。

Let's have the meeting on Thursday, September 10th at 3:00 p.m.
我們就在 9 月 10 日週四下午 3 點開會吧。

3. at 用於提及時間或夜晚（night）時。

at 3:30, at noon, at 6 p.m., at night

在同時提到時間、星期和日期的情況下，可以用以下方式表達，此時時間的位置可以放在星期和日期的前面或後面。

Let's have the meeting on Thursday, September 10th at 3:00 p.m.
將時間放在星期和日期的後面

Let's have the meeting at 3:00 p.m. on Thursday, September 10th.
將時間放在星期和日期的前面

接下來，讓我們重新檢視下面這幾個句子。提及月份（month）時要用 in，而不是 on。

×   We're going to launch the new product on October.
○   We're going to launch the new product in October.
我們將在十月推出新產品。

在表示準確的時間時，記得要用時間介系詞 at。

×   The meeting will be on February 14th 9:30 a.m.
○   The meeting will be on February 14th at 9:30 a.m.
會議將於 2 月 14 日上午 9 點 30 分舉行。

3 for / since

（以 2021 年為基準，說話者是在 2009 年移居美國。）

I'm Korean, but I have lived in the US since 12 years.

除了時間介系詞 in、on、at 之外，for / since 也經常令人混淆。

雖然 for 和 since 都是用來表示時間長度的介系詞，但重要的是後面出現的單字是什麼。舉例來說，假如你從早上 9 點開始工作，而現在是下午 4 點，你就可以說「I have been working for 7 hours.」或「I have been working since 9 a.m.」。區別在於 since 後面接的是開始行動的時間點。

這不僅適用於短時間，也適用於長時間。例如，假如你從 2007 年到 2021 年一直從事金融工作，你就可以這樣造句。

I have been working in the financial industry for 14 years.
我在金融領域工作了 14 年。
I have been working in the financial industry since 2007.
我自 2007 年以來，一直在金融領域工作。

現在讓我們重新檢視一開始的句子。since 後面要接開始的時間點，但這裡卻出現 12 years 這個時間長度，因此應該改成 for 12 years；由於是 2009 年去美國的，所以也可以説 since 2009。

✗   **I'm Korean, but I have lived in the US ~~since 12 years~~.**

○   **I'm Korean, but I have lived in the US** for 12 years.

        雖然我是韓國人，但我在美國住了 12 年。

○   **I'm Korean, but I have lived in the US** since 2009.

        雖然我是韓國人，但我自 2009 年開始一直住在美國。

Ⓓetails

since 後面通常會接時間點，但有時候也會接年齡。

I'm Korean, but I have lived in the US since I was 23 years old.
雖然我是韓國人，但我從 23 歲開始就住在美國了。

此外，它也可能會接某種狀態或某個行為的開始。

I'm Korean, but I have lived in the US since graduating college.
雖然我是韓國人，但我從大學畢業後就一直住在美國。

應用

I've worked for this company since 2006, but I've only been a member of this team for three years.
雖然我從 2006 年就開始在這家公司工作，但我加入這個小組才 3 年。

4 this / last / next replacing on / in

I started working here in last August.

I have a really important interview on this Thursday.

有些人會在表示時間的 this / next / last 前面加 on 或 in。

this、last、next 是用來代替加在時間前面的介系詞 in 和 on 。因此，如果已經出現 this、last、next，就不需要再用 in 或 on。讓我們來看看幾個錯誤的句子。

✗	I sent you the email on last Friday.
○	I sent you the email last Friday.
	我上週五寄了電子郵件給你。

✗	The meeting is on next Tuesday.
○	The meeting is on Tuesday.
○	The meeting is next Tuesday.
	會議時間是下週二。

✕   **The store will open** ~~in this July~~**.**

○   **The store will open** in July**.**

○   **The store will open** this July**.**

那家店將在今年七月開幕。

讓我們重新檢視下面這幾個句子。

✕   **I started working here** ~~in last August~~**.**

○   **I started working here** last August**.**

我從去年八月開始在這裡工作。

✕   **I have a really important interview** ~~on this Thursday~~**.**

○   **I have a really important interview** this Thursday**.**

我這週四有個非常重要的面試。

應用

We decided to divide the Zoom conference into three different meetings. The first Zoom meeting was last Wednesday. We'll have the second meeting this Wednesday, and the final meeting next Wednesday.

我們決定分三次舉行 Zoom 會議。第一次 Zoom 會議於上週三舉行。第二次會議將在這週三舉行，最後的會議將在下週三舉行。

5 a / an

He is incredibly skilled, organized, and efficient manager.

I hope to work for an US company someday.

雖然是很基本的內容，但有時候還是會出現錯誤使用 a / an 的情況。

1. 即使名詞前面加了再多的形容詞、副詞等修飾語，也不可以漏了 a / an。

× He is ~~really talented and confident salesman~~.

O He is a really talented and confident salesman.
他是個非常有才能又有自信的業務員。

當名詞前面的修飾語變多，大家經常會忘了加冠詞。請注意。即使前面的修飾語變得再長，只要該名詞為單數，就不可以漏掉冠詞。

讓我們重新檢視下面的句子。這句話的重點內容是「He is manager.」，中間的 incredibly skilled, organized, and efficient 全都是修飾語。因此，我們必須將可數名詞 manager 所需的冠詞以適當形態放在第一個修飾語前面。

✕　　　He is ~~incredibly skilled, organized, and efficient manager.~~

○　　　He is an incredibly skilled, organized, and efficient manager.
　　　　他是個非常熟練、有條理又有效率的主管。

2. 冠詞 a、an 的使用取決於發音，而非名詞的拼寫。

以母音 a、e、i、o、u 開頭的單字前面用 an，其餘的單字用 a。但是也有與拼寫無關，發音以母音開頭的情況。

>　　I'll meet you in an hour.
>　　一小時後見。

>　　I'm going back to school to get an MBA.
>　　我要重返校園取得 MBA 學位。

相反的，也有拼寫以 a、e、i、o、u 開頭，但發音卻不是以母音開頭的情況。

>　　My brother studies at a university in London.
>　　我哥哥正在倫敦的一所大學就讀。

根據上述內容，讓我們重新檢視下面這個句子。US 的 U 和 university 一樣發 [ju] 的音，因此其冠詞應該用 a，而非 an。

✕　　　I hope to work for ~~an~~ US company someday.

○　　　I hope to work for a US company someday.
　　　　我希望有一天能在美國公司工作。

6 using 'the'

I usually work from home, but I'm going to office today.

The Coupang has become very popular in Korea recently.

→ 許多人經常對冠詞的正確用法感到混淆。

在本節，除了一般的規則之外，我將告訴各位幾個原則，可用來應對這些常見錯誤。

1. 在團隊（team）、部門（department）、辦公室（office）、產業／工作領域（industry）前面要加 the。

Talk to the purchasing team.
請與採購組洽談。

We want to be one of the top companies in the e-commerce industry.
我們想成為電商業的佼佼者。

2. 在單數專有名詞（特定人物、國家、城市、公司名稱等）前面不加 the。

除了如 the United States、the Dominican Republic、the Czech Republic 等習慣性加 the 的情況之外，專有名詞前面不加 the。

3. 單一建築物前面大部分會加 the。

> I had an appointment at the hospital this weekend.
> 我這個週末預約了要去醫院。
>
> I usually go to the gym after work.
> 我通常下班之後會去健身房。
>
> Can you please take these checks to the bank later today?
> 你能在今天稍晚的時候，把這些支票拿去銀行嗎？

現在，讓我們重新檢視下面的句子。因為我要去的是特定公司，所以必須說 the office。

✗　　I usually work from home, but I'm going to office today.
○　　I usually work from home, but I'm going to the office today.
　　　我通常都居家上班，但今天我會去公司。

Coupang 是專有名詞，所以必須去掉前面的 the。

✗　　The Coupang has become very popular in Korea recently.
○　　Coupang has become very popular in Korea recently.
　　　Coupang（電商公司）最近在韓國大受歡迎。

I'll pass your suggestion on to the HR team. The HR manager isn't working from the office today, but she'll email you in a few hours.

我會將你的建議轉達給人資部。人資經理今天沒有進辦公室工作，但她幾個小時之後會寄電子郵件給你。

7 on the Internet

I saw that story at the Naver.

I saw that story on online.

→ 提到網路（Internet）或網站（website）時，大家對於介系詞的正確用法經常感到混淆。

這個問題的解決方法意外地簡單，只要加介系詞 on 就行了，如 on the Internet、on Naver、on YouTube、on Instagram。此外，在 Naver、YouTube、Instagram 等平台名稱前面不加 the。

I read that on Naver. 我在 Naver（韓國入口網站）讀過那個。
I read that on the Internet. 我在網路上讀過那個。

但是，當提及網站內的特定部分時，如論壇、聊天室、留言、私訊（DM, direct message）、電子郵件等，介系詞要用 in。

I read that in an email. 我在電子郵件中讀過那個。
I read that in a chat room. 我在聊天室裡讀過那個。
I read that in a Facebook comment. 我在 Facebook 留言中讀過那個。

另外，由於 online 一詞本身就包含了 on，所以不需要另外加介系詞。

✕　　　I saw that news story through online.

○　　　I saw that news story online.
　　　　我在網路上看過那篇新聞報導。

✕　　　You can order through online.

○　　　You can order online.
　　　　你可以在網路上訂購。

現在我們回頭去看前面的句子，只要將 at the Naver 改成 on Naver 即可。

✕　　　I saw that story at the Naver.

○　　　I saw that story on Naver.
　　　　我在 Naver 上面看過那個故事。

online 可不加介系詞單獨使用，所以應該將句子裡的 on 去掉。

✕　　　I saw that story on online.

○　　　I saw that story online.
　　　　我在網路上看過那個故事。

應用

My company does a lot of paid marketing on the Internet.
We run English ads on Facebook, Instagram, and YouTube
as well as Korean ads on Naver.
我們公司在網路上做了大量的付費行銷。我們在 Facebook、Instagram 和
YouTube 上播放英文廣告，在 Naver 播放韓文廣告。

8 similar with / to, different from / than

> We want our company to seem unique and different to all our competitors.
>
> 當我們使用 similar 和 different 比較兩件事，有時會對於該用什麼介系詞感到困惑。

similar 和 different 可以用以下兩種句型來表達。

1. X is similar to Y.

I've worked at both of our offices. They're very similar to each other.　我在我們的兩個辦公室都工作過，兩處非常相似。

2. X is different from Y.

This job is quite different from my old job.
這份工作跟我之前的工作截然不同。

similar 和 different 也經常放在名詞前面，作為修飾名詞的形容詞使用。在這種情況下，不需要加介系詞。

I had a similar problem last year. 我去年也有過類似的問題。
Because I'm a salesman, I talk to many different customers each day. 因為我是業務員，所以每天都要跟不同的顧客交談。

作為參考，compared to ～ 的用法也很常見，意思是「與～相比」，句型為 X is Y compared to Z.。

This computer is great <u>compared to</u> yours.
= This computer is better than yours.
這台電腦比你的電腦更好。

This question is hard <u>compared to</u> the last one.
= This question is harder than the last one.
這個問題比上次的問題更難。

讓我們重新檢視下面的句子。正如前面所說，我們必須以 different from 為一個單位來記憶。

✗ We want our company to seem unique and <s>different to</s> all our competitors.

○ We want our company to seem unique and different from all our competitors.
我們希望本公司有別於所有的競爭者，看起來與眾不同。

應用

I recently moved from my company's R&D department to sales. It was a big adjustment because talking to customers all day is very <u>different from</u> doing solo research. The work I do now is actually more <u>similar to</u> my first job when I was a sales representative at a retail store.

我最近從公司的研發部門調到了銷售部門。由於整天和客戶交談與獨自進行研究截然不同，所以我需要一些時間適應。我現在所做的工作，其實更接近我在零售商店當銷售員的第一份工作。

9 by / until

I have to finish sending these emails until 3:00 p.m.

I have to work overtime by 10:30 p.m. tonight.

→ 對於要如何使用表示「到～為止」的 by 和 until，經常令人感到混淆。

by 一般都用於訂定 deadline（期限）時，通常會與 start、over、done、complete、finish 等動詞一起使用。

Please finish the report by Friday.
請在週五之前完成報告。

until 意味著持續進行的活動在某個時間點發生變化。通常會與 continue、stay、work、study、sleep、remain 等動詞一起使用。

I have to work until 8 p.m. today.
我今天必須工作到晚上 8 點。

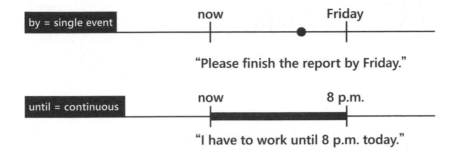

在下面的句子裡，動詞是 finish，而且後面出現 3 點這個截止時間，所以應該要用 by。

✗   I have to finish sending these emails until 3:00 p.m.

○   I have to finish sending these emails by 3:00 p.m.

      我必須在下午 3 點之前寄出這些電子郵件。

✗   I have to work overtime by 10:30 p.m. tonight.

○   I have to work overtime until 10:30 p.m. tonight.

      我必須加班到今天晚上 10 點半。

應用

My boss gave me a bunch of work last week and said it all had to be done by Friday. I had to stay up until 2 or 3 in the morning every night to get it all finished in time.

我老闆上週分派很多工作給我，而且說全部都要在週五之前完成。為了按時完成所有工作，我每天都得熬夜到凌晨兩三點。

10 still / until

I love working here until now.

有時候會出現在應該使用 still 的時候，卻使用 until 的情況。

正如前面所見，until 指的是考量某個特定時間的情況。在過了那個時間點之後，情況就會改變。請注意，只有當情況在特定時間點發生變化時，才能使用 until。也就是說，如果情況沒有改變，就要使用 still，而非 until，就像下面的句子一樣。

✕   I started working at Samsung in 2013 and work there until now.

○   I started working at Samsung in 2013 and still work there now.
     我從 2013 年開始在三星工作到現在。

下面的句子如果用了 until now，聽起來就像「雖然我到目前為止喜歡所有的課程，但以後不知道會怎麼樣」的意思。事實上，這裡想表達的是從一開始到現在都對課程感到很滿意，所以應該去掉 until now，只說「I have liked all of our classes.」就好了。

✕   I have liked all our classes until now.
○   I have liked all of our classes.
     我喜歡所有的課程。

讓我們重新檢視下面的句子。這裡要說的是仍然喜歡在這裡工作，並不是在說未來會改變的事，因此只要用 still 就可以了。

✕   I love working here until now.

○   I still love working here.

○   I love working here.

我一直很喜歡在這裡工作。

如果要表達到目前為止都喜歡在這裡工作，但事情發生變化，已經不再喜歡了，這個時候就可以使用 until now。不過，此時需要注意的是，因為前面的情況已經結束，所以必須用過去式表示。

I loved working here until now.
直到現在，我都喜歡在這裡工作。

應用

I got my MBA from Columbia Business School in the United States, then got a job on Wall Street. I lived and worked in New York until 2017. Now I'm back in Korea, but I still stay in contact with a lot of my old coworkers and plan on moving back to America in the future.

我在美國哥倫比亞大學商學院取得 MBA 學位後，在華爾街找到了一份工作。直到 2017 年，我一直在紐約生活和工作。雖然現在我回到了韓國，但仍然與許多以前的同事保持聯繫，並計劃將來要再回美國。

11 during / for / while

I met my recruiter during networking at a tech conference.

This client was pretty rude. He kept interrupting me while my presentation.

→ during、for 和 while 都被認為是「在～期間」的意思,往往無法仔細區分其中的差別。

during、for 和 while 在意義上並無區別,但在用法上有下列區別。

during　後面通常是表示事件(event)

for　　　後面是表示明確時間長度(如 2 hours、3 days、4 weeks、one year 等)

while　　後面是有主詞 + 動詞的句子,或是省略主詞,動詞改 V-ing 型態

I took notes <u>during the meeting</u>. 我在會議期間做了一些記錄。

I lost my phone <u>during the concert.</u>
= <u>During the concert</u>, I lost my phone.
我在演唱會期間遺失了手機。

I took notes for 2 hours straight.

我在兩小時內一直在做筆記。

I talked to my boss for half an hour to explain why I was
late.

為了解釋我遲到的原因，我跟老闆談了 30 分鐘。

I took several notes while I attended the meeting.
= I took several notes while attending the meeting.

我在參加會議的期間做了一些筆記。

✗ I met my recruiter during networking at a tech conference.
○ I met my recruiter while networking at a tech conference.
○ I met my recruiter during a networking event at a tech
conference.

我在一次科技會議的社交活動中，認識了我的招聘人員。

✗ He kept interrupting me while my presentation.
○ He kept interrupting me during my presentation.
○ He kept interrupting me while I gave my presentation.

他在我進行簡報的時候一直打斷我。

應用

I have a hard time paying attention during really long
business meetings. I want to improve this, so I started
taking notes while everyone else talks because this forces
me to pay closer attention.

我很難在長時間的商務會議上集中精神。為了改進這一點，我開始在別人說
話的時候做筆記，這樣子能讓我更集中注意力。

12 another / other / the other

We're planning to hire other HR manager.

My company wants to gain many another client in Korea this year.

Can you please send this package to other office?

許多人經常分不清楚 another、other 和 the other 的區別。

another 可以照字面上的意思,想成是 a(n)+ other。a(n) 是用於不限定單數名詞的冠詞,因此 another 必須用在不限定單數名詞的前面。

We opened another office last week.
我們上週設立了另一個辦公室。

Let's have another meeting next week.
我們下週再開一個會吧。

另一方面,other 則用於下列情形。

1. other + 複數名詞

Our cloud service does a lot more than just organize your files. There are tons of other useful features.

我們的雲端服務不僅能幫你整理檔案，還提供其他許多有用的功能。

This is my only meeting. I don't have any other meetings today.

這是我唯一的會議。我今天沒有其他會議行程。

2. the other + 限定的單／複數名詞（可用其他限定詞代替 the）

I'll ask the other members of my team about this.

我會向其他組員詢問這件事。

We released two new products this year. Our first product didn't sell well, but our other product was really popular.

我們今年推出兩款新產品。雖然第一款新產品銷售不佳，但另一款頗受歡迎。

讓我們重新檢視下面的句子。從前後文來看，是要招聘一位經理，所以應該說 another HR manager 才對。

✕　　We're planning to hire ~~other~~ HR manager.

○　　We're planning to hire another HR manager.

我們計劃再招聘一名人資經理。

因為是想要吸引很多（many）客戶，所以應該說 many other clients。

✕　　My company wants to gain many ~~another~~ client in Korea this year.

○ **My company wants to gain many other clients in Korea this year.**
我們公司今年想在韓國吸引更多其他的客戶。

提到限定的名詞時，一定要加限定詞。也就是要採用「限定詞 + other + 限定的名詞」的句型。當我們提到公司內的其他辦公室的時候，可以用下列限定詞來表示。

✕ **Can you please send this package to ~~other~~ office?**
○ **Can you please send this package to the other office?**
○ **Can you please send this package to our other office?**
能否請你將這個包裹送到另一個辦公室？

應用

Our main projector broke, so you'll need to use the other projector for the sales meeting. I think it's in the supply closet.
主投影機故障了，所以你必須用另一台投影機進行銷售會議。我想它應該在儲物櫃裡。

Our previous business consultant didn't have a lot of industry knowledge, so we're currently looking for another consultant to help our startup expand.
我們之前的商業顧問缺乏業界知識，現在我們正在尋找另一位顧問來幫助我們新創公司擴張。

13 besides / except

There are three other women on the team except Michelle.

有時候我們會不知道該如何使用 besides 和 except。

首先，讓我們來看一下它們各自的定義。兩者最大的不同在於 besides 有「包含、補充」的意思，而 except 則有「除外」的意思。

besides prep. adv. in addition to, as well 而且、還有
except prep. not including 不包括～、除外

> **I talked to everyone on the team except for John.**
> 除了 John 之外，我已經告訴所有組員了。
>
> **Besides John, I also talked to Sam and Jade.**
> 不只 John，我還告訴了 Sam 和 Jade。

不過，except 和 besides 有時候也會用來表示相同的意思，因此很容易混淆。

> **Besides Tim, everyone showed up to the meeting.**
> =
> **Everyone showed up to the meeting except for Tim.**

上面的例句可以解讀為「除了 Tim，所有人都參加了會議。」總而言之，besides 原則上是「包含」的意思，但有時候也會像 except 一樣，解讀為「除外」的意思，所以需要特別留意。besides 的意思必須通過掌握前後文來區分，通常如果句子裡面出現 too、also 的話，此時 besides 就是「包含（in addition to）」的意思。

Besides Korea, I've also been to Vietnam, China, and Japan.
不只韓國，我還去過越南、中國和日本。

相反的，如果句子裡面出現 every、each、all、the entire 的話，此時的 besides 大部分都是作「除外（except for）」的意思。

I've been to every country in Asia besides Korea.
我去過亞洲的所有國家，除了韓國。

在下面的句子裡，使用 besides 來表達除了 Michelle 之外，還有 3 名女性的意思就行了。

✗　　**There are three other women on the team except Michelle.**

○　　**There are three other women on the team besides Michelle.**
除了 Michelle 之外，那一組還有另外三名女性成員。

> 應用
>
> **We work with many other companies besides Pentatonix.**
> 除了 Pentatonix 之外，我們也跟很多其他公司有業務往來。

All of our business partners are based in Korea except for Lighthouse Communications. It's based in the US.

除了 Lighthouse Communications 之外，我們所有的商業合作夥伴都在韓國。Lighthouse Communications 位於美國。

下面是針對前面介紹過的 with Error 部分，修正錯誤用法後的內容，你可以在劃底線的部分確認正確的表達方式。

Michelle	It's great to meet you, Jiwon. We're very happy to have you on our team. 智媛，很高興見到你。很開心你能加入我們的團隊。
智媛	It's great meeting you too! I'm really excited to join the team. I've been looking forward to this all week. 我也很高興見到你。非常開心能加入這個團隊。我期待了一整週。
Michelle	This morning I thought I could introduce you to the team and explain some of our policies around the office. Then in the afternoon I wanna get you started contacting some of our customers. 今天早上我想向銷售組介紹智媛，並且稍微說明一下公司政策。然後下午我想讓你開始聯繫我們的顧客。
智媛	Sounds great! 聽起來很不錯！
Michelle	Most of the sales team are actually in client meetings right now, but they should be finished in about an hour. I'll show you your desk ... 銷售組大部分的人目前正在與客戶開會，但大約一小時就會結束了。我帶你去看你的辦公桌…… (walks into desk area) （走向辦公桌的地方）

Okay, here's where you'll be. You're sharing a cubicle with Sanghyeon Kim. He's a really experienced salesman and is head of the sales team. He's been working with us for almost three years and will be happy to help you out if you have any questions.

好，這裡就是你以後辦公的地方。你和金尚賢共用一個隔間。尚賢是經驗豐富的銷售員，也是銷售組的主管。他已經和我們一起共事了近 3 年的時間，如果你有任何問題，他會很樂意幫助你。

智媛　Great! At my previous job I had to share a cubicle with another coworker but it was half this size. I'm glad I'll have more space to work!

太好了！在我之前的公司，我必須和另一位同事共用一個隔間，但它只有這裡的一半大。能擁有更寬敞的工作空間真是太好了！

Michelle　Yeah, I really like how open and spacious our office is. We remodeled it last year and this new layout is so much better. It's a lot different from before!

是，我真的很喜歡我們辦公室開放又寬敞的空間。我們去年改造了辦公室，新的布局好多了。變得跟以前截然不同！

Here let's get you logged in and registered on the computer. Do you have your company ID yet?

現在試著登入電腦並註冊帳號。你拿到你的員工識別證了嗎？

智媛　Yep, got it right here.

拿到了，在這裡。

Michelle　Okay, enter your employee email and 10-digit employee ID number here to log in to the company portal.

好，在這裡輸入你的員工信箱和 10 位數的員工識別證號碼，然後登入公司入口網站。

The first thing to do at the start of each shift is to check our sales team alerts by clicking here. It usually doesn't take that long, so if you get to the office at 8:00 a.m. you should be able to finish by around 8:10. I usually send a short sales team agenda so whatever you do after that will depend on the agenda for the day. And... Sanghyeon, you're back already? I thought you would be in meetings until 10:00.

每一次輪班時，你必須做的第一件事是點擊這裡，確認銷售組的提醒事項。這通常不會花很久的時間，如果你在早上 8 點進公司，大概 8 點 10 分左右就能完成了。通常我會將銷售組的大概待辦事項寄給你們，所以之後該做什麼事就取決於當天的日程。尚賢，你這麼快就回來了？我以為你要開會開到 10 點。

尚賢　Yeah, the purchasing team from Apex Apparel actually contacted me a few weeks ago. They read about us on the Internet and were really interested in our AI marketing systems, so it was a really easy sell. They actually placed their first purchase order during the meeting. We signed a one-year contract that will start in two weeks.

對，其實 Apex Apparel 採購組幾週前就聯絡我了。他們在網路上看到我們的資料，並對 AI 行銷系統表現出極大的興趣，所以交易過程非常順利。事實上，他們在開會時就下了第一筆採購訂單，並且簽訂了自兩週後開始，為期一年的合約。

Michelle　Great! I've heard that their culture is pretty similar to ours so they should be a really good long-term client. I'm glad we can get that partnership started. By the way, this is Jiwon, your new cubicle mate.

太好了！我聽說他們的公司文化跟我們很像，應該會是很好的長期客戶。我很高興能跟他們建立合作關係。另外，這位是要和你共用隔間的智媛。

尚賢 Hey Jiwon, I heard really good things about you. Welcome to the team.
智媛，你好。我聽說了很多關於你的事。歡迎你加入我們。

智媛 Yeah, it's great meeting you, too. I'm excited to be here.
是，我也很高興認識你。能來到這裡我很開心。

Michelle Besides Sanghyeon there are 3 other members on your sales team. They should be back in about 45 minutes. Sanghyeon, can you explain a little more about the company portal?
除了尚賢之外，銷售組還有其他 3 名成員。他們大約 45 分鐘後會回來。尚賢，能請你幫忙介紹一下公司的入口網站嗎？

尚賢 Yeah, no problem.
好，當然可以。

Michelle Perfect, I'll leave you to it then. Jiwon, if you have other questions, feel free to send me a quick Hangouts message. Again, it was great meeting you.
太好了。那就交給你囉。智媛，如果你有任何問題，隨時傳 Hangouts 訊息給我。讓我再說一次，很高興認識你。

智媛 Great meeting you, too. Thank you!
我也很高興認識你。謝謝你！

Chapter 3

近似表達的誤用 1

Word Set Mistakes 1

1   take care of / care for / care about

2   wish / hope

3   similar / same

4   price / cost / fee

5   revenue / profit

6   convenient / comfortable

7   economy / finance

8   company / office / industry

9   believe / believe in / trust

以下的敘述中包含錯誤的用法。請閱讀一遍，並試著找出不自然的表達方式。在各章節的最後會提供修正後的正確表達。

智媛正在向潛在客戶 Green Light Electronics(GLE) 進行銷售簡報。她在介紹高度發展的人工智慧系統 Synthesis Marketing AI，這套人工智慧系統可以監控公司網路廣告活動與行銷預算，從而創造最佳的行銷投資報酬率。

Jiwon　　Alright, it's great to be with you all today. I'm looking forward to sharing how Synthesis can help your business grow.

Today I thought I could tell you a little more about what Synthesis is and how it works, then share a few examples of other Korean businesses that have really benefited from using Synthesis. It's a pretty short agenda, so I think we should be finished within 30 or 40 minutes. Does anyone have any questions before we begin?

GLE　　Nope.

Jiwon　　Okay great, so first let me explain a little more about what Synthesis is and why we believe in it will change online marketing forever. We know how important data analytics is in today's business world, and how much companies care of really understanding their target customers. We developed Synthesis to make effective advertising as easy and comfortable as possible. Synthesis is an AI system that can monitor and analyze the performance of all your online marketing campaigns.

Synthesis tracks the performance of every online advertisement your company is running. Synthesis uses this data to find out not only which ads are most effective, but also the times when and websites where your ads are performing best. Synthesis can then actually change when and where your ads are shown to maximize your advertising ROI.

Not only that, but Synthesis can analyze historical data to predict how you should change your advertising strategies in the future. There are some pretty same AI products on the market right now, but none of them have this key feature. The advices Synthesis gives has increased sales profit by 15% for our ten largest clients YOY, and actually reduced advertising prices by 27%.

One thing that makes Synthesis very comfortable to use is that you can access it anywhere you have an Internet connection. Whether you're at the company or working from home. Synthesis also comes with a group chat feature so your marketers will be able to conversation with each other based on what's happening in Synthesis. Before moving on, does anyone have any questions?

GLE   Yes, does Synthesis only track advertisements in Korea? Or can it track advertisements in other countries as well?

Jiwon   Great question. Synthesis can monitor your advertisements anywhere in the world. Wherever your country does business, Synthesis can help your ads perform better and help your company make more money.

GLE   That's great to hear. Right now we have many European business partners and advertise a lot in France, Germany and Switzerland. We wish to expand to the UK and Spain by the end of the year.

Jiwon   Perfect, we have a few other clients advertising in Europe and using Synthesis has not only improved their company economy, but saved them a lot of time as well.

GLE   Excellent. How much is the fee for using Synthesis?

Jiwon   It will really depend on your advertising budget, how many team members you have, and how much data your plan on using. Once we have all that information, we'll email you a quote.
I'd be happy to have a conversation with a member of your marketing team to discuss the details as well.

GLE   That would be great. Would you be available to meet with one of our marketers sometime next week?

Jiwon   Sure! Let me check my schedule ... how about next Thursday afternoon at 2 p.m.?

GLE   That sounds great. I'll communicate this with the marketing team and someone from that department will email you later this week.

Jiwon   Perfect! Looking forward to that. Thank you for your time! I wish you have a great rest of your day.

1 take care of / care for / care about

I am very close to my coworkers. I care of them a lot.

很多人並不清楚 take care of、care for 和 care about 的區別。

care about 是認為某事物很重要、有價值。對象可以是人,也可以是意見或感受。

> **I really care about my customers.**
> 我非常重視我的顧客。
> **I don't care about other people's opinions.**
> 我不在意別人的想法。

take care of 和 care for 基本上是同樣的意思,指的是照顧某人,或細心維護以使某物維持良好的狀態。

> **If you take care of this product, it will work for years.**
> 如果你好好維護,這個產品可以使用好幾年。

take care of 也有「解決困境或問題」的含義,此時它可以換用 handle、deal with、manage 來表達。不過,比起前面提到可以和 care for 替換使用的「維護」之意,「解決困境或問題」這個含義較少使用。

The store manager asked if I could take care of the angry customers at the customer service desk.

店經理問我能否在顧客服務台應付那些生氣的顧客。

最常見的錯誤是在必須使用 care about 的情況下，使用 take care of 或 care of。take care of / care for 是指照顧好某人或某種情況，使之維持良好狀態；care about 則是指關注並珍惜重要、有價值的事物。接著讓我們試著修改下面的句子。

✗　　I am very close to my coworkers. I care of them a lot.

○　　I am very close to my coworkers. I care about them a lot.

　　我和同事們的關係很好。我非常重視他們。

應用

Our store manager really cares about having very professional-looking displays in our stores. We make sure we take good care of all our product displays so they look clean and attractive to our customers.

我們店經理非常重視店內陳列展示的專業性。因此我們會確保商品陳列的良善，以讓顧客覺得商品看起來整潔又吸引人。

2 wish / hope

We're planning to launch our second Android application next week. I wish it gets lots of downloads.

wish 和 hope 都表示「期望、希望」的意思，但所期盼的對象有所不同。

一般來說，動詞 wish 用於實現可能性較低的事情。

I wish I could help you, but I'm stuck at work.
我想幫你，但我有很多工作要做。
I wish I had studied harder when I was in college.
真希望我大學時學習再認真一點。

另一方面，hope 則用於表達對未來的期盼。

I have a big presentation next week. I really hope it goes well!
下週我有個重要的簡報。我真心希望一切順利！

總結來說，wish 是用於因事與願違而感到惋惜，或是想表達對過去的遺憾時；hope 則是用來表示未來要實現的計劃、目標、希望等。

讓我們重新檢視下面這個句子。這裡說希望會有很多人下載，是一種對未來的期盼，因此最好使用 hope，而非 wish。

✕　　We're actually planning to launch our second Android application next week. I ~~wish~~ it gets lots of downloads.

○　　We're actually planning to launch our second Android application next week. I hope it gets lots of downloads.
　　　我們計劃在下週推出第二款 Android 應用程式。希望會有很多人下載。

> 應用
>
> I really wish I had studied coding when I was in college because that's such a useful skill in today's business world. I'm actually taking classes at a programming academy now, so I hope I can gain the skills to enter that industry in the future.
>
> 我真希望大學時學過怎麼寫程式。因為它是近來在業界非常有用的技能。我最近在程式補習班上課，希望未來能掌握這項技術並進入這個行業。

3 similar / same

（正在談論工作經歷）

I started out as a junior web developer. I'm a senior developer now, but my overall job duties are still pretty same.

有些人會在應該使用 similar 的情況下，卻用了 same。

the same 代表 100% 相同。而 similar 則用來表示雖然非常類似，但仍存在差異的情況。

I take the same subway route to work every morning.
我每天早上搭相同的地鐵路線去上班。
This project should be pretty similar to what we did last year.
這個項目應該跟我們去年做過的非常相似。

在幾乎沒有差別的情況下，可以用 almost the same 或 very similar 來表達。

=　　My current job is almost the same as my previous job.
My current job is very similar to my previous job.
我現在的工作跟之前的工作差不多。

作為參考，由於 same 是 100% 相同的意思，因此不能使用 more same、less same 等說法。也不能用 pretty same、very same 等說法。這是因為除了一樣和不一樣這兩種情形之外，不可能有第三種情形。

常見的錯誤是將與 similar 一起使用的 very / more / pretty 等詞，與 same 一起使用。讓我們重新檢視下面這個句子。

✗　　I started out as a junior web developer. I'm a senior developer now, but my overall job duties are still pretty same.

○　　I started out as a junior web developer. I'm a senior developer now, but my overall job duties are still pretty similar.

我一開始是初級網站開發人員。現在是資深網站開發人員，但整體上做的工作是差不多的。

應用

There are a lot of very similar products in the fashion industry. The other day, I saw two jackets from different retailers that were almost the exact same. That's why we hired new designers. We really want our brand to be different and unique.

在時尚產業中有許多非常相似的產品。前幾天，我在不同的商店裡看到兩件幾乎一模一樣的夾克。所以我們聘請了幾位新的設計師。我們希望自己的品牌是獨特且與眾不同的。

4 price / cost / fee

> Our latest desktop computers' fee is $1,000 each.
> However, if you're interested in buying computers
> for your entire office, we can sell you a set of 20
> computers for $15,000. This is really an unbeatable
> cost for this high-quality of a product. Plus, if you
> want, we can take care of shipping and install all the
> computers in your office for you for an additional
> price of $500.

→ price、cost、fee 都是跟金錢有關的單字，但它們有明顯的區別。

price

n. the amount of money required as payment for something 支付某物所需的金額

v. to decide the price of an item 決定商品的價格

The price of our newest AI smart speaker is $350.
本公司最新型 AI 智慧音箱的售價為 350 美元。

We priced our newest AI smart speaker at $350.
本公司將最新型 AI 智慧音箱的價格定為 350 美元。

cost

n. the expense incurred for creating a product or operating a business
製造產品或商務經營的成本

v. 1. has a price of 價格為～

    2. (of a product / service) to require a specific amount of payment
       to be purchased 費用為～

> **Our company is trying to lower production costs so we can increase profits.**
> 我們公司嘗試透過節省成本來提高收益。
>
> **These jeans cost $45.**
> 這件牛仔褲要 45 美元。
>
> **These shoes cost $30 to make.**
> 這雙鞋子的製作成本是 30 美元。

fee

n. a required payment to a person in exchange for a service / advice
作為提供服務 / 諮詢而需收取的費用

> **The tutor charges a fee of $40 per hour.**
> 那個家教每小時收取 40 美元的費用。

另外，fee 也用來表示小額的額外費用。例如，運費叫作 shipping fee，停車費叫作 parking fee，信用卡滯納金叫作 late fee。

讓我們重新檢視下面這段話。unbeatable price 是「最低價」的意思。另外，最後一句話提到如果需要宅配和安裝，要額外支付 500 美元的費用，這裡最好用 fee 比較恰當。

✕   **Our latest desktop computers' fee is $1,000 each.**

However, if you're interested in buying computers for your entire office, we can sell you a set of 20 computers for $15,000. This is really an unbeatable **cost** for this high-quality of a product. Plus, if you want, we can take care of shipping and install all the computers in your office for you for an additional **price** of $500.

○ **Our latest desktop** computers only cost **$1,000 each.** However, if you're interested in buying computers for your entire office, we can sell you a set of 20 computers for $15,000. This is really an unbeatable price for this high-quality of a product. Plus, if you want, we can take care of shipping and install all the computers in your office for you for an additional fee of $500.

我們最新的桌上型電腦單價為 1,000 美元。但是，如果您正在考慮採購公司用的電腦，我們可以用 20 台 15,000 美元的價格出售。這是這種高規格產品可提供的最低價格。此外，如果額外支付 500 美元，我們會將產品送到您的公司並協助安裝。

應用

Right now our latest computer model costs only 1.2 million won. If you order online, there will also be a 30,000 shipping fee. They won't be at this price for long, so I definitely recommend buying now if you're interested in this model.

目前我們最新款的電腦只要 120 萬韓元。若您在網路上訂購，將加收 3 萬韓元的運費。這個優惠價格不會持續太久，因此若您對此款感興趣，我強烈建議您立即購買。

5 revenue / profit

My company is really trying to reduce expenses this quarter so we can maximize revenue.

儘管 revenue 和 profit 是不同的概念，但有時候會被混用並解釋為「利潤」。

revenue n. the money earned/generated from something 從某事物中賺來的錢

profit n. the amount of money earned after subtracting all expenses from revenue 從收入中扣除所有花費後的金額

revenue - expenses = profit

根據上述公式，從收入（revenue）中扣除人力成本、租金等費用（expense）後，就剩下收益（profit）了。revenue 可以用來指整個公司的銷售額，也可以用來指銷售特定產品或服務所帶來的收益。

Samsung generated 100 billion dollars in revenue last year.
三星去年的銷售額達到 1,000 億美元。

My company's newest app is generating around $25,000 in sales revenue each month.
我們公司最新的應用程式每個月可創造約 25,000 美元的收入。

如同上面的例句，revenue 通常會與動詞 generate 一起使用，結構為「主詞 generate + 金額 + in revenue.」。而 profit 可以分為 gross profit（毛利）和 net profit（淨利）兩種。

total revenue（總銷售額）– cost of goods sold（銷售成本）
= gross profit（毛利）
total revenue（總銷售額）– all expenses（所有費用）
= net profit / income（淨利）

revenue 一向用金額表示，但 profit 可以用金額或總收益的百分比來表示。又稱為 profit margin（淨利率）。

The company generated $1 million in revenue and $100K in profit last month. They achieved a 10% net profit margin.
該公司上個月的銷售額為 100 萬美元，利潤為 10 萬美元。達到 10% 的淨利率。

在下面的句子裡，是要藉由縮減 expense 使 profit 最大化，所以應該改成 profit 才對。

✗   My company is really trying to reduce expenses this quarter so we can maximize revenue.

○   My company is really trying to reduce expenses this quarter so we can maximize profit.
我們公司這一季正在努力縮減成本以實現利潤最大化。

（經理在向團隊說明公司的財務狀況）

Alright everyone, now let's talk about our finances for this quarter. Our team generated $2.0 million in revenue, which was a 9% increase from this quarter last year. Our gross profit was 70%, which is great because I know we've been trying to reduce our production costs. However, because of all our operating expenses, net profit is actually slightly down from last year. We only earned about $150,000 in net income. Next quarter, let's make it our main objective to increase net income. I think $200,000 and at least 8% of total revenue are realistic goals for us.

各位，現在讓我們來談談本季度的財務狀況。我們團隊創造了兩百萬美元的銷售額，比去年同期增長了 9%。毛利為 70%，這個數字很棒，因為我知道我們為了降低生產成本做了很多努力。然而，因為經營成本導致淨利比去年小幅縮減，只賺了大約 15 萬美元。我們團隊下一季度的主要目標是提高淨利。我認為 20 萬美元，也就是相當於總收入 8% 的金額是可能實現的目標。

6 convenient / comfortable

Hello team,

If you would like to continue working from home, please message me whenever it is comfortable for you. If you feel more convenient returning to the office, we will open our offices back up next month. Please email me if you have any questions.

convenient 和 comfortable 乍看之下意思差不多，但其實用法有所區別。

1. convenient 在商務情境中，通常作以下兩種意義。

convenient　　adj. fitting well with your schedule, needs, or plans 符合行程安排、需求或計劃的

convenient　　adj. involving little / less time and effort 省時省力的

> I need to schedule our monthly meeting. When is a convenient time for us to meet?
> 我要安排月例會的時間，什麼時候方便呢？

> I used to walk to work, but now I take the bus because it's much more convenient.
> 我之前都是走路上班，現在搭公車比較方便，所以就改成搭公車了。

作為參考，at your earliest convenience 是一種禮貌的表達方式，意思是「盡快」，在寫電子郵件時很有用。

> **Please send the payment information at your earliest convenience.** 請盡快寄出您的付款資訊。

2. comfortable 是在身體或精神上感到舒適時使用的。另外，也可用來形容整體的氣氛（atmosphere）。

comfortable　　adj. providing physical relaxation and feeling good on your body / not causing any pain 身體上舒適的、不累的

comfortable　　adj. not causing stress or fear in your mind 精神上沒有壓力或沒有不安的

> **I wish our office chairs were more comfortable.**
> 我希望辦公室的椅子能更舒服一點。
>
> **Our old boss was so demanding. Everyone was stressed all the time. I'm really glad he left, because the office environment is so much calmer and more comfortable now.**
> 我們之前的上司真的非常難搞，每個人都一直處於壓力之下。我很開心他離開了，因為辦公室的氣氛變得更加平靜，也更加自在了。

✕　　Hello team,
　　If you would like to continue working from home, please message me whenever it is comfortable for you. If you feel more convenient returning to the office, we will open our offices back up next month. Please email me if you have any questions.

○ Hello team,

If you would like to continue working from home, please message me whenever it is convenient for you. If you feel more comfortable returning to the office, we will open our offices back up next month. Please email me if you have any questions.

各位夥伴：

如果你想繼續居家上班，請在你方便的時間留言給我。如果你覺得來公司工作更方便，公司將於下個月重新開放。如果你有任何問題，請寄電子郵件給我。

應用

Hello team,

I hope you're all doing well. It seems like everyone is really enjoying working from home. After discussing this with the other managers, we've decided we will allow people to continue to do so. If you would like to continue working from home, please message me whenever is convenient for you. If you feel more comfortable returning to the office, we will open our offices back up next month. Please email me if you have any questions.

大家好：

希望各位一切安好。大家似乎都非常享受在家工作。對此，經過與其他主管商議後，我們決定延長遠距辦公的時間。有意繼續居家上班的人，請在你方便的時候寄電子郵件給我。另外，覺得在公司工作更自在的人，我們將於下個月重新開放公司。如果你有任何疑問，請寄電子郵件給我。

7 economy / finance

> The hurricane caused billions of dollars in damages and really hurt the country's finances.
>
> The company's economic situation isn't great. They haven't been profitable in over 3 years.
>
> → **economy 和 finance 都和金錢有關,但適用的語境不同。**

首先,我們先來看 finance 和 finances 的區別。

finance n. the study of how money is managed and the activities associated with managing money 金融學或與資金管理相關的活動

finances n. all of the money a person or company owns 資金、財政

I majored in corporate finance.
我主修公司金融學。

My first job was in my company's finance department.
我第一份工作是在我們公司的財務部門。

I'm writing a report about my company's finances.
我正在寫一份有關本公司財務狀況的報告。

與管理資金的規模大小無關，不管是個人、公司或政府等，都可以使用 finance 和 finances。不過，在提到地區、產業或整個國家時，一般不會用 finance。

economy n. all the wealth and resources of a country or region, especially related to the production and usage of goods and services
國家或地區的財富與資源，特別是與商品和服務的生產及運用有關

> **Korea's economy has grown significantly over the past 50 years.**
> 在過去 50 年，韓國經濟實現了高度成長。

finance 和 economy 最大的區別在於，finance 是用於個別的家庭、公司、政府和個人，而 economy 則是用於整個國家、整個產業和大區域。

讓我們重新檢視以下句子。既然影響了整個國家，就應該使用 economy，而非 finances。

✗ **The hurricane caused billions of dollars in damages and really hurt the country's finances.**

○ **The hurricane caused billions of dollars in damages and really hurt the country's economy.**
颶風造成數十億美元的損失，並給國家經濟帶來嚴重損害。

✗ **The company's economic situation isn't great. They haven't been profitable in over 3 years.**

○ **The company's financial situation isn't great. They haven't been profitable in over 3 years.**
公司的財務狀況不佳。已經超過 3 年沒有盈餘了。

（科技公司 Versacore 寄給投資者的季度財務報告）

As you know, the economy was not in a good place for most of this year. Many other companies in our industry incurred a loss this quarter. However, despite the economic downturn, Versacore had a very strong quarter. Financially, our profits are up 14% compared to this time last year. We also opened three new offices: two new domestic offices and one foreign office in Taiwan.

正如各位所知，今年的經濟狀況普遍不好。同業的許多其他公司在本季度都出現了虧損。然而，儘管經濟不景氣，Versacore 在木季度仍然表現強勁。在財務方面，利潤比去年同期增長了 14%。我們也開設了三個新的辦事處，兩個在國內，一個是在臺灣的海外辦事處。

8 company / office / industry

> Even though it's Saturday, I have to go to my company today.

↳ 很多時候，我們只知道 company 是公司，公司裡的辦公室是 office，產業是 industry，但各個單字其實有著細微語感差異。

company　n. a business organization that makes or sells goods or services 販售商品或服務的單一事業體

> **Veratech is one of the largest tech companies.**
> Veratech 是最大的科技公司之一。

company 之中規模特別大的公司稱為 corporation（企業、法人）。

office　n. a room or set of rooms used as a place for business or professional work 用於處理業務的辦公室

你可以把 office 想成辦公室，也就是上班族工作的場所。office 可以是一整棟建築，也可以是建築物裡的空間。

> **Veratech has offices all over the world.**
> Veratech 在世界各地都設有辦事處。

industry n. a specific group of similar businesses or a specific part / section of the economy 相似企業的特定群體或經濟的特定領域

industry 通常會在提及特定產業群時使用。教育產業叫作 education industry，人工智慧產業叫作 artificial intelligence industry。

> **Veratech is a leader in the electronics industry.**
> Veratech 是電子產業的領頭羊。

讓我們重新檢視下面的句子。company 指的是公司 / 企業本身，而非地點。很多人會説錯，用「I go to my company.」來表示要去上班的意思，但 company 並不是一個地點，所以應該改用 go to my office 或 go to work 來表達。

✗　**Even though it's Saturday, I have to go to my company today.**

○　**Even though it's Saturday, I have to go to my office today.**

○　**Even though it's Saturday, I have to go to work today.**
　　雖然今天是週六，但我還是得去上班。

（科技新創公司的 CEO 在說明公司的願景）

Our company has been in operation for three years now. We've grown a lot during that time. We went from two friends working together in our apartments to having 80 employees and 9 offices all over the city. Our vision for the next 10 years is to continue our growth, expand into new domestic and international markets, and become a major company in the tech industry.

我們公司至今已營運 3 年，並且大幅成長。我們從兩個夥伴一起在公寓裡工作，發展到在這座城市擁有 80 名員工和 9 處辦公室。我們公司未來 10 年的願景是持續成長，開拓新的海內外市場，成為科技領域的重要企業。

9 believe / believe in / trust

> My boss always supports me and is honest with me.
> I believe him a lot.
> Good sales people have to believe the products
> they're selling.

> believe、believe in 和 trust 這三種表達方式分別用於不同的
> 情況。

believe v. to accept or think that something is true 接受或認為某件事為事實

> **My colleague missed our virtual meeting earlier today. He said it was because his computer broke down, but I don't believe him. I think he just forgot about the meeting.**
> 我同事今天早上錯過了一場虛擬會議。他說因為他的電腦壞了,但我不相信他的話。我認為他只是忘記了。

trust v. to have faith in the truth, reliability, and accuracy of someone or something 相信人 / 事物的真實性、可靠性和準確性

Every product I've ever bought from them has been excellent, so I really <u>trust</u> this brand.

我購買過所有來自這家的產品都很棒,所以我很信任這個品牌。

believe 是相信特定資訊為事實。如果 believe 的對象是人,就代表相信那個人說的話是事實。另一方面,trust 的情感色彩比較強烈。無論相信的對象是事物或人,都表示相信那個對象的誠實與真實性。

在下面的句子裡,要表達的意思是因為上司是個真誠的人而信任他,所以這裡應該要用 trust。

✗	My boss always supports me and is honest with me. I ~~believe~~ him a lot.
○	My boss always supports me and is honest with me. I trust him a lot.

我的上司總是支持我,對我真誠以待,所以我非常信任他。

believe in

1. to think something is real or actually exists 認為某種事物是真的或實際存在的

I don't <u>believe in</u> ghosts.

我不相信有鬼。

2. to support or agree with something 支持或同意某事

I <u>believe in</u> my company's core values.

我支持公司的核心價值。

3. to think someone or something will be great / successful and have confidence in them / it 對某事 / 某人成功的可能性有信心

> （對面臨重要面試的朋友說）
> I believe in you. You're going to do great!
> 我相信你。你一定會表現得很好！

讓我們再重新檢視下面這句話。這裡要表達的是銷售員必須對自己賣的產品有信心，所以應該要用 believe in 才對。

✗   Good salespeople have to ~~believe~~ the products they're selling.

○   Good salespeople have to believe in the products they're selling.
好的銷售員必須對自己販賣的產品有信心。

應用

Believe me, after just a few uses you'll know how effective our product is. Our brand believes in producing the highest-quality products possible, so you can trust that anything you purchase from us will be incredibly well made.
相信我，只要用過幾次，您就會知道我們的產品有多有效。我們品牌的信念是生產最高品質的產品，所以您可以相信從我們這裡購買的產品都是品質優良的。

下面是針對前面介紹過的 with Error 部分，修正錯誤用法後的內容，你可以在劃底線的部分確認正確的表達方式。

智媛   Alright, it's great to be with you all today. I'm looking forward to sharing how Synthesis can help your business grow.
很高興今天能與各位共聚一堂。我想和各位分享 Synthesis 如何能夠幫助你們拓展業務。

Today I thought I could tell you a little more about what Synthesis is and how it works, then share a few examples of other Korean businesses that have really benefited from using Synthesis. It's a pretty short agenda, so I think we should be finished within 30 or 40 minutes. Does anyone have any questions before we begin?
今天我將向各位介紹 Synthesis 系統及其運作原理，再以一些其他韓國企業的實際案例，幫助各位了解採用 Synthesis 系統可以獲得的許多好處。由於議程很簡短，我想大約能在 30 到 40 分鐘內結束。在開始之前，各位有什麼疑問嗎？

GLE   Nope.
沒有。

智媛   Okay great, so first let me explain a little more about what Synthesis is and why we believe it will change online marketing forever. We know how important data analytics is in today's business world, and how much companies care about really understanding their target customers. We developed Synthesis to make effective advertising as easy and convenient as possible. Synthesis is an AI system that can monitor and analyze the performance of all your online marketing campaigns.

好。首先，讓我稍微解釋一下 Synthesis 是什麼，以及為什麼我們認為它會徹底改變網路行銷。我們都知道數據分析在現今商務世界中的重要性，以及企業對於了解目標客群有多在乎。為了盡可能簡單、方便地做出有效的廣告，我們開發出 Synthesis 系統。Synthesis 是一套能監控並分析所有網路行銷活動成果的 AI 系統。

Synthesis tracks the performance of every online advertisement your company is running. Synthesis uses this data to find out not only which ads are most effective, but also the times when and websites where your ads are performing best. Synthesis can then actually change when and where your ads are shown to maximize your advertising ROI.

Synthesis 會追蹤貴公司所有正在進行的網路廣告表現。利用這些數據，Synthesis 不僅能確定哪些廣告是最有效的，還能知道效果最好的時段是什麼時候，以及在哪些網站的表現比較好。接著，Synthesis 可以實際更改廣告曝光的時間和地點，最大化你的廣告 ROI（投資報酬率）。

Not only that, but Synthesis can analyze historical data to predict how you should change your advertising strategies in the future. There are some pretty similar AI products on the market right now, but none of them have this key feature. The advice Synthesis gives has increased sales revenue by 15% for our ten largest clients YOY, and actually reduced advertising costs by 27%.

不僅如此，Synthesis 還能透過分析歷史數據，預測未來應該如何改變你的廣告策略。雖然目前市面上有幾款類似的 AI 產品，但它們都不具備這種核心功能。根據 Synthesis 的建議，已經幫助我們的前十大客戶營收年增 15%（YOY, Year-Over-Year, 年增率），而且廣告成本實際減少了 27%。

One thing that makes Synthesis very <u>convenient</u> to use is that you can access it anywhere you have an Internet connection. Whether you're at the <u>office</u> or working from home. Synthesis also comes with a group chat feature so your marketers will be able to communicate with each other based on what's happening in Synthesis. Before moving on, does anyone have any questions?

Synthesis 非常便利的一點在於，你可以在任何有網路的地方連上 Synthesis 系統。不管你是在公司或在家裡工作都無所謂。Synthesis 也提供群組聊天的功能，所以行銷人員可以根據 Synthesis 的內容進行交流。在進入下一個部分之前，請問各位有任何問題嗎？

GLE

Yes, does Synthesis only track advertisements in Korea? Or can it track advertisements in other countries as well?

是的，我有問題。Synthesis 只能追蹤在韓國進行的廣告嗎？或者也能追蹤在其他國家進行的廣告呢？

智媛

Great question. Synthesis can monitor your advertisements anywhere in the world. Wherever your country does business, Synthesis can help your ads perform better and help your company make more money.

這個是好問題。Synthesis 可以從全球的任何地方監控你的廣告。無論你的公司位於何處，Synthesis 都可以幫你提升廣告效益並創造更多收益。

GLE | That's great to hear. Right now we have many European business partners and advertise a lot in France, Germany and Switzerland. We hope to expand to the UK and Spain by the end of the year.
這真是令人開心的消息。我們目前有許多歐洲的商業夥伴，所以在法國、德國和瑞士有很多廣告正在進行中。我們希望今年年底前可以擴展到英國和西班牙。

智媛 | Perfect, we have a few other clients advertising in Europe, and using Synthesis has not only improved their company finances but saved them a lot of time as well.
太好了，我們也有幾位客戶正在歐洲打廣告，使用 Synthesis 不僅幫助他們提高公司營收，也讓他們節省了很多時間。

GLE | Excellent. How much does it cost to use Synthesis?
太棒了。Synthesis 的費用是多少？

智媛 | It will really depend on your advertising budget, how many team members you have, and how much data your plan on using. Once we have all that information, we'll email you a quote. I'd be happy to have a conversation with a member of your marketing team to discuss the details as well.
這取決於你的廣告預算、團隊成員人數和計畫使用的數據等。在確認所有資料後，我們會用電子郵件將報價單寄給你。我也很樂意與你的行銷團隊成員討論相關細節。

GLE | That would be great. Would you be available to meet with one of our marketers sometime next week?
聽起來很不錯。下週你可以找個時間跟我們的行銷人員見面嗎？

智媛	Sure! Let me check my schedule ... how about next Thursday afternoon at 2 p.m.?
	當然可以！讓我確認一下我的行程。下週四下午 2 點可以嗎？

GLE	That sounds great. I'll communicate this with the marketing team and someone from that department will email you later this week.
	好。我會與行銷組討論這些內容，該部門的人會於這週寄電子郵件給你。

智媛	Perfect! Looking forward to that. Thank you for your time! I hope you have a great rest of your day.
	太好了！我很期待。感謝你抽出寶貴的時間！祝你有個愉快的一天。

Chapter 4

近似表達的誤用 2
Word Set Mistakes 2

1   fun / funny

2   hear / listen / understand

3   say / talk / tell / speak / discuss /
    debate

4   toilet / restroom / bathroom

5   trip / travel / tour / journey / vacation

6   remember / remind / memory /
    memorize

7   lend / loan / borrow

8   wage / salary / income / paycheck

9   complain / criticize / confront

以下的敘述中包含錯誤的用法。請閱讀一遍，並試著找出不自然的表達方式。在各章節的最後會提供修正後的正確表達。

下班後，智媛為了和新同事們拉近關係，和他們一起去吃晚餐和喝酒。尚賢與智媛先抵達了餐廳，他們的外國同事隨後也加入了。

Sanghyeon	I heard you met with Green Light Electronics earlier today. How'd your first sales presentation go?
Jiwon	I think it went well! They seemed interested in the product and I'll have a follow-up meeting with their marketer and purchase team to discuss about pricing.
Sanghyeon	Nice! I was really nervous before my first sales presentation. That's impressive that you already have a follow-up scheduled!
Jiwon	Thanks! Yeah, they talked that they want to expand into Europe and they really like that Synthesis works anywhere in the world.
Sanghyeon	Great. Sales presentations are one of my favorite parts of the job. It's really funny to connect with new businesses.
Jiwon	Yeah, I'm excited to keep learning and getting better. (two Americans walk up to the table)
Sanghyeon	Ah, hey guys, glad you could make it! This is Jiwon, the newest member of the sales team.
Mike	Hey, Jiwon, I'm Mike. Good to meet you.

Jiwon	Good to meet you too! Sorry, can you say your name again? I didn't listen you.
Mike	Yeah, it's louder in here than usual! We come here all the time and it's usually pretty quiet. I'm Mike.
Jiwon	Mike, got it.
Charlie	And I'm Charlie. Welcome to the team.
Jiwon	Thanks!
Charlie	Hey, Sanghyeon, do you know where the restroom is? I'll be right back.
Sanghyeon	Yeah, it's just around that corner. (Mike sits down at the table)
Sanghyeon	Mike just got back from a business travel in Singapore. How was the conference, Mike?
Mike	It was really interesting. They had a lot of really good marketing and sales ideas. I wrote most of what they said down so I remind it. I think we can lend some of these strategies and use them here. I'll share my notes during the team meeting next Monday. So how was your first week, Jiwon?

Jiwon	It was really good! I had my first sales presentation and am learning about how the portal system works. I think Ill really like it here … I already like it a lot better than my old job at Nexus!
Mike	Ahh yeah, I've heard mixed reviews about working there. Why did you leave?
Jiwon	Well, I don't mean to criticize, but the senior managers were really demanding and unreasonable. They set really high sales quotas that almost nobody could reach, then complained everyone who didn't meet the quotas and blamed us for everything. There was a lot of pressure on us and I really didn't like it.
Sanghyeon	That sounds rough. I'm glad you're here. We work hard obviously, but things are a lot more relaxed. Kangmin is a great boss.
Jiwon	Yeah, it seems that way from my perspective. That wasn't the worst part about Nexus though. They actually forced me to transfer to one of their new offices even though I really didn't want to. I had to move to a new neighborhood that was way more expensive, but they didn't increase my paycheck. Like 40% of my wage went to rent every month and I couldn't save any money.
Mike	Wow, that's ridiculous! Yeah, don't worry there won't be anything like that here.

(waiter walks up to the table)

Mike   Anyway, let's get some drinks ... first round is on me. Jiwon, you good with Budweiser?

Jiwon   Sure!

Sanghyeon   You're in Korea, still going Budweiser?

Mike   Ahh come on, it remembers me of home!
(pours drinks)

Sanghyeon   Cheers! To Jiwon's first week here!

1 fun / funny

> We really want to create a relaxed, funny shopping experience for our customers.
>
> I wish I could've attended the company workshop last weekend! I heard it was really funny.
>
> → **fun** 和 **funny** 經常令人感到混淆。

fun 是用在享受某事和對某事感興趣的時候,而 funny 則是用於某人在開玩笑或描述搞笑的情況時。有些事可以同時既 fun 又 funny,有些事雖然 fun 卻不 funny,還有一些情況是雖然不 fun 卻很 funny。總而言之,fun 涵蓋的情緒和狀況更廣泛,因此在使用上更為普遍。

根據上述內容,讓我們重新檢視下面的句子。購物通常是我們享受並感興趣的事,所以用 fun 來描述是很自然的。

✗   We really want to create a relaxed, ~~funny~~ shopping experience for our customers.

○   We really want to create a relaxed, fun shopping experience for our customers.
我們希望能為顧客提供舒適且愉快的購物經驗。

如果很多人在研討會中感受到整體愉快的氛圍，我們就可以說「It was fun.」。

✗   I wish I could've attended the company workshop last weekend! I heard it was really <u>funny</u>.

○   I wish I could've attended the company workshop last weekend! I heard it was really fun.

真希望我有參加上週末的公司研討會！聽說真的很有趣。

Ⓓetails

與 funny 意思相近的 hilarious（搞笑的）一詞，也是母語人士愛用的一種表達方式。他們也經常使用 crack (sb) up 這個說法，當有人說「You cracked me up.」時，它的意思是「你讓我捧腹大笑」。

┌─────┐
│ 應用 │
└─────┘

The office environment has become much friendlier and more <u>fun</u> since David took over as manager. People are more relax and feel less pressure. David is a really <u>fun</u> boss. He even throws a few jokes into his daily team emails that are actually really <u>funny</u>!

自從 David 接任經理後，辦公室的氣氛就變得更加友善和愉快。大家變得更放鬆，壓力也變小了。David 是個非常有趣的上司。他甚至會在每日寄給組員的電子郵件裡開一些玩笑，真的非常搞笑。

2 hear / listen / understand

（當有人說話而你聽不懂的時候）
Sorry, I didn't hear what you said.

（在 Zoom 會議中連線狀態不佳）
Can you say that again? The connection was bad so I couldn't listen you.

→ hear 和 listen 適用於不同的情況。

首先，讓我們來看一下各單字的定義。

hear   v. to notice or receive a sound 察覺或聽到聲音
listen   v. to pay attention to a sound 仔細聆聽聲音
understand v. to hear a sound and know what it means 聽到聲音並了解其含義

要表達集中注意力聽某個聲音的時候，用 listen 會比較自然；如果僅僅是聽到聲音，就應該使用 hear。

Can you turn the microphone volume up? The people in the back can't hear what the speaker is saying.
可以請你將麥克風的音量調大嗎？後面的人聽不清楚演講者在說什麼。

It's important to pay attention and listen closely to what your customers want.

留意並聽取顧客意見是很重要的。

有些人會在聽不懂說明的時候，說「I didn't hear.」或「I didn't listen.」。當我們無法理解的時候，應該要說「I didn't understand it.」、「I didn't get it.」，或是「I didn't catch it.」才對。

從下面的例句來看，是沒有理解對方所說的話，因此應該使用understand才對。

✕　　**Sorry, I didn't hear what you said.**

○　　**Sorry, I couldn't understand what you said.**

　　　對不起，我沒聽懂你說的話。

下面的情況是聽不清楚對方的聲音，所以可以改成「I couldn't hear you.」，或是改成「I couldn't understand you.」，用以表示因對方聲音中斷而無法理解對方在說什麼的意思。

✕　　**Can you say that again? The connection was bad so I couldn't listen you.**

○　　**Can you say that again? The connection was bad so I couldn't hear you.**

○　　**Can you say that again? The connection was bad so I couldn't understand you.**

　　　可以請你再說一次嗎？由於連線狀態不好，我聽不懂你在說什麼。

讓我們再多看幾個例句。

Can you speak louder? I can't hear you.

你可以講大聲一點嗎？我聽不清楚。（對方說話聲音太小時）

Working with Mike is really frustrating because he never listens.

Mike 完全不聽別人講話，跟他一起工作很辛苦。（不專心聽對方說話的情況）

Communicating with our Chinese colleagues is difficult, because I don't understand Chinese.

由於我不懂中文，所以很難跟我們公司的中國同事溝通。（聽不懂意思的情況）

Ｄetails

「Can you hear me?」這種說法是在詢問對方能否聽清楚。當我們說「Don't be late again. Do you hear me?」意思是「別再遲到了。聽懂了嗎？」

「Do you hear me?」可以用在表達強烈語氣的時候。另外，「Hear me out!」是當對方在我說話時插嘴，或是說出對方有可能誤解的話時，用來表示「（別打斷我的話）聽好了！」的意思。

┌─────┐
│ 應用 │
└─────┘

It's really important that we have a stable Wi-Fi connection because we have to video chat with our colleagues in Los Angeles almost every day. If the connection isn't good it's really hard to understand what they're saying even when you're listening really closely.

穩定的無線網路連線之所以重要，是因為我們幾乎每天都與在洛杉磯的同事進行視訊通話。如果連線品質不良，即使再怎麼仔細聆聽，也很難聽懂他們在說什麼。

3 say / talk / tell / speak / discuss / debate

（跟上司說同事 Jason 今天沒來上班）
I talked that Jason can't work today because he's sick.

（回答同事關於日後會議主題的提問）
We can discuss about this in more detail during the next meeting.

我們通常很難區分表示「說話」的 say、talk、tell、speak，以及表示「討論」的 discuss、debate 之間確切的語感差別。

say 用於直接引用某人的話，或間接傳達別人所說的話或意見時。

John said "Pizza is my favorite food. I really like it."
John 說：「披薩是我最喜歡的食物。我真的很喜歡。」（直接引用）

John said (that) he really likes pizza.
John 說他真的很喜歡披薩。（間接傳達意見）

talk 用於與某人對話（conversation）時，以 talk to、talk with 來呈現，兩者意思上並沒有太大的差別。談論某個主題時，可以用 talk about 來表示。

Peter talks too much during the workday. It's honestly pretty distracting.

Peter 在工作時話太多了，老實說有點讓人分心。

I talked to / with my boss yesterday.

我昨天跟我老闆談過了。

We talked about the new company policies.

我們談到了公司的新政策。

tell 的意思是「向～傳遞資訊」，所以接收資訊的對象總是緊接在 tell 的後面。

Don't worry. I won't tell anyone about it.

別擔心。我不會告訴任何人。

speak 可以用於說特定語言或單方面說話的情形。

Do you speak English?

你會說英文嗎？

I'm going to speak in front of 100 people at the conference.

我將在會議上，在 100 個人面前發言。

I will speak to him tonight. = I will talk to him tonight.

我今晚會告訴他。

I want to speak with the manager. = I want to talk with the manager.

我想跟經理說話。

discuss 用於提到討論主題的時候，雖然它與 talk about 的意思相同，但 discuss 後面不加 about。不過，如果使用 discuss 的名詞型

discussion，通常必須在後面加 about，如「Let's have a discussion about it.」。debate 也是一樣，我們可以説「We should debate the issue.」，或是「We should have a debate about the issue.」。

> **During the meeting, we discussed our marketing budget for next quarter.**
> 我們在會議中討論了下一季度的行銷預算。

debate 通常作名詞使用。就像總統候選人辯論（presidential debate）一樣，debate 通常是指分成正反兩方辯論對錯。

> **There has been a heated debate about abortion.**
> 關於墮胎曾經有過一場激烈的爭論。

讓我們根據上述內容，重新檢視下面的句子。因為是告訴上司 Jason 生病的事，所以最好用 I told my boss that 的句型來表示。

✕　　**I talked that Jason can't work today because he's sick.**
○　　**I told my boss that Jason can't work today because he's sick.**
　　　我告訴我的上司，Jason 今天因為生病不能來上班。

正如前面所説，discuss 後面不加 about。

✕　　**We can discuss about this in more detail during the next meeting.**
○　　**We can discuss this in more detail during the next meeting.**
　　　我們可以在下次的會議上，更詳細地討論這個問題。

4 toilet / restroom / bathroom

（與同事一對一開會時）

Can we start in a few minutes? I have to go to the toilet really quickly.

（向新員工介紹公司時）

The men's toilet is at the end of the hall on the right.

→ 許多人無法準確區分 toilet 和 bathroom 的不同。

表示洗手間的說法有很多種。在美式英文中，公共廁所一般稱為 restroom 或 bathroom，家裡的洗手間稱為 bathroom。在英國，說到洗手間時會用 toilet，不過美國人一提到 toilet 就會想到馬桶，所以要謹慎使用。在加拿大通常會使用 washroom，男廁叫作 men's room，女廁叫作 ladies' room。另外，飛機上的廁所被稱為 lavatory。

讓我們一起重新檢視下列句子。在美國，要去洗手間的時候不會說 go to the toilet，要說 go to the restroom / bathroom。如果是工作上的場合，比起直接提到洗手間，用「I'll be right back.（我馬上回來）」的委婉說法會更自然。

✗　　　Can we start in a few minutes? I have to ~~go to the toilet~~ really quickly.

○　　　Can we start in a few minutes? I have to go to the restroom / bathroom really quickly.

我們可以等一下再開始嗎？我需要去一下洗手間。

回頭來看下面這個句子，男廁可以用 men's restroom 或 men's room 來表示。

✗　　　The ~~men's toilet~~ is at the end of the hall on the right.

○　　　The men's restroom is at the end of the hall on the right.

男廁在走廊盡頭的右手邊。

應用

We actually don't have restrooms on this floor, but you can take the elevator or stairs down to floor 3, and the bathrooms are right there.

這一層樓沒有洗手間，不過你搭電梯或走樓梯下去 3 樓就有洗手間了。

5 trip / travel / tour / journey / vacation

（與同事談論關於休假的事）
I can't wait for this upcoming vacation.
I will trip all over Southeast Asia with my family.

（上司寄給小組的電子郵件）
We need two team members to take a short business travel to Busan this weekend for the tech conference.

由於 **trip**、**travel**、**tour**、**journey** 都被解釋為「旅行」，所以大家往往分不清楚它們確切的區別。

trip

n. the act of going to another place (often for a short period of time) and returning （短時間內）去了其他地點再回來的行為

You're back from vacation! How was your trip?
你休假回來啦！這次的旅程怎麼樣啊？

I went on business trips to Singapore and Vietnam last month.
我上個月去新加坡和越南出差。

需要注意的是，trip 不作動詞使用，因此必須使用 take a trip 或 go on a trip 來表達，還有在 a、the、所有格後面不能用 travel，必須用 trip。

I got really sick on the trip to Busan.
我去釜山旅行的時候病得很嚴重。

Our trip to Florida was very memorable.
佛羅里達之旅真的很令人難忘。

vacation

n. a single, specific journey to a place and then returning 訪問特定地點後返回的單次旅行

vacation 和 trip 在字典上的意思幾乎相同。兩者的不同點在於，trip 也可以用在與工作相關的出差上，而 vacation 只能用來表示玩樂的旅行或假期。如果你正在出差，你可以說「I'm on a business trip.」，卻不能說「I'm on a business vacation.」。另外，由於意味著工作或學業上的休息，所以暑假也可以用 summer vacation 來表示。

travel

v. go from one place to another, often to a place that is far away 從一個地點移動到另一個地點，特別是指移動到很遠的地方

I will travel to Singapore for a business conference.
我將出差去新加坡參加商務會議。

My work involves a lot of travel.
My work involves a lot of traveling.
我的工作經常需要出差。

從文法上來看，上面的兩個句子都是正確的表達，但實際上當 travel 作名詞使用時，更常使用像下面那一句加 -ing 的用法，這種表達方式也比較自然。

tour

n. an organized trip that people go on to several different places 遊覽許多地點的計劃性旅行

按照事先規劃好的行程移動的旅行，稱為 tour。

BTS is on a world tour.
BTS 正在進行世界巡迴演出。

I'm not a big fan of guided tours.
我不喜歡跟導覽行程。

journey

n. the act of going from one place to another, usually a long distance 從一個地點移動到另一個地點，通常是指移動到很遠的地方

journey 是從一個地方移動到另一個地方，通常用來表示長距離移動或旅行。

The journey takes 8 hours by plane or 12 hours by bus.
那趟旅程搭飛機要花 8 小時，如果搭巴士要花 12 小時。

He made the 300-mile journey by bike.
他騎自行車完成了 300 英里的旅程。

事實上，在一般對話中，journey 不常作「旅行」的意思使用，比較常用的是以下的說法。

life journey 人生旅程
career journey 職業歷程、職涯

讓我們重新檢視下面的句子。由於 trip 是名詞，所以只要改成 take a trip 或 travel 就可以了。

✕　　I can't wait for this upcoming vacation. I will **trip** all over Southeast Asia with my family trip.

◯　　I can't wait for this upcoming vacation. I will take a trip all over Southeast Asia with my family.
　　　我非常期待這次的假期。我要跟我的家人一起環遊東南亞。

為了特定目的而短期訪問某個地點，會用 trip 表示，通常出差叫作 business trip。

✕　　We need two team members to take a short **business travel** to Busan this weekend for the tech conference.

◯　　We need two team members to take a short business trip to Busan this weekend for the tech conference.
　　　我們需要兩位組員短期出差，到釜山參加這個週末的科技會議。

應用

In addition to virtual meetups, a few members of our team take a business trip to attend the yearly Fintech conference in Singapore. I really enjoyed it last year. I actually travelled there with my wife and kids. They enjoyed a really fun vacation while I attended the conference.

除了虛擬會議之外，我們的幾位組員還要出差去參加於新加坡舉行的年度金融科技會議。我非常喜歡去年的行程。事實上，我和我的妻子還有孩子們一起去那裡。在我參加會議的期間，我的家人度過了非常愉快的假期。

6 remember / remind / memory / memorize

（人資經理在面試中提到應徵者的履歷）
If I memory correctly, you said you got your MBA in America, right?

（在公司裡，經理對櫃台人員說）
Please remember everyone to scan their thumb prints when they leave today.

remember、remind、memory、memorize 的含義與用法經常被混淆。

remember

remember 是用來表示「記住某事不忘記」的意思。

Please remember to email me the report tomorrow.
= Please don't forget to email me the report tomorrow.
明天請一定要用電子郵件把報告寄給我。

It's important to write an outline before any business presentation to make sure you remember everything you want to say.
如果不想忘記發表內容，最好在進行簡報之前寫下大綱。

memory

通常在說記憶力好的時候，會用 memory 來表示。

> **I set alarms on my phone for all important deadlines because if I don't, I will forget. My memory isn't very good.**
> 我為所有重要的截止日設定了手機鬧鈴。因為如果不這麼做，我會忘記。我的記憶力不太好。

過去的回憶也可以用 memory 來表示。幸福的回憶叫 happy / fond memories，歷歷在目的回憶叫 clear / vivid memories，不好的回憶叫 bad memories。

> **Playing on the beach with my parents is one of my favorite childhood memories.**
> 與父母去海邊玩是我最喜歡的童年回憶之一。
>
> **I have a clear memory of the first time I went to the Philippines.**
> 對於第一次去菲律賓的事，我記憶猶新。

remind

remind 是「提醒、讓人想起」某事的意思。舉例來說，如果上司說「Please don't forget to email me the report tomorrow.」，就是在提醒你明天要記得寄電子郵件。因此，我們可以改寫成「The boss reminds you to email him the report tomorrow.」。另外，remind 的主詞也可能是情況或物品，當你看到去世的媽媽的戒指並想起她時，你可以說「The ring reminds me of my mom.」。

> **I think you probably know this, but let me remind you how lucky you are.** 我想你應該也知道，但讓我再次提醒你，你有多麼幸運。

`memorize`

memorize 是 memory 的動詞型，意思是「記住」。 如果説 remember 是記住過去的事情，那麼 memorize 指的就是背誦。背數學公式、背單字、記電話號碼、記名字等，都要用 memorize 來表示。

銷售術語必須背很多次，才能 100% 記住（memorize）吧。然而在大多數的情況下，memorize 是學習或讀書時所需的技能，因此它可能不是在一般商務情境中會使用的説法。

> **Each salesman needs to <u>memorize</u> the entire sales pitch so they can say it perfectly without looking at the script.**
> 每個銷售員都必須記住所有的銷售術語，這樣他們才能在不看稿的情況下完美表達。
>
> **I want to increase my English vocabulary, so I try to <u>memorize</u> the definitions of 20 new English words each week.**
> 我想增加我的英文字彙量，所以打算每週背 20 個新的英文單字的解釋。

現在讓我們重新檢視下面的句子。首先，在 memory 的位置上應該填入動詞，變成「假如我沒記錯」的意思，所以這裡必須用表示「記住」的 remember 才對。

× **If I memory correctly, you said you got your MBA in America, right?**

○ **If I remember correctly, you said you got your MBA in America, right?**
假如我沒記錯，你說你在美國取得了 MBA 學位，對嗎？

在下面的句子裡，從前後文來看是在提醒櫃台人員交辦事項，所以應該使用 remind，而不是 remember。

✕　　　Please **remember** everyone to scan their thumb prints when they leave today so they can officially clock out using our new system.

○　　　Please remind everyone to scan their thumb prints when they leave today so they can officially clock out using our new system.

請記得告訴員工在今天下班的時候掃描拇指指紋。那樣才能用新系統記錄下班時間。

┌─ 應用 ─────────────────────────────────────╮

One of my weaknesses is that I'm sometimes not a very good multi tasker. I tend to focus very intensely on my major work tasks but occasionally don't remember to do the smaller, more minor tasks. To fix this, I started writing a weekly to-do list every Sunday and continuing to check it throughout the week. It helps remind me to get everything done on time.

我的弱點之一是有時候不擅長一心多用。我傾向專注於我的主要工作，所以偶爾無法記住那些瑣碎的小事。為了解決這個問題，我開始在每週日列一份當週待辦事項清單，並於當週持續確認清單上的事項。這樣做能提醒我按時完成所有事情。

7 lend / loan / borrow

My company had to lend some money from the bank to finance our new office.

很多人會搞混 lend 和 borrow 的意思。

lend v. to GIVE something to someone with the agreement that they will return it later 將某物交給借方

borrow v. to RECEIVE something from someone with the agreement that you will return it to them later 從被借方那裡收到某物

讓我們通過以下對話來了解 lend 和 borrow 的不同。

A:Oh my god. My bike just broke down. Can I <u>borrow</u> your bike for a week?
哎呀，我的自行車剛才故障了。我可以借你的自行車一週嗎？

B:I'm sorry to hear that. Sure, I can <u>lend</u> you my bike. I take a bus to work so I don't need it for now.
那真是太糟糕了。當然可以，我可以把自行車借給你。因為我都搭公車上班，現在不需要用到。

A:Thanks a lot. I'll return it in a week.
真是謝謝你。我會在一週後還你。

loan　v. to GIVE something to someone with the agreement that they will return it later 將某物交給約好日後償還者

lend / borrow 和 loan 的區別在於 loan 還可以作名詞使用。

loan　n. a thing / object that is borrowed, usually a sum of money that will be paid back over time, sometimes with interest 過一段時間後償還的錢（有時會連同利息一起）

> **The bank gave us a $50,000 loan.**
> 銀行借我們 5 萬美元的貸款。
>
> **We took out a $50,000 loan from the bank.**
> 我們從銀行那裡拿到 5 萬美元的貸款。

現在讓我們重新檢視前面出現過的句子。向銀行借錢可以用動詞 borrow，或是用 take out a loan、get a loan 來表示「得到貸款」的意思。

✗　**My company had to ~~lend some money~~ from the bank to finance our new office.**

○　**My company had to** borrow some money **from the bank to finance our new office.**

○　**My company had to** take out a loan **from the bank to finance our new office.**
　　我的公司為了籌措新辦公室的資金，不得不向銀行貸款。

8 wage / salary / income / paycheck

（聽到自己被提升為區域經理後）
I'll work more hours but I also get a big wage increase.

用來表示「收入」的 wage、salary、income、paycheck 各有不同的用途。

wage

wage 的概念通常是指從事體力勞動的非技術勞工（unskilled workers），以日薪 / 時薪的方式領取的工資。由於兼職人員（part-timer）也是按時數領取薪資，因此也可以視為 wage，以 $19/hour（時薪 19 美元）、$200/day（日薪 200 美元）的形式表示。

salary

salary 的概念通常是指有一定教育程度的工作者所領取的月薪及年薪。salary 會以 $30,000/year（年薪 3 萬美元）、$4,000/month（月薪 4000 美元）的形式表示。

income

income 是做某事所賺取的所有收入之總稱。

My salary is actually lower this year than last year, but my total income is higher because I'm making a lot of money investing.

事實上，我今年的薪水比去年低，但因為投資賺了很多錢，所以總收入反而更高。

paycheck

paycheck 是指公司在支付 salary 或 wage 時，直接提供的支票（check）。在韓國，薪水通常都是直接存入（direct deposit）帳戶，所以較難理解這種概念。不過，近來美國企業也偏好直接轉帳。

下面的句子是期待晉升為 country manager 之後，年薪會調漲，所以應該使用可表示年薪的 salary 才對。

✕　**I'll work more hours but I also get a big wage increase.**

〇　**I'll work more hours but I also get a big salary increase.**

雖然我要多工作幾個小時，但也會得到更高的年薪。

Ｄetails

薪水（wage、salary）的多寡可以用 high / low、higher / lower 來表示。

✕　**I really want to earn more salary this year.**

〇　**I really want to earn a higher salary this year.**

我希望今年的年薪會調漲。

I really want to earn more income this year.

＝　**I really want to earn higher income this year.**

我希望今年能有更多收入。

I can't wait for my next paycheck. My boss actually increased my salary last month, and because it's December I'll also get my end-of-the-year bonus.

我等不及下次的發薪日了。我老闆上個月幫我加薪,而且現在是 12 月,還可以領年終獎金。

9 complain / criticize / confront

> The guests criticized to the hotel manager about the condition of their room.
>
> My boyfriend complained my looks so I just dumped him.
>
> 有些人會分不清楚 complain、criticize 和 confront 的細微差異。

complain (n. complaint)

v. to voice anger, annoyance, or dissatisfaction with something 表達對某事的憤怒、厭惡或不滿

criticize (n. criticism, adj. critical)

v. to notice, point out the flaws / weaknesses of someone or something 察覺並指出某人或某事的缺點 / 弱點

根據不同情況，criticism 可能是正面的，也可能是負面的。constructive criticism 指的是有建設性的批評。complain 和 criticize 最大的區別在於，complain 偏向情緒化地表達對某事的不滿，而 criticize 則偏向理性地説明某事的缺點。我們也可以説，criticism 通常是由地位高的人或專家所提出的。

Your coworker is always talking to you about how he
doesn't like his job because the boss is mean. ◀ complain

如果你的同事總是跟你說因為上司很刻薄，所以他很討厭他的工作，這就是
complain。

Your boss pointing out the flaws / weaknesses of your sales
pitch. ◀ criticize

上司指出你在銷售話術中的問題點或缺點，這就是 criticize。

confront (n. confrontation, adj. confrontational)

v. 1. (about a person) to meet someone face to face in a hostile /
argumentative manner 以敵對 / 爭論的態度一對一地對抗某人
2. (about a situation) to face and try to deal with a difficult / tough
situation or problem 面對並試圖努力處理困難的 / 辛苦的狀況或問
題

confront 某人指的是直接說出那個人行為上的問題。根據爭論的理由
是否合理，confront 可能是正面的，也可能是負面的。另一方面，形
容詞 confrontational 通常都帶有貶義，指的是頻繁與他人對立，過於
激進和易怒的情況。

讓我們試著修改以下例句。顧客對酒店房間表達不滿。通常在物品不
良或服務不佳的時候，我們會情緒化地 complain。

✕   The guests criticized to the hotel manager about the
       condition of their room.
◯   The guests complained to the hotel manager about the
       condition of their room.
       客人們向飯店經理抱怨客房的狀態。

當我不喜歡自己的外表時，我會 complain，但如果是「批評」別人的
外表，就要用 criticize 來表達比較自然。

×   My boyfriend ~~complained~~ my looks so I just dumped him.

○   My boyfriend criticized my looks so I just dumped him.
     男朋友批評我的外表，所以我就把他甩了。

應用

Our customer service team has been receiving a lot of
complaints about our new salesmen. Apparently, they're
way too aggressive.
A few customers said salesmen confronted them and really
pushed them to make a purchase even after they said they
weren't interested. Let's call a meeting with the entire sales
team next week so the lead sales manager can give some
firm, constructive criticism.

我們的客服組收到許多關於新進銷售人員的投訴。我認為銷售人員的態度顯
然太過強硬了。根據一些顧客的說法，儘管他們已經明確表示不感興趣，銷
售人員仍然一直催促他們購買。讓我們在下週召開一次銷售組全體會議，首
席銷售經理可以提出一些強而有力、有建設性的批評。

下面是針對前面介紹過的 with Error 部分，修正錯誤用法後的內容，你可以在劃底線的部分確認正確的表達方式。

尚賢　　I heard you met with Green Light Electronics earlier today. How'd your first sales presentation go?
聽說你今天稍早的時候去了 Green Light Electronics。第一次的銷售簡報情況還好嗎？

智媛　　I think it went well! They seemed interested in the product, and I'll have a follow-up meeting with their marketer and purchase team to discuss pricing.
我認為進行得很順利！他們看起來對我們的產品有興趣。後續我會再跟他們的行銷人員及採購組開會，商討價格事宜。

尚賢　　Nice! I was really nervous before my first sales presentation. That's impressive that you already have a follow-up scheduled!
太好了！我第一次進行銷售簡報之前，緊張得不得了。沒想到你連後續會議都安排好了，真令人訝異！

智媛　　Thanks! Yeah, they said that they want to expand into Europe and they really like that Synthesis works anywhere in the world.
謝謝！他們說想將業務拓展到歐洲，使用 Synthesis 可以在世界任何地方工作的這一點令他們很滿意。

尚賢　　Great. Sales presentations are one of my favorite parts of the job. It's really fun to connect with new businesses.

太好了。做銷售簡報是我最喜歡的工作之一。與新的公司建立關係真的很有趣。

| 智媛 | Yeah, I'm excited to keep learning and getting better. (two Americans walk up to the table)
沒錯，持續學習和進步是一件很開心的事情。
（兩名美國人走向桌邊） |

| 尚賢 | Ah, hey guys, glad you could make it! This is Jiwon, the newest member of the sales team.
你們好！很高興你們來了！這位是銷售組的新進人員，智媛。 |

| Mike | Hey, Jiwon, I'm Mike. Good to meet you.
你好，智媛。我是 Mike。很高興認識你。 |

| 智媛 | Good to meet you too! Sorry, can you say your name again? I didn't hear you.
我也很高興認識你。不好意思，可以請你再說一次你的名字嗎？我沒聽清楚。 |

| Mike | Yeah, it's louder in here than usual! We come here all the time, and it's usually pretty quiet. I'm Mike.
這裡比平常還要吵！我們經常來這裡，平常這裡很安靜。我的名字叫 Mike。 |

| 智媛 | Mike, got it.
原來是 Mike，我知道了。 |

| Charlie | And I'm Charlie. Welcome to the team.
我是 Charlie。歡迎你加入這個團隊。 |

智媛   Thanks!
      謝謝你！

Charlie Hey, Sanghyeon, do you know where the restroom is? I'll
         be right back.
         尚賢，你知道這裡的洗手間在哪裡嗎？我馬上回來。

尚賢   Yeah, it's just around that corner.
      (Mike sits down at the table)
      知道，就在那個轉角處。
      （Mike 在桌邊坐下）

尚賢   Mike just got back from a business trip in Singapore.
      How was the conference, Mike?
      Mike 剛從新加坡出差回來。這次的會議怎麼樣，Mike ？

Mike   It was really interesting. They had a lot of really good
       marketing and sales ideas. I wrote most of what they said
       down so I'll remember it. I think we can borrow some of
       these strategies and use them here. I'll share my notes
       during the team meeting next Monday. So how was your
       first week, Jiwon?
       非常有趣。他們有很多不錯的行銷和銷售創意。為了記住這些，我
       幾乎把他們說的話全寫下來了。我認為我們可以借用其中的一些策
       略。我會在下週一的小組會議上分享我的筆記。智媛，你上班的第
       一週過得怎麼樣？

智媛   It was really good! I had my first sales presentation and
      am learning about how the portal system works. I think I'll
      really like it here ... I already like it a lot better than my
      old job at Nexus!

非常好！我進行了第一次的銷售簡報，現在正在學習入口網站系統的操作方式。我覺得我會非常喜歡這裡……已經喜歡到勝過我之前在 Nexus 的工作了！

Mike

Ahh yeah, I've heard mixed reviews about working there. Why did you leave?

對了，我聽說過關於在 Nexus 工作的各種評價。你為什麼會離開那裡？

智媛

Well, I don't mean to complain, but the senior managers were really demanding and unreasonable. They set really high sales quotas that almost nobody could reach, then criticized everyone who didn't meet the quotas and blamed us for everything. There was a lot of pressure on us and I really didn't like it.

好吧，我並不是要抱怨，但是資深經理要求苛刻又不講道理。他們設定幾乎不可能實現的銷售目標，然後指責每個沒有達到目標的人，並將所有責任都推給我們。我們承受了很大的壓力，我真的很不喜歡那樣。

尚賢

That sounds rough. I'm glad you're here. We work hard obviously, but things are a lot more relaxed. Kangmin is a great boss.

一定很辛苦吧。我很高興你能來我們公司。我們當然也很努力工作，不過從容多了。姜敏是個好上司。

智媛

Yeah, it seems that way from my perspective. That wasn't the worst part about Nexus though. They actually forced me to transfer to one of their new offices even though I really didn't want to. I had to move to a new neighborhood that was way more expensive, but they didn't increase my <u>salary</u>. Like 40% of my <u>paycheck / salary / income</u> went to rent every month and I couldn't save any money.

是的，我也這麼認為。不過剛剛說的還不是最糟的。即使我不願意，他們也強迫我調到新的辦公室。我必須搬到生活成本高出許多的地區，但是薪水卻沒有調漲。我月薪的 40% 都用來付每個月的房租了，根本無法儲蓄。

Mike   Wow, that's ridiculous! Yeah, don't worry there won't be anything like that here.
(waiter walks up to the table)
哇，太離譜了！別擔心。在我們這裡不會發生那種事。
（服務生來到桌邊）

Mike   Anyway, let's get some drinks ... first round is on me. Jiwon, you good with Budweiser?
好了，我們來喝點東西吧……第一輪我請客。智媛，百威啤酒可以嗎？

智媛   Sure!
當然可以！

尚賢   You're in Korea, still going Budweiser?
這裡是韓國，你還在喝百威啤酒？

Mike   Ahh come on, it <u>reminds</u> me of home!
(pours drinks)
喔，別這樣。它讓我想起我的故鄉啊！
（倒飲料）

尚賢　　　　　Cheers! To Jiwon's first week here!
　　　　　　　乾杯！敬智媛的第一週！

Chapter 5

不自然的表達
Unnatural Mistakes

1   I am sorry / I feel sorry for

2   answering 'or' questions

3   How's your condition?

4   I am (name)

5   I am okay / That's okay / It's okay

6   Do you know ~?

7   negative questions

8   I don't care

9   as soon as possible

10   in touch

11   take a rest

12   I understand well.

13   I'm waiting for your response.

14   have a good time

以下的敘述中包含錯誤的用法。請閱讀一遍，並試著找出不自然
的表達方式。在各章節的最後會提供修正後的正確表達。

週四下午銷售簡報結束後，為了召開第二次會議來討論細節，智媛聯
繫了 Green Light Electronics 的行銷組。

Message sent: Friday morning, 8:45 a.m.

Hello Park Taeho,
I am Jiwon Lee, one of the sales representatives for Onward Tech. It's
good to meet you. I hope your condition is great.
I met with some of your colleagues yesterday afternoon to discuss
how our Synthesis marketing AI system can help Green Light
Electronics grow. Kim Donghwi told me to get touch with you about
having a follow up meeting.
I'd love to meet with you sometime next week if you're available. Let
me know as soon as possible. You can also look at the attachment I
added to this email. It explains more about Synthesis.
I will wait for your reply.

Have a good time,
Jiwon Lee

Message sent: Tuesday morning, 9:30 a.m.

Hi Jiwon,

Thank you for getting back to me. Also I feel sorry for the late reply. I had a lot of work last Friday, last weekend, and on Monday. Looking forward to next weekend already so I can finally take a rest!

I read your email and looked at the Synthesis attachment. I understand it well. I would be happy to have a follow-up meeting this week. I am available tomorrow any time 2:00-4:00 p.m. or Thursday 1:00-5:00 p.m. Let me know which time works for you.

Thanks Jiwon!
Taeho

Message sent: Tuesday morning, 11:05 a.m.

Hey Taeho,

I'm okay! I've been pretty busy the past few days as well. That sounds great. I think Thursday afternoon at 3 p.m. would be perfect. We usually have our follow-up meetings virtually on Webex. Do you know Webex? However, I don't mind coming to your office to meet in person. Would you prefer a virtual meeting or a face-to-face meeting?

Take care,
Jiwon

Message sent: Tuesday afternoon, 1:43 p.m.

Hi Jiwon,
Yes! I'm looking forward to meeting you. Is there anything I need to prepare for our meeting?

Taeho

Message sent: Tuesday afternoon, 4:20 p.m.

Sounds good, Taeho!
Here's a Webex meeting link:
www.webex/meeting57189282711

If you could have some information ready about your recent / planned advertising campaigns (for example: your latest budget, analytics, and plans for next quarter) that would be great.
See you Thursday at 3!

Take care,
Jiwon

1 I am sorry / I feel sorry for

（因沒接到客戶來電而寄電子郵件致歉）
Hi Mark,
I feel sorry for missing your phone call.

（事後向同事說明情況）
I felt sorry about missing Mark's phone call, so I sent him an email.

許多人會將 I'm sorry 和 I feel sorry for 當作相同的意思使用。

I'm sorry 和 I feel sorry for 都是正確的英文用法，但是使用時的語境有所不同。I'm sorry 大致可用於以下兩種情形。

1. 道歉時

（直接與上司交談）
<u>I'm really sorry</u> I was late for the meeting. It won't happen again.
很抱歉我開會遲到了。我保證不會再發生這種事了。

我們也可以用動詞 apologize 來表示較為正式的說法。上面的句子可以改成「I apologize for being late for the meeting. It won't happen again.」。

I am sorry 或 I apologize 只能用在與想道歉的對象直接交談時。當你告訴別人你犯了錯或是做了不好的事情時，你可以用 I feel bad for / about 的說法來表達，意思是「我因為～而感到難過、心情不好」。

（當天稍晚跟同事說話時）

I feel really bad for being late to the meeting this morning.

今天早上開會遲到讓我心情很糟。

I feel bad for him because he failed the test.

我很遺憾他沒有通過考試。

2. 當對方發生不好的事時

（從朋友口中聽到她失業的消息）

I'm so sorry to hear that. I hope you find a new job soon. If you need any help please let me know.

我很遺憾。希望你能早日找到新工作。如果需要幫忙就告訴我。

I feel sorry for 可以用於當對方發生不好的事情時，也可以用在對該消息感到遺憾並將其轉達給別人的時候。讓我們把上面的例句改一下。

（跟同事談到朋友失業的事）

My friend Min told me she lost her job this week. I feel so sorry for her.

我朋友小敏跟我說她這個禮拜失業了。我真為她感到難過。

只能用 I feel sorry for [sb] 的句型，不能用 I feel sorry to。另外，由於 I feel sorry 並非完整的句子，所以不能只說 I feel sorry，sorry 可以用 bad 代替。

現在讓我們重新檢視下面的句子。這裡是因為沒接到客戶 Mark 打來的電話，親自向他道歉的情況，因此可以直接用 I am sorry 或 I apologize。

    Hi Mark,

✕   **I feel sorry for missing your phone call.**

○   I'm sorry **for missing your phone call.**

○   I apologize **for missing your phone call.**
    很抱歉沒接到你的來電。

下面是向其他同事描述因沒接到 Mark 的電話而寄電子郵件過去的情況，所以用 I feel bad 比較恰當。

✕   **I felt sorry about missing Mark's phone call, so I sent him an email.**

○   I felt bad **about missing Mark's phone call, so I sent him an email.**
    沒接到 Mark 的電話讓我很過意不去，所以我寄了電子郵件給他。

2 answering 'or' questions

A: Should I email the clients or call them?
B: Yes.

很多人無法正確回答包含 or 在內的選擇疑問句。

以錯誤的方式回答選擇疑問句,可能會導致溝通出現問題並使對方感到困惑。回答選擇疑問句的正確方式是說出你同意的觀點或選項,而不是回答 Yes 或 No。

> **We can have our Zoom call today or tomorrow. Which would you prefer?**
> 我們可以今天或明天用 Zoom 通話。你比較喜歡什麼時候?

由於是在詢問你要選哪一個選項,所以不能用 Yes / No 回答。你可以說「Let's have the Zoom call today.」,或是「Let's have the Zoom call tomorrow.」。也可以簡短回答「Today.」或「Tomorrow.」。

讓我們重新檢視下面的對話。A 在詢問要寄電子郵件,還是打電話給客戶。所以 B 不該回答 Yes or No,應該在兩個選項中選擇符合情況的答案。

A: Should I email the clients or call them?

我該寄電子郵件還是打電話給客戶呢?

✗ B: Yes.

○ B: You should call them. If they don't answer, you can send a follow-up email tomorrow.

你應該打電話給他們。如果他們沒接電話,明天再寄跟進郵件就可以了。

應用

A: So I haven't heard from the prospect I met with last week yet. Should I follow up with him or just move on to new prospects?

B: I would move on and try to schedule some sales meetings with new prospects. If he's interested in buying, he'll contact you.

A:我上週見的潛在客戶還沒有聯絡我。我該主動聯絡那位客戶?還是繼續尋找其他新客戶呢?

B:我會繼續尋找新的潛在客戶並試著安排銷售會議。如果那個人有意購買,他就會聯絡你。

3 How's your condition?

A: How's your condition today?

B: My condition is great today.

在提到自己的狀態時使用 condition 一詞，雖然並非錯誤的用法，卻是不自然的表達方式。

在美式英文中，condition 通常用於以下情況。

1. 表示特定物品的狀態

This car is 10 years old but is still in good condition.

這輛車的車齡已經 10 年了，但狀態還是很好。

2. 在醫院裡談到患者的心情或狀態時

（護理師對醫生說）

The patient took the medicine, and his condition quickly improved.

患者吃了藥之後，病情迅速好轉了。

因此，如果是一般問候，用「How are you?」或「How's it going?」會更加自然。如果你真的想要詢問某人的「狀態」，可以用 feel 取代 condition 來詢問，如「How are you feeling today?」或是「How do you feel today?」。

如果你想要回答「我的狀態很好」，你可以説「I feel good.」（也可以用 great、fantastic、awesome 等各種説法取代 good）。相反的，如果你今天身體不太舒服，你可以用「I'm not feeling well today.」、「I don't feel well today.」、「I feel under the weather.」等説法來回答。

現在讓我們重新檢視下面的對話。

✗　　A: How's your condition today?
○　　A: How are you feeling today?
○　　A: How do you feel today?
　　　你今天的心情如何？

✗　　B: My condition is great today.
○　　B: I feel great / awesome / fantastic today.
　　　我今天的心情很好。

應用

Hey Jihyun, I heard you've been kind of sick lately. How are you feeling today?

智賢，聽說你最近不太舒服。你今天感覺還好嗎？

4 I am (name)

（第一次寄電子郵件給外國同事）
Hi Sam,
I am Jiwon.

在提及名字的自我介紹中，有些問候方式不自然。

通常我們會用以下三種方式來介紹自己。

1. I am + 名字
2. This is + 名字
3. My name is + 名字

讓我們來看一下它們各自用在什麼情況下。

「I am + 名字」是直接或透過影像與初次見面的人面對面做自我介紹時使用的表達方式。在寫自傳或電子郵件等書面文章時，不會用「I am + 名字」的方式來表達。

（與初次見面的新同事握手）
Hi, I'm Jiwon.
你好，我是智媛。

在書面、電話、簡訊等非面對面的情況下，可以用「My name is + 名字」或「This is + 名字」的句型來做自我介紹。順帶一提，介紹其他

人的時候也可以用「This is + 名字」，意思是「這位是～」。

「My name is + 名字」通常用於在正式場合第一次見面的情況。這種表達方式不僅適用於面對面的情況（直接見面、視訊通話等），也適用於非面對面的情況（電話、電子郵件、簡訊等）。一般在商務情境中，除了名字之外，最好連同自己的職業、所屬公司和聯絡的理由也一併表明。

> （開始進行銷售簡報時）
> Thank you all for taking the time to meet with me today.
> My name is Jiwon Lee. I'm a sales rep for Onward Tech.
> 感謝各位今天抽出寶貴的時間。我是 Onward Tech 的銷售代表李智媛。

「This is + 名字」可用於開始透過新管道對話時，例如之前見過面或曾透過電子郵件交流，在交換電話號碼後，打電話或傳簡訊給對方的情況。

> Hello Mr. Park,
> This is Jiwon Lee. We met at the Seoul AI tech conference
> last week. I am emailing you to see if your company
> is interested in using our new online data platform to
> organize and grow your business.
> 朴先生，您好：
> 我是李智媛。上週我們在首爾 AI 科技會議中見過面。我寄這封電子郵件，是為了了解貴公司是否有興趣使用我們新的網路數據平台，來幫助您組織與發展業務。

由於是已經跟對方見過面，但第一次用其他方式（此處為寄電子郵件）聯絡對方的情況，所以這裡用的是「This is Jiwon Lee.」。

現在讓我們重新檢視下面的句子。由於是智媛第一次用電子郵件向外國同事 Sam 問候的情況，所以應該用「My name is Jiwon.」。

但是，如果智媛之前曾經跟 Sam 交談過，或是用電子郵件聯絡過，就必須把「I am Jiwon.」改成「This is Jiwon.」才行。

Hi Sam,

× **I am Jiwon.**

○ My name is **Jiwon.**

我的名字叫智媛。

應用

（與新同事交談時做自我介紹）

Hey Yoojin, I'm John. Nice to meet you. Welcome to our team.

柳真，我是 John。很高興見到你。歡迎你加入我們的團隊。

（寄電子郵件給之前見過面，但很久沒聯絡的區域經理）

Hello Mr. Kim,

This is John Park from the marketing department. I'm emailing you because ...

你好，金先生：

我是行銷部的 John Park。我寄這封電子郵件是為了⋯⋯

（在正式發表會上向觀眾們自我介紹）

My name is Jonathan Park. I'm the lead product developer here at Seoul AI, and today I want to talk to you about ...

我的名字叫 Jonathan Park。我是首爾 AI 的首席產品開發人員。我今天要跟各位談論關於⋯⋯

5 I am okay / That's okay / It's okay

A: Are you ready to start the meeting?
B: I am okay.

A: Why don't we have a follow-up call tomorrow at
4 p.m. Does that work with you?
B: Yes, I am okay! Talk to you then.

A: Sorry I missed your phone call!
B: I am okay! What did you need to ask me?

在某些情況下,使用「I'm okay.」顯得不自然又尷尬。

「I am okay.」通常作下列三種意思使用。

1.(生理上、精神上)我沒事。

I lost my job, but I'm okay.
雖然失業了,但我沒事。
I was in a car accident, but I'm okay.
雖然出了車禍,但我沒事。

相反的，如果說「I'm not okay.」，意思就是「生理上、精神上的狀態不好」。

> A: I heard your grandmother passed away. I'm so sorry. Are
> you okay?
>
> 聽說你的祖母過世了。我很遺憾。你還好嗎？
>
> B: No, I'm not. I've been crying all day. I can't stop thinking
> about her.
>
> 不，我不好。我哭了一整天。無法停止想她。

2. 我（實力或能力）一般、還可以。

> I am really good at Korean, but just okay at English.
>
> 雖然我的韓語很好，但英文實力一般。

3. 行為（I am okay with）

當 I am okay 後面接 with + 行為時，表示那個行為是可行的、沒問題的。

> When are you available to meet? I'm okay with meeting
> any time 12-5 p.m.
>
> 你什麼時候有時間見面？我中午 12 點到下午 5 點都可以。

現在讓我們重新檢視前面出現過的句子。在下面的句子裡，「I'm okay.」被誤用為「我準備好了」的意思。

> A: Are you ready to start the meeting?
>
> 你準備好開始會議了嗎？
>
> ✗ B: I am okay.
>
> ○ B: I am ready. Let's start.
>
> 我準備好了。我們開始吧。

對於對方提出的問題或請求給予肯定答覆時，用「I'm okay.」是不自然的表達方式。

A: Why don't we have a follow-up call tomorrow at 4 p.m.?
Does that work with you?
我們明天下午 4 點再通話怎麼樣？你可以嗎？

✗ B: Yes, I am okay. Talk to you then.

○ B: Yes, that works fine. Talk to you then.
是，沒問題。那就到時候再聊。

接受道歉時，回答「I'm okay.」也是不恰當的表達。

A: Sorry I missed your phone call!
很抱歉沒接到你的電話！

✗ B: I am okay! What did you need to ask me?

○ B: That's no problem! What did you need to ask me?
沒關係！你要問我什麼事？

如果想用 okay 來表示「That's no problem.」的意思，你可以説「It's okay.」或「That's okay.」。

┌─────┐
│ 應用 │
└─────┘
A: I'm really sorry about postponing our meeting. Thank
you for being flexible.

B: It's okay! This meeting time actually works a little better
for me, so I don't mind at all.

A：我很抱歉會議延期了。感謝您的配合。
B：沒關係！我也覺得這個時間更好，真的沒關係。

6 Do you know ~?

I took a trip to Jeju last weekend. Do you know Jeju?

My coworkers and I play Go after work. Do you know Go?

Next weekend is Chuseok. Do you know Chuseok?

這裡用了很多「Do you know ~?」的表達方式，但其實它用在其他情況感覺才自然。

首先，讓我們來了解一下，「Do you know ~?」應該使用在什麼情況下。

1. 與疑問句一起

在 Do you know 後面接的間接問句，詞序為「疑問詞 + 主詞 + 動詞」。

Do you know where John went?
你知道 John 去了哪裡嗎？
Do you know what time the workshop ends?
你知道研討會幾點結束嗎？
Do you know how to fix this computer error?
你知道怎麼修正這個電腦錯誤嗎？

2. 與明確的資訊或事實一起

Do you know Tony's email address?

你知道 Tony 的電子郵件地址嗎？

Do you know this product's release date?

你知道這個產品的上市日期嗎？

Do you know that Seoul is one of the largest cities in the world?

你知道首爾是全球最大的城市之一嗎？

3. 與人一起

「Do you know + [sb]?」基本上是在問你是否認識或熟悉那個人。

A: **Do you know** John?

你認識 John 嗎？

B: He's the new head of the HR department.

他是新來的人資部主管。

一般在工作的正式場合，建議可用「Have you met [sb]?」代替「Do you know [sb]?」。

那麼，誤用了「Do you know ~?」的句子，應該要如何修改呢？通常我們可以改用下列三種句型來表達。

1. Do you know about ~?（使用 about）

當我們說「Do you know about ~?」時，意思是「你知道～（相關資訊）嗎？」

Do you know about the new work policy?

你知道新的工作方針嗎？

Do you know about our latest products?

你知道我們公司的最新產品嗎？

2. Have you heard of ~?

當我們說「Have you heard of ~?」時，是在問對方「你聽過（知道）～嗎？」

Have you heard of the band BTS?

你聽過 BTS 這個團體嗎？

3. Have you + 連綴動詞的過去分詞 ~?

要詢問對方是否有過某種經驗，可以用「Have you (ever) + 連綴動詞的過去分詞 ~?」來表達。如下面的句子，因為 BTS 是做音樂的團體，所以動詞可以用 listen。

Have you ever listened to BTS?

你聽過 BTS 的音樂嗎？

接著就讓我們試著用這三種方法來修改下列句子。

1	I took a trip to Jeju this weekend. ~~Do you know~~ Jeju?
方法 1	Do you know about Jeju?
＝	**Do you know information about Jeju?**
方法 2	Have you heard of Jeju?
＝	**Are you aware of the existence of Jeju?**
方法 3	Have you been to Jeju?
＝	**Have you ever actually visited Jeju?**

我這個週末去濟州島出差。你知道濟州島嗎？

2　My coworkers and I play Go after work. ~~Do you know~~ Go?

方法 1　Do you know about **Go?**

=　**Do you know information about the game Go?**

方法 2　Have you heard of **Go?**

=　**Are you aware of the existence of the game Go?**

方法 3　Have you ever played **Go?**

=　**Have you performed the action of playing a game of Go?**

我同事和我工作結束後會下圍棋。你知道圍棋嗎？

3　Next weekend is the Moon Festival. ~~Do you know~~ the Moon Festival?

方法 1　Do you know about **the Moon Festival?**

=　**Do you know information about the Moon Festival?**

方法 2　Have you heard of **the Moon Festival?**

=　**Are you aware of the existence of the Moon Festival?**

方法 3　Have you ever celebrated **the Moon Festival?**

=　**Have you ever actually participated in the Moon Festival?**

下週就是中秋節了。你知道中秋節嗎？

7 negative questions

Do you not want to stay?

Would it be bad if I left the meeting early?

Are they not finished with the project yet?

在回答否定疑問句時，許多人會感到混亂。

否定疑問句指的是包含 no、not 或其他否定詞在內的所有疑問句。讓我們依序來看上列否定疑問句的正確回答方式。

1. Do you not want to stay?

如果用 Yes 來回答這個問題，從意義上來看，似乎很自然地是指「Yes, I do not want to stay. We should leave.」的意思；但在實際對話中，我們通常會說「No, I really don't want to stay. We should leave.」。

比 Yes / No 更重要的是後面出現的「I don't want to stay.」。所以我們只要把它想成肯定疑問句去回答的話，就不會出錯了。你可以試著把「Do you not want to stay?」想成和「Do you want to stay?」一樣，然後用「Yes, I want to stay.」或「No, I don't want to stay.」來回答。

2. Would it be bad if I left the meeting early?

No, we have a lot to cover today. I don't think you should leave early.

不，今天要處理的事情很多。我不認為你可以提早走。

Yes, this meeting is really important. Please stay for the whole thing.

是的，這次的會議非常重要。請你留到最後。

3. Are they not finished with the project yet?

（如果那個專案已經完成了）

No, they're finished! You can ask them about it later.

不，已經完成了！你晚一點可以跟他們確認關於專案的事。

Yeah, they actually finished last week.

是的，其實上週就已經完成了。

通過以上的例句，你會發現 Yes 或 No 並不重要。為了傳達確切的意思，在 Yes / No 後面做補充說明更為重要。

8 I don't care

A: Which prototype should we choose?
B: I don't care.

A: Would you be interested in moving to sales team C?
B: I don't care.

I don't care 使用不當可能會引起誤會。

A: Do you want to cook dinner at home tonight or get a takeout?
今天的晚餐你想在家自己煮，還是外帶回來吃？
B: I don't care. Whatever you want is fine.
我無所謂。你想怎麼樣都行。

「I don't care.」用在對於對方的決定沒有特別提出個人意見的情況。基於這個理由，在做重要的決定或是必須向職場上司提出意見的情況下，說「I don't care.」是不自然的，甚至可能會給人無禮的感覺，這點必須特別留意。

一般來說，最好用以下句子加上原因說明來代替「I don't care.」，才是較為正式的說法。

對某件事沒有特別的意見，覺得不錯的時候

○   **I don't have a preference.**

不管是否做出選擇，那些選項大致上都不錯的情況

○   **I can't choose.**

○   **It's hard / impossible to choose.**

現在讓我們假設某種特定情況，再用上述兩種表達方式來重新檢視下面的句子。

（從專案設計小組那裡拿到關於產品雛型的兩種提案，兩者都很不錯的情況。）

A: **Which prototype should we choose?**

我們該選擇哪一種雛型呢？

B: **They're both so good,** it's honestly really hard to choose. **I'm going to check with senior managers and see if we can produce both.**

這兩種都很不錯，老實說真的很難選。我去向資深經理確認一下，能不能兩種產品都生產。

（與上司一對一面談時，對於組織改造沒有特別意見的情況。）

A: **I know you've been part of sales team A for nearly a year now. We're moving some of our sales associates around. Would you be interested in moving to sales team C?**

我記得你加入銷售 A 組快滿一年了吧。我們準備讓一些銷售人員輪調。你有意願調到銷售 C 組嗎？

B: Thank you for the opportunity. I honestly don't have a preference. I like my team now, but am totally open to switching teams if you think that move makes sense.

謝謝您給我這個機會。老實說，我沒有特別的意見。我喜歡我的團隊，但如果您認為我調到別組比較好，那也無妨。

應用

Which of these website designs do you like better? I honestly can't choose.

這些網站設計之中，你喜歡哪一個？老實說，我無法抉擇。

9   as soon as possible

（寄電子郵件向客戶詢問一個並不重要的問題）

Please let me know your answers as soon as possible. Thank you!

→ 明明並非緊急要求，有些人還是會使用 as soon as possible 來表達。

大多數人都知道 as soon as possible 的意思是「盡快」。但是，當我們在對話中用 as soon as possible 這種表達方式，告訴對方某事必須「盡快」發生時，聽起來就像在強調事情的急迫性，要求或表示某事一定要立刻發生。

因此，as soon as possible 最好只在非常重要和緊急的情況下使用。如果是在沒有設定截止日等非緊急狀況下，想要用相對鄭重又比較不會帶來壓力的方式表達，你可以用 whenever you have time、whenever you get the chance、whenever is convenient for you 等説法。

Please fill out this questionnaire whenever you have time. Thanks!

請您有空時幫忙填寫這份問卷。謝謝！

還有另一種方法，就是提出期限（deadline）。即使情況並不緊急，這樣做也可以達到提醒對方的效果。在這種情況下，建議使用「by + 期限（deadline）」的句型。

> Please let me know by Friday morning if you'll be able to attend the weekend conference. Thanks!
>
> 請於週五上午之前告知我們，您是否能出席週末的會議。謝謝！

你也可以用以 could、would 開頭的疑問句去詢問對方。這種疑問句通常會用在有禮貌地與上位者交談時，如上司或老師等。

> Could you send me that report by the end of the day? Thanks!
>
> = Would it be possible to send me that report by the end of the day? Thanks!
>
> 請問您能否於今天之內將報告寄給我？謝謝！

接著就讓我們分成兩種情況，重新檢視下面的句子。

1. 沒有設定期限的情況

× Please let me know your answers as soon as possible. Thank you!

○ Please let me know your answers whenever you have time. Thank you!

請您有空時給我答覆。謝謝！

2. 有設定期限的情況

✗   Please let me know your answers **as soon as possible**. Thank you!

○   Could you **send me your answers** by next Monday? We'll **need them for the meeting Tuesday afternoon**. Thank you!

能否請您於下週一之前給我答覆？我們下週二下午的會議需要用到。謝謝！

Ⓓetails

對別人使用 as soon as possible 可能是不禮貌的，但站在本人的立場使用 as soon as possible 卻是很自然的。就像我們會很自然地說「我會盡快處理這件事」一樣。

（上司剛才分派了幾項任務給我）

No problem. I'll get these done as soon as possible.

沒問題。我會盡快處理這幾件事情。

應用

If you have any additional questions, please email me at your earliest convenience. Have a great day!

如果您有其他問題，請於您方便的時候寄電子郵件給我們。祝您有美好的一天！

10 in touch

（一名員工對經理說）

Is there a way for me to touch with the marketing director? I have a really good idea for an advertisement.

（B2B 銷售人員與新的潛在客戶開完會要離開的時候）
Have a great rest of your day. Let's get in touch. Hopefully we can have a follow-up meeting sometime next week.

→ 有些人在使用 in touch 時，會漏掉介系詞 in，或是誤用一起使用的動詞（get、keep、stay）。

in touch　to be in communication or to have communication with someone 與某人交流

當我們說某人與其他公司 in touch，意思就是你們之間有聯繫往來。

使用 in touch 時，絕對不能漏掉介系詞 in。因為當 touch 單獨使用時，就會變成物理上的接觸的意思。此外，in touch 的含義也會根據一起使用的動詞而改變。

get in touch　to first start having communication 首次開始交流

> I heard a new business just opened in Gangnam. We should get in touch with them and see if they're interested in buying some of our office supplies.
> 我聽說江南那裡新開了一間公司。我們應該主動聯繫他們，看看他們是否有興趣購買我們的辦公用品。

keep / stay in touch　to maintain communication 保持交流
與某人已經是彼此聯繫的狀態，要表達持續保持此狀態時，便可使用 keep in touch、stay in touch 的説法。

> I use Facebook and KakaoTalk to stay in touch with my friends and family back in Korea.
> 我用 Facebook 和 KaokaoTalk 與我在韓國的朋友與家人保持聯繫。

be in touch　to be communicating 正在進行交流
我們也可以使用 be 動詞來説明交流的整體情況。

> I'm in touch with several prospective customers right now. I think I should be able to close at least 2 deals by the end of the week.
> 我現在正在與一些潛在顧客聯繫。在這週末之前，我想我應該可以完成至少兩筆交易。

讓我們以上述內容為基礎，重新檢視下面的句子。

（員工正在與經理交談）

✗ Is there a way for me to **touch** with the marketing director?
I have a really good idea for an advertisement.

○ Is there a way for me to get in touch with the marketing
director? I have a really good idea for an advertisement.

有什麼方法可以讓我聯絡到行銷總監嗎？我有一個非常好的廣告創意。

在下面的句子裡，是與已經認識的人持續保持聯繫，所以必須用 stay
/ keep in touch。get in touch 是用於第一次開始聯繫的情況。另外，
也可以用 contact 取代 touch，寫成 get in contact、stay in contact、
keep in contact 等，意義是相同的。

（B2B 銷售人員與客戶開完會要離開時）

✗ Have a great rest of your day. Let's get in touch. Hopefully
we can have a follow-up meeting sometime next week.

○ Have a great rest of your day. Let's stay / keep in touch.
Hopefully we can have a follow-up meeting sometime next
week.

祝你今天過得愉快。讓我們保持聯繫。希望我們能在下週找個時間進行後續
會議。

11 take a rest

I've been working for 6 hours straight. I really need to take a rest.

It's been a very hectic week. I'm looking forward to taking a rest this weekend.

➤ **要自然地使用 take a rest 比想像中困難。**

take a rest 雖然並非錯誤的說法，但有其他更普遍、更自然的表達方式可以取代 take a rest。根據情況不同，最適合的表達方式也可能會有所不同。

take a break to have a short pause / rest from working, then resume working later 暫停工作、稍後再開始工作

通常我們可以用 take a break 代替 take a rest，用來表示在工作中暫時休息一下的情況。假如是固定的例行休息時間，就可以用 have a break 來表達。舉例來說，如果工作時間是上午 9 點到下午 2 點，以及下午 5 點到 9 點，我們就可以說 have a 3-hour-break，來表示從 2 點到 5 點休息 3 個小時的意思。

讓我們重新檢視下面的句子。這句話的意思是需要暫時休息一下，再回來開始工作。

✗   I've been working for 6 hours straight. I really need to ~~take a rest~~.

○   I've been working for 6 hours straight. I really need to take a break.

我已經連續工作 6 小時。我真的需要休息一下。

如果是離開工作崗位享受自由時間，或是在工作時間之外休息的話，可以用 rest / relax 取代 take a rest 會更自然。

✗   It's been a very hectic week. I'm looking forward to ~~taking a rest~~ this weekend.

○   It's been a very hectic week. I'm looking forward to resting / relaxing this weekend.

真是忙碌的一週。我希望這個週末可以好好休息。

應用

In addition to lunchtime, most employees take a 15-minute break in the afternoon around 3 p.m.

除了午餐時間之外，大部分員工還會在下午 3 點左右休息 15 分鐘。

I just relaxed at home this weekend because I was so burnt out from the workweek.

這週的工作太累了，我週末就待在家休息。

12   I understand well.

I read your email and I understand it well. I will discuss this with my team and get back to you.

Thank you for your email. I understand it well. Unfortunately, I don't think your suggestions will work because ...

「I understand well.」如果使用不當，在某些情況下可能會給人無禮的感覺。

當你說「I understand your email well.」時，可能會讓對方認為你只是在表達你理解電子郵件的內容，卻沒有表明你是否同意電子郵件中提到的內容，也讓人覺得沒有親切感。

另一種可以代替「I understand well.」，並且又更自然的說法是 make sense。當我們使用 make sense 時，不僅給人更親切的感覺，還可以表達肯定或同意電子郵件內容或對方所說內容的意思。

讓我們假設適當的情境，試著修改前面的句子。

✕   I read your email and I understand it well. I will discuss this with my team and get back to you.

○   **Thanks for your response. I think your suggestions make complete sense. I will discuss this with my team and get back to you.**

    感謝你的回覆。我認為你的建議非常有道理。我會與組員商議後再聯絡你。

雖然只用 make sense 也可以，但是利用形容詞和副詞，如 totally makes sense、makes complete sense 等，可以使表達語氣更加豐富。與表示同意對方的 make sense 相反，若是不同意對方的意見時，我們該怎麼說呢？在這種情況下，與其使用和「理解（understand）」有關的說法，不如對對方的建議或努力（idea、effort）表達感謝之意。

×   **Thank you for your email. I understand it well. Unfortunately, I don't think your suggestions will work because ...**

○   **Thank you for your email. I appreciate your suggestions, but unfortunately I don't think they'll work because ...**

    感謝你的來信。謝謝你的建議，但很遺憾，我不認為這樣子會有用，因為……

應用

Hey John,
I read your email and everything makes total sense to me. I think your plan sounds great.

你好，John：
你寄來的電子郵件我已經看過了，我完全同意你所說的內容。我認為這是一個很棒的方案。

13 I'm waiting for your response.

（為寄給潛在商務合作夥伴的電子郵件做結尾）

... You can use my online calendar to confirm the meeting time. I think next week would work best for me. I'll be waiting for your reply.

Thanks, Jiwon Lee

在訊息的最後用「I'm waiting for your response.」做結尾，會給人有點無禮又生硬的感覺。

當我們說「I'm waiting for your response.」的時候，會給人一種在催促對方的感覺。感覺就像你坐在電腦前面苦苦等待，想著對方為什麼還沒有回信，所以這並非恰當的說法。若是改用 look forward to ~ 來表達，不僅語氣較委婉，也可以給人比較專業的形象。

在撰寫正式的電子郵件時，可以用「I look forward to hearing back from you.」，如果關係比較親近的話，可以用「Looking forward to hearing back from you.」。

... You can use my online calendar to confirm the meeting time. I think next week would work best for me.
你可以用我的線上行事曆來敲定會議時間。我認為下週是最好的時間。

✗　　**I'll be waiting for your reply.**

○　　**I look forward to hearing back from you!** (formal)

　　　Looking forward to hearing back from you! (casual)

　　　期待收到你的回覆！

ⓓetails

「收到回覆」不一定要用 hearing back from you 來表示，可以根據不同情況使用不同說法。

舉例來說，如果你在期待 networking event，那你就可以說「Looking forward to the event.」。如果你在期待與某人的初次會面，那你就可以說「Looking forward to meeting you.」。

應用 ─────────────────────

（為電子郵件做結尾）

... We can start moving forward with our project then.

Looking forward to hearing back from you! Have a great day,

Jiwon

……然後我們便能推動我們的專案。

期待您的回覆。祝您度過美好的一天。

智媛

14   have a good time

（結束一天的工作，離開辦公室時向同事說）
Have a good time

（電子郵件的結尾問候語）
Have a good time.

（對即將進行重要簡報的同事說）
I hope you have a good time.

如果沒有在適當的情況下使用 have a good time，可能會顯得很尷尬。

have a good time   (about a specific situation) have fun / enjoy yourself during this situation

如何在適當的情況下正確使用 have a good time，關鍵在於將 have a good time 用於特定的事件或情況（specific situation）。

Did you have a good time at the party last night?
(specific situation = party)
昨天晚上的派對，你玩得開心嗎？

Unfortunately I won't be able to come to the team dinner tonight, but I hope everyone has a good time.

(specific situation = the team dinner)

可惜我沒辦法參加今晚的聚餐，祝大家度過愉快的一晚。

在非特定的情況下，如果要表達「祝你度過愉快的時間」，可以改用 day、night、week 等來取代 have a good time 裡面的 time，這樣會顯得更加自然。

讓我們根據上述內容，重新檢視下面的句子。因為下班後就是晚上了，所以只要改成「Have a good night.」就行了。也可以加上 rest of your，變成「Have a good rest of your night.」。

✗　　　Have a good time.

○　　　Have a good night.

就像我們傳訊息或寄電子郵件時，會說「祝你今天一切順利」一樣，寄英文電子郵件時，也經常使用「Have a good / great day.」。

✗　　　Have a good time.

○　　　Have a good / great day.

另外，必須牢記的一點是，have a good time 簡單來說就是「玩得開心（have fun）」的意思，所以它可能不適合作商務英义使用。如果你想向對方說「祝你發表或協商成功」，你可以用下面的句子表達。

I hope (situation) goes well.

Best of luck with (situation).

希望（情況）一切順利。

下面的句子是對即將進行重要簡報的同事說的話，所以可以修改如下。

×   I hope you have a good time.

○   I hope your presentation goes well.

○   Best of luck with your presentation.

應用

Best of luck with your interview tomorrow! I'm sure you'll do great.

祝你明天面試順利！你一定會做得很好。

I'm about to leave the office. Have a good night!

我先下班了。祝你有個愉快的夜晚！

I heard you just got back from a vacation in Hawaii! How was it, did you have a good time?

聽說你從夏威夷度假回來了！怎麼樣，玩得開心嗎？

下面是針對前面介紹過的 **with Error** 部分，修正錯誤用法後的內容，你可以在劃底線的部分確認正確的表達方式。

Message sent: Friday morning, 8:45 a.m.
傳送訊息：週五上午 8 點 45 分

Hello Park Taeho,
您好，朴泰浩：

This is Jiwon Lee, one of the sales representatives for Onward Tech.
It's good to meet you. I hope you're doing well.
我是 Onward Tech 的銷售代表李智媛。很高興認識您。您過得好嗎？

I met with some of your colleagues yesterday afternoon to discuss
how our Synthesis marketing AI system can help Green Light
Electronics grow. Kim Donghwi told me to get in touch with you
about having a follow-up meeting.
昨天下午，我與您的同事見面討論過 Synthesis 行銷 AI 系統要如何幫助 Green
Light Electronics 的發展。金東輝讓我與您聯絡，討論關於後續會議的事宜。

I'd love to meet with you sometime next week if you're available. Let
me know at your earliest convenience. You can also look at the
attachment I added to this email. It explains more about Synthesis.
如果時間允許的話，我希望能在下週與您見個面。請在您方便的時候聯繫我們。另
外，您可以在附檔中看到關於 Synthesis 的詳細說明。

Looking forward to meeting you!
希望能快點與您會面！

Have a great day,
祝您有美好的一天。

Jiwon Lee
李智媛

Message sent: Tuesday morning, 9:30 a.m.
傳送訊息：週二上午 9 點 30 分

Hi Jiwon,
您好，智媛：

Thank you for your message. Also I apologize for the late reply. I had a lot of work last Friday, last weekend, and Monday. Looking forward to next weekend already so I can finally relax!
謝謝您的來信。很抱歉這麼晚才回覆您。我上週五、上週末和週一的工作量太多了。真希望週末快點到來，那樣我就能休息了。

I read your email and looked at the Synthesis attachment. I think Synthesis sounds like a great product.
I would be happy to have a follow-up meeting this week. I am available tomorrow any time 2:00-4:00 p.m. or Thursday 1:00-5:00 p.m. Let me know which time works for you.
我已經看過您寄來的電子郵件與關於 Synthesis 的附加檔案。我認為 Synthesis 是非常出色的產品。我希望我們可以在本週進行後續會議。我明天下午 2 點到 4 點，還有週四下午 1 點到 5 點有空。請告訴我您方便的時間。

Thanks Jiwon!
謝謝智媛！

Taeho
泰浩

Hey Taeho,

您好，泰浩：

It's okay! I've been pretty busy the past few days as well.

沒關係。我前幾天也很忙。

That sounds great. I think Thursday afternoon at 3 p.m. would be perfect. We usually have our follow-up meetings virtually on Webex. Are you familiar with Webex? However, I don't mind coming to your office to meet in person.

太好了，我認為週四下午 3 點不錯。我們通常會在 Webex 上面以虛擬會議的方式進行後續會議。您熟悉 Webex 嗎？不過，我也可以親自去拜訪您，與您面談。

Would you prefer a virtual meeting or a face-to-face meeting?

虛擬會議和當面開會，您認為哪種方式比較好呢？

Take care,

保重。

Jiwon

智媛

Message sent: Tuesday afternoon, 1:43 p.m.

傳送訊息：週二下午 1 點 43 分

Hi Jiwon,

您好，智媛：

I'm totally fine with meeting on Webex! I'm looking forward to
meeting you. Is there anything I need to prepare for our meeting?
我可以接受用 Webex 開會。我期待與您的會面。在開會之前我需要準備什麼嗎？

Taeho
泰浩

Message sent: Tuesday afternoon, 4:20 p.m.
傳送訊息：週二下午 4 點 20 分

Sounds good, Taeho!
太好了，泰浩！
Here's a Webex meeting link:
下面是 Webex 會議連結：
www.webex/meeting57189282711

If you could have some information ready about your recent /
planned advertising campaigns (for example: your latest budget,
analytics, and plans for next quarter) that would be great.
如果您能準備最近或是之前企劃過的廣告活動相關資料（例如最新預算、分析、下
一季度的計劃等），那就太好了。
See you Thursday at 3!
週四下午 3 點見！
Take care,
保重。

Jiwon
智媛

Chapter 6

文法錯誤PART 1
Grammar Mistakes Part 1

1   comparative sentences

2   I am difficult / hard / easy /
    convenient / inconvenient

3   seem / seem like

4   passive sentences

5   using intransitive verbs

6   using transitive verbs

7   including questions in statements

8   first / at first / the first time

9   each / every

10 all the time / every time

11 gerunds and infinitives

12 adjectives involving numbers

13 using size adjectives

以下的敘述中包含錯誤的用法。請閱讀一遍，並試著找出不自然的表達方式。在各章節的最後會提供修正後的正確表達。

智媛成功與 Green Light Electronics 簽訂了合約，並做過多次業務成果發表。現在智媛正在與 Michelle 進行她第一個月的績效考核面談。

(Jiwon knocks on Michelle's office door)

Michelle Hey, Jiwon! Come on in.

(Jiwon comes in and sits down)

Michelle Alright, so first of all, I'd love to hear your perspective on how this month has been.

Jiwon Yeah, I'm really enjoying things so far! I was kind of difficult the first time, because I don't have a lot of B2B sales experience, but I'm already more confident in my sales skills and am working hard to get better. I think I'm improving with every presentations.

Also, everyone's been really friendly and helpful. I knew the office environment was good here, but it's even great than I expected.

Michelle Great! Do you have any questions or anything you aren't sure about?

Jiwon Yeah, last sales meeting they asked a lot of really technical programming questions. I did my best, but I wasn't totally sure how should I answer. Should I just

	connect them with one of our engineers in those cases?
Michelle	Yeah, that is happen pretty often. Jaemin handles a lot of the more technical questions from prospects and customers. Just say you'll connect them with him. After the meeting, send a group email connecting them and briefly explain the questions so Jaemin can understand.
Jiwon	Okay, got it. I've also noticed that some people seem a little hesitant to sign up for our 1 year subscription plan. Do we ever offer a 3 months plan or 6 months plan?
Michelle	Most of the time no, simply because the 1-year plan is by far the best value for them and us. What made people seem like hesitant about the 1-year plan?
Jiwon	I met with Daylight Nutrition last week. They're a health supplement startup and want to start marketing their vitamins online. They interested in using Synthesis, but they just spent huge money opening their second offline store. They said they really want to balancing their budget and cutting costs right now.
Michelle	Ahhhhh okay, that makes sense. We'd had a few different situations like that in the past. Usually in those situations we offer a delayed billing plan. We break the price up into multiple installments and allow them to start using the product before we start billing them. We can put a clause into the contract that they have to cover our installment costs if they terminate the contract early. If

they really are interested in using Synthesis but don't have the cash up front, the delayed billing plan works almost all the time.

Jiwon   Great. I'll offer that next time. Is there a standard delayed payment option or would it be case by case?

Michelle   Talk to Sanghyeon about that and follow his suggestions. He does a lot of custom contracts and contract negotiations.

Jiwon   Okay! I'll do that later today.

Michelle   Great. Alright, let's get started with your evaluation ...

1 comparative sentences

This week is much busy than last week.

Our June sales were much more bigger than our May sales.

I prefer work from home over go to the office.

My boss prefers having morning meetings than afternoon meetings.

依照正確文法使用各種比較句是很困難的。

比較兩個對象時，我們可以用幾種句型來表示比較的概念。首先，最基本的句型如下。

X is + 比較級 + 'than' Y

Our newest product is more popular than our previous product.
我們的新產品比之前的產品受歡迎。

此外，拿來比較的兩個對象之中，有一方不一定非得是事物，它可能
是一個想法或意見。

That test was easier than I expected.
那個測驗比我想的還簡單。

在這裡，比較的對象是「對測驗的期待」。

讓我們重新檢視錯誤的例句。第一句應該要用 busy 的比較級 busier 來
表達才對。

✗　　**This week is much busy than last week.**
○　　**This week is much busier than last week.**
　　　這週比上週忙多了。

在第二個錯誤的例句中，由於已經用了比較級的 bigger，所以不必再
加上放在三音節以上的形容詞前面的 more。

✗　　**Our June sales were much more bigger than our May sales.**
○　　**Our June sales were much bigger than our May sales.**
　　　我們在 6 月的銷售額明顯高於 5 月。

prefer 的意思是「更喜歡～」，可以用下列例句的句型來表達。prefer
這個動詞本身就帶有比較（than）的意思，所以必須要用 to / over 來
取代 than。

**Most customers preferred product model 2 to / over
product model 1.**
與型號 1 的產品相比，大部分顧客更喜歡型號 2。

如果在前面已經提到過比較的對象，也可以簡短地說「主詞 + prefer X.」就好。

> A: Which product model did the customers like more?
> 顧客們偏好哪個型號的產品？
> B: They liked both models, but most customers preferred product model 2.
> 他們兩個都喜歡，但大部分的顧客更喜歡型號 2。

如果 X 和 Y 是動作動詞（action verb）的話，則必須在每個動詞後面加上 ing。

> I prefer calling customers to / over emailing customers.
> 比起寄電子郵件，我更偏好打電話給顧客。

讓我們來看一下，大家最常犯與 prefer 相關的錯誤。

1. 使用動詞原形作為比較對象

╳　　I prefer **work** from home to / over **go** to the office.
○　　I prefer working from home to / over going to the office.
　　　比起去公司，我更喜歡居家上班。

2. 使用不是 to / over 的介系詞來進行比較

╳　　My boss prefers having morning meetings **than** afternoon meetings.
○　　My boss prefers having morning meetings to / over afternoon meetings.
　　　我老闆比起下午開會，更喜歡上午開會。

在對話中，比起 prefer，更常用的說法是「I'd rather X than Y.」（X、Y 是動詞），或是「I like X more than Y.」（X、Y 是名詞）。

I prefer working from home to / over going to the office.
= I'd rather work from home than go to the office.
= I like working from home more than going to the office.
比起去公司，我更喜歡居家上班。

應用

The career opportunities for me are much bigger in the US than in Korea. Plus, I actually prefer American culture. Those are the main reasons I'm looking for work abroad.
對我來說，在美國的工作機會比在韓國多很多。此外，其實我更喜歡美國文化。那些是我尋找海外工作的主要原因。

2 I am difficult / hard / easy / convenient / inconvenient

I was really difficult this week because I had to work overtime every day.

I am easy to speak English casually, but I am hard to give formal presentations in English.

有些人會用 difficult、hard、easy、inconvenient 來形容人。

這些形容詞大多是用來描述狀況（situation）或執行的任務（task），不是用來形容人（person）的。

讓我們重新檢視下面的句子。這裡應該用讓人感到辛苦的狀況（this week）取代人（I）來作為 difficult 的主詞。

×   I was really difficult this week because I had to work overtime every day.

○   This week was really difficult for me because I had to work overtime every day.
     我這週真的很辛苦，因為每天都要加班。

由於主詞必須為名詞，所以當狀況（situation）或任務（task）為動詞時，必須在後面加 ing，使其變成名詞。在下面的句子裡，讓人感到辛苦（hard）的不是人（I），而是狀況（finish all my work on time），因為 finish 是動詞，所以必須加 ing，以 finishing all my work on time 作為主詞使用。

✗　　**My boss gives me so much work. ~~I am very hard to finish all my work on time.~~**

○　　**My boss gives me so much work.** Finishing all my work on time is very hard for me.
　　　老闆給我太多工作，要按時完成實在太難了。

當狀況或任務如上述例句一樣為動詞時，我們可以用「It（虛主詞）be easy / difficult for 人 to 不定詞（真主詞）」的句型來表達。

讓我們根據上述內容再來重新檢視下面的句子。

✗　　**~~I am easy to speak English casually, but I am hard to give formal presentations in English.~~**

○　　**It is easy for me to speak English casually, but it is hard for**
　　　虛主詞　　　　　　　　　真主詞　　　　　　虛主詞

　　　me to give formal presentations in English.
　　　　　　　　真主詞

　　　對我而言，要用英文隨意交談很容易，但要用英文做正式簡報很難。

Ｄetails

如果你在談論的對象是自己，就可以省略 for me，因為大家都很清楚說話者是誰。當然，若是加上 for me，整個句子在表達上會更清楚。

229

Finishing all my work on time is very hard for me.
= Finishing all my work on time is very hard.

It is easy for me to speak English casually, but it is hard for me to give formal presentations in English.
= It is easy to speak English casually, but it is hard to give formal presentations in English.

應用

I had an incredibly difficult week. I had several important meetings all over Seoul, but my car broke down so I had to use public transportation. It was really inconvenient for me, but thankfully my meetings went well and our company secured two new clients.

我度過了非常難熬的一週。我在首爾有幾個重要的會議，但我的車子故障了，我只好搭乘大眾交通工具。雖然很不方便，但幸好會議進行得很順利，我們公司又多了兩個新客戶。

3 seem / seem like

> These goals seem like very difficult. You look like really tired today. Are you okay?
>
> → 有些人會分不清楚何時要在動詞後面加上 like。

在 look、seem、taste 等感官動詞後面加 like，可以表示「與～相似」或「具有～的特徵」之意。所以 look like 的意思是「看起來與～相似」或「看起來具有～的特徵」。

是否需要加 like，取決於動詞後面單字的詞性。當動詞後面出現與句子主詞相似或具有類似特徵的名詞或代名詞時，就應該要加 like。

He seems like a really hard worker.
他似乎是個很努力工作的人。
This project seems like it will be impossible.
這個項目似乎不可能實現。

上述例句也可以改成在 seem 後面直接加形容詞，如下所示。

He seems like a really hard worker.
= He seems very hardworking.

This project <u>seems like</u> it will be impossible.

=   This project seems <u>impossible</u>.

如果 seem 的後面出現形容詞或副詞,且沒有加 like,我們便可得知它不是在説主詞與什麼相似,而是在描述主詞的性質。

讓我們重新檢視下面的句子。由於 seem like 後面不接形容詞,所以當形容詞出現時,只要單獨使用 seem 即可。

✗   These goals ~~seem like~~ very difficult.

○   These goals seem very difficult.
　　　　這些目標看起來很困難。

同樣地,下面的句子出現 tired 這個用來説明主詞狀態或情況的形容詞,所以不可以加 like。

✗   You ~~look like~~ really tired today.

○   You look really tired today.
　　　　你今天看起來真的很累。

應用

Our office <u>feels like</u> a ghost town now that over 80% of the staff is working remotely. Sometimes I'm the only one there for a majority of the stay. That might <u>seem</u> kind of isolating, but I actually really like it. I can concentrate easily and there are no interruptions.

由於現在有 80% 以上的員工採取遠距辦公,所以公司感覺像座鬼城。有時候甚至只有我一個人在辦公室。也許看起來有點像被孤立,但我非常喜歡這樣。因為這樣子很容易專心,而且不會被干擾。

4 passive sentences

I surprised how well our product sold!

The payment received our sales team last Tuesday.

要在適當的脈絡中自然地使用被動句是很困難的。

讓我們重新檢視上面出現的句子。被嚇到的人是我,而使我感到驚訝的是 how well our product sold,因此應該改用 be p.p by 句型的被動語態。

✗　　　**I ~~surprised~~ how well our product sold!**

○　　　**I was surprised by how well our product sold!**
　　　　我很驚訝我們的產品賣得這麼好!

此外,在被動語態的句子結構中,如果能根據前後文確實掌握 by 之後的行為者或原因,則可以省略不提。

讓我們來看第二個句子。收到貨款的對象是 our sales team。如果用主動語態來説,是「Our sales team received the payment last Tuesday.」;但若是將 the payment 移作主詞,改成被動語態的話,動詞的形式就要改成 was received by。

✗	The payment **received** our sales team last Tuesday.
○	The payment was received by our sales team last Tuesday.

上週二，我們銷售組收到貨款了。

總而言之，練習如何在主動句與被動句之間自由切換是非常重要的。

被動	I was surprised by how well our product sold!
主動	How well our product sold surprised me!
被動	The payment was received by our sales team last Tuesday.
主動	Our sales team received the payment last Tuesday.

應用

The latest Marvel Avengers movie quickly broke most box office records.

最新的漫威復仇者聯盟電影，迅速打破了大部分的電影票房記錄。

Most box office records were quickly broken by the latest Marvel Avengers movie.

大部分的電影票房記錄都被最新的漫威復仇者聯盟電影迅速打破了。

5 using intransitive verbs

> You're right, that could be happened!
>
> Two weeks ago, I didn't even know this product was existed. Now I absolutely love it!
>
> → 沒有受詞的不及物動詞不能作被動式使用。

及物動詞（transitive verbs）是需要受詞（對象）的動詞，而不及物動詞（intransitive verbs）是說明主詞行為或狀態的動詞，不需要受詞。當然，它的後面可以接形容詞、副詞、介系詞片語等修飾語，但不能出現直接受詞（對象）。

因此，不及物動詞只能用於主動語態。尤其是使用動詞 happen 時，經常出現使用被動式表達的錯誤，happen 是意指「發生」的不及物動詞，所以一定要作主動式使用。

✗   You're right, that could ~~be happened~~!
○   You're right, that could happen!
      你說得對，那是有可能發生的！

exist 也是不及物動詞，同樣也經常被誤用為被動式。

✗   Two weeks ago, I didn't even know this product ~~was existed~~.
      Now I absolutely love it!

235

○ **Two weeks ago, I didn't even know this product** existed.
Now I absolutely love it!

兩週前，我甚至不知道這個產品的存在。但現在我超愛它的！

Details

想要確認動詞屬於及物動詞或不及物動詞，可以在 Google 上搜尋「Is 動詞 transitive or intransitive?」，大部分的字典也有標明及物動詞與不及物動詞。另外，也有同時可作及物動詞和不及物動詞使用的情況，此時兩者的解釋是不同的，必須特別注意。

應用

Please wait for the customer to arrive**. After they** arrive, **be friendly and smile.**

請你等到顧客來為止。待顧客抵達後，請親切接待並保持微笑。

6 using transitive verbs

I sent this morning.

Please open on your computers and scroll down to page five.

完全及物動詞一定要加受詞（對象）。

如果及物動詞沒有加直接受詞，從文法上來看，會變成不完整且不自然的句子。

✗ Everyone should **bring** to the meeting.

在這個句子裡，bring（帶來）這個動詞後面沒有加受詞（對象），所以是錯誤的句子。必須像下面的句子一樣，明白地寫出受詞才行。

○ Everyone should bring their laptops as well as a pen and paper to the meeting.
每個人都得帶著紙筆和筆記型電腦出席會議。

讓我們重新檢視下面的句子。sent 後面的 this morning 是時間副詞，不能當作受詞（對象）。所以 sent 後面必須多加一個受詞才行。

✗   I **sent** this morning.

○   I sent the report **this morning**.

我今天早上把報告寄出去了。

在下面的句子裡，應該改成打開電腦裡的某個東西，這樣子語意表達才自然，所以必須在 open 後面多加一個受詞。

✗   Please **open** on your computers and scroll down to page five.

○   Please open the excel file on your computers and scroll down to page five.

請打開電腦裡的 excel 檔，並向下滑動到第 5 頁。

應用

My company sells AI technology that helps small businesses grow. We also offer many great products for companies in all industries.

我們公司銷售幫助小公司發展的 AI 科技，並且也為各領域的企業提供許多出色的產品。

7 including questions in statements

I'm not sure what does it mean.

I don't know what is it.

用在直述句中間的間接問句，其語序經常令人感到混亂。

疑問句與用在直述句中間的間接問句，在語序上有所不同。假設我們要將「Where did I put my phone?」這個問句變成直述句中的間接問句，就必須把語序按照「疑問詞－主詞－動詞」的順序排列，變成「I can't find where I put my phone.」（我找不到手機放在哪裡）。

讓我們重新檢視下面的句子。

× I'm not sure **what does it mean**.

○ I'm not sure what it means.

我不確定這是什麼意思。

× I don't know **what is it**.

○ I don't know what it is.

我不知道這是什麼東西。

I sent a bunch of follow-up emails to all our customers today. I'm not sure <u>how many I sent</u>, but it must have been at least 100.

我今天寄了很多跟進的電子郵件給所有顧客。我不確定寄了多少封,但至少也有 100 封。

8 first / at first / the first time

At first I gave a business presentation, I was really nervous.

The first time, it was difficult adjusting to the work culture.

→ first、at first、the first time 的用法有時會令人感到混淆。

首先，first 是用來表示事件的清單或順序，可在說明某事或決定順序時使用。

There are three main things we still need to do before launching the application. First, we need to finish beta testing and collect reviews. Second, we need to finish designing our online store. Third, we need to plan out our social media advertisements.

在推出應用程式之前，我們有三件重要的事情要做。首先，我們必須完成 Beta 測試並蒐集評價。其次，我們必須完成網路商店的設計。第三，我們需要規劃社群媒體廣告。

at first 用於表示特定情況或持續的行為開始的時間點。另外，它也暗示了從開始到現在，情況已經發生某種變化。所以當某人說 speaking

English was very difficult at first，那就意味著現在說英文已經變簡單了。如果情況並未改變，最好去掉 at first，並且將句子改成現在式。

Speaking English was very difficult at first. But now it's really fun.
一開始，說英文真的很難，但現在變得很有趣。
Speaking English is very difficult for me.
對我而言，說英文非常困難。

the first time 用於重複的（repeatable）、可數的（countable），且有明確開始與結束的行為，通常是用來表示第一次經歷某事的時候。

The first time I went to my English class, I was very nervous.
我第一次上英文課的時候，真的非常緊張。

英文課的出席次數很容易計算，而且有動詞 went，是有明確開始和結束的情況，所以用 the first time 來表達是很自然的。作為參考，the first time 是意指「第一次」的副詞片語。

My company is offering a 50% discount on all products for the first time ever.
我們公司在進行首次全品項打五折的優惠活動。

現在，讓我們重新檢視下面的句子。由於是回想著第一次做簡報的經驗而說出的話，所以應該使用 The first time。

✗	**At first** I gave a business presentation, I was really nervous.
○	The first time I gave a business presentation, I was really nervous.

我第一次做商務簡報時，真的非常緊張。

從上下文來看，下面要表達的意思是一開始很難適應職場文化，但最近有所改善了，所以應該要用 at first。

✗	**The first time**, it was difficult adjusting to the work culture.
○	At first, it was difficult adjusting to the work culture.

起初，我很難適應職場文化。

應用

The first time I developed an application was such a learning experience for me. I didn't know what to do at first, but by the end of the project I was a much better developer.

對我來說，第一次開發應用程式是很好的學習經驗。起初我不知道該怎麼做，但到了專案要結束時，我已經是個能力更好的開發人員。

9 each / every

- **Each team members should review the monthly company newsletter.**

  Every information you need is on our company website.

將 each 和 every 作複數使用，或是與不可數名詞一起使用的情形經常發生。

當 each 或 every 用在名詞前面時，該名詞必須是單數的可數名詞。

Our sales numbers have improved every month this year.
今年以來，我們的銷售業績每個月都在成長。

這裡指的不是一個月，而是好幾個月，看似該作複數使用，但 each 和 every 都被視為單數。因為它們是用來表示特定群體中的個別對象。相反的，all 指的是整個群體的集合。

every person / each person / all people

另外，each 和 every 必須與可數名詞一起使用。在不可數名詞之前，請一律使用 all。

讓我們重新檢視下面的句子。當句子裡出現 each，只要記住「視為單數」和「可數名詞」這兩個重點即可。所以這裡必須將 members 改為 member。

✗　**Each team members** should review the monthly company newsletter.

○　Each team member should review the monthly company newsletter.
　　每一位組員都應該查看公司的每月通訊。

下面句子裡的 every 也和 each 一樣，必須視為單數並放在可數名詞前面。由於 information 為不可數名詞，所以必須將 every 改成 all，此處指的並非需要的特定資訊，所以只要說 all of the information 即可。

✗　**Every information** you need is on our company website.

○　All of the information you need is on our company website.
　　你需要的資訊在我們的公司網站上全都有。

Ｄetails
有些情況並不適用上述的一般原則，必須特別注意。

1. every + 數字（number）+ 複數名詞（plural noun）
通常用於表示時間。

My company allows employees to take a break every four hours.
我們公司允許員工每 4 個小時休息一下。

2. each of + 限定詞（determiner）+ 複數名詞（plural noun）

The company assigned a specific quarterly goal to <u>each of</u> <u>the employees</u>.
公司給每個員工指派了具體的季度目標。

3. every one of + 限定詞（determiner）+ 複數名詞（plural noun）

<u>Every one of my teammates</u> skipped the meeting today.
我們的組員今天全都沒去參加會議。

應用

Each salesperson should offer discounts to <u>all the</u> <u>customers</u> on their contact list. We want <u>every customer</u> to know about this deal.
每一個銷售人員都得向通訊錄中的所有顧客提供折扣。我們希望每位顧客都知道這個優惠。

10 all the time / every time

> All the time we have a group project, Mark forgets to do his part.
>
> My coworkers gossip every time at work. It's really annoying.
>
> → all the time 和 every time 適用的情況不同。

every time 是用來表示在可數並重複的情況下，某件事 100% 會發生。

He is late every time we have a meeting.
我們每次開會時他都遲到。

上面那句話意味著公司舉行很多會議，而那個人所有會議都 100% 遲到。在這裡，他在可數且一再重複的會議中 100% 遲到，所以用 every time 來表達是很自然的。

all the time 的意思與 constantly、very often 相近，用於持續進行中或頻繁發生的情況。

I have my accounting exam next week, so I've been studying all the time.
下週有會計學測驗，所以我一直在唸書。

這句話的意思是，我為了下週的會計學測驗一直在學習，而學習本身是不可數的。這裡因為想要表達努力不懈地學習，所以使用 all the time 來強調。使用更明確的時間表達方式，如 all day long、all week long、all year long 等，也可以傳達類似的感覺。

讓我們重新檢視下面的句子。group project 是可數名詞，這裡要表達的意思是每次做 group project 的時候，他100% 會忘記自己負責的事，所以應該要改成 every time 才對。

✗　**All the time we have a group project, Mark forgets to do his part.**

○　Every time we have a group project, Mark forgets to do his part.
　　每次做分組報告時，Mark 總是忘記自己負責的部分。

下面要表達同事們在公司裡說別人的閒話（gossip）是常有的事情，所以應該要用 all the time。

✗　**My coworkers gossip every time at work. It's really annoying.**

○　**My coworkers gossip all the time at work. It's really annoying.**
　　我的同事們總是在公司裡說長道短的。真的很討厭。

Ｄetails
1. 使用 every time 的時候，可以用實際發生的事件來取代 time。

I feel nervous before every job interview.

= I feel nervous every time I have a job interview.

我每次面試的時候都很緊張。

2. time 也可以換成特定期間或特定星期/月份。

The regional manager visits our office every quarter.

區域經理每一季都會訪問我們的辦公室。

There's a big international conference every July.

每年 7 月都會舉行一次大型國際會議。

應用

I really wish HR would do something about Mark. He's a
terrible employee. He's late every time we have a meeting,
he surfs the web all the time instead of working, and he
doesn't contribute anything to our group projects.

我希望人資部能對 Mark 做出處置。他是個糟糕的員工。我們每次開會他都遲
到,不工作一直在上網,而且對我們的小組專案一點貢獻也沒有。

11 gerunds and infinitives

> We need to gathering more customer data.
>
> My team wants increasing our sales.
>
> 動名詞和 to 不定詞是相當棘手的部分，連母語人士也會用錯。

我們必須確實區分動名詞與 to 不定詞。

> 動名詞的形式－動詞（V）+ ing：studying, finishing, paying
> to 不定詞的形式－ to + 動詞原形：to study, to finish, to pay

正如字面上的意思，動名詞是將動詞名詞化。因此它雖然具有動詞的性質，但在句子裡扮演著名詞的角色，通常作主詞和受詞使用。而不定詞在句子裡不僅能當名詞，還可以扮演形容詞和副詞的角色。

〔一般原則〕
1. to 不定詞和動名詞通常不會同時使用。有一些例外的情形將另外說明。

○ I like working from home.
○ I like to work from home.

✗   I like ~~to working~~ from home.

2. like、love、hate、start 的後面可以接動名詞，也可以接不定詞。

I like meeting our customers.

我喜歡見顧客。

I like to meet our customers.

我喜歡見顧客。

3. choose、decide、get、want、need、plan 後面要接不定詞。

I need to finish this project by tomorrow.

我必須在明天之前完成這個專案。

We're planning to open a new office in Ulsan.

我們計劃在蔚山開設新的辦事處。

4. quit、finish、enjoy、practice 後面要接動名詞。

I practice giving my speech each night before bed.

我在每晚睡前練習演講。

We need to quit wasting time.

我們必須停止浪費時間。

〔動名詞出現的情況〕

1. 動名詞作主詞使用

Reaching our sales goals will be difficult.（自然）

To reach our sales goals will be difficult.（不自然）

要達成我們的銷售目標會很困難。

Planning the team workshop was a lot more difficult than I anticipated. （自然）

To plan the team workshop was a lot more difficult than I anticipated. （不自然）

規畫小組工作坊比我預期的困難多了。

2. 動名詞作介系詞的受詞使用

1) 介系詞後面必須接名詞，所以要將動詞改為動名詞。

I'm thinking about starting my own company.
我正在考慮要不要自己開公司。
I'm really tired of working overtime every night.
我真的厭倦了每晚加班的生活。

2）前面曾提過，原則上 to 不定詞與動名詞不會同時使用，但也有例外的情形。當動名詞作介系詞 to 的受詞使用時，就是例外的情形。

I am close to finishing the report.
我幾乎快完成那份報告了。
I am looking forward to seeing you.
我真的非常想見到你。

〔不定詞出現的情況〕

1. 形容詞 + 不定詞

It's hard to remember all of the new work policies.
要記住所有新的工作方針是很難的。
It's always important to follow up with customers after a sales session.
重要的是在銷售會議後持續與顧客聯繫。

2. 名詞 + 不定詞

當動詞後面出現名詞時，用 to 不定詞來補充説明該名詞是很自然的。

> **Our team leader wants us to email every customer.**
> 組長要我們寄電子郵件給所有顧客。
> **I do yoga to relax my body after work.**
> 我下班後會做瑜珈來放鬆身體。

讓我們重新檢視下面的句子。儘管有例外會用動名詞作介系詞 to 的受詞使用，但一般不會這樣用。因此，這裡應該用 need to 的不定詞形式。

× **We need to gathering more customer data.**

○ **We need to gather more customer data.**
我們必須蒐集更多顧客資料。

want 是以 to 不定詞為受詞的動詞，因此這裡應該改成 to increase。

× **My team wants increasing our sales.**

○ **My team wants to increase our sales.**
我們的團隊想要增加銷售額。

應用

My boss likes taking us all out for drinks after work on Friday. It's a really nice gesture, but it's kind of annoying when I just want to go home and relax after a long workday.
我的老闆喜歡在週五工作結束後帶我們去喝一杯。雖然是件好事，但在我結束一天漫長的工作，只想回家休息時，就會覺得有點煩人。

12　adjectives involving numbers

> My company has a very clear five years business plan.
>
> We are hoping to start building small two people cars next year.
>
> 這裡犯了把限定形容詞的名詞部分寫成複數形的錯誤。

限定形容詞的作用是在名詞前面修飾並說明該名詞。

> **The tall building**
> **A motivated employee**

有時候會結合多個單字組成限定形容詞，在這種情況下，即使組成形容詞的名詞部分代表兩個以上的數量，也不會使用複數形表示。

回頭看前面第一個句子，會發現它將「五年事業計劃」說成 five years business plan，five years 是在修飾緊隨在後的 business plan。在這種情況下，我們不該將用來修飾名詞的限定形容詞變成複數形，應該在限定形容詞的組成單字之間加上 -（hyphen），改為 5-year business plan 才對。

✗　　　　My company has a very clear **five years** business plan.

○　　　　My company has a very clear five-year business plan.
　　　　我們公司有非常具體的五年事業計畫。

「My company has a very clear five-year business plan.」也可以改寫如下，在這裡 five years 用複數形表示也無妨。

○　　　　**My company has a very clear** business plan for the next five years.
　　　　我們公司往後五年的事業計畫非常具體。

下面的句子也一樣，two people 是用來修飾後面的 cars，表示「兩人座汽車」的意思，由於這裡的 two people 是限定形容詞，所以必須用單數。因此應該使用 people 的單數形 person，改成 two-person cars 才對。

✗　　　　We are hoping to start building small **two people** cars next year.

○　　　　We are hoping to start building small two-person cars next year.
　　　　我們希望能從明年開始生產兩人座小型車。

應用

After saving for years, I finally was able to afford a two-story luxury apartment in New York City.
經過多年的儲蓄，我終於買得起在紐約的豪華雙層公寓了。

13 using size adjectives

The product premiere was a total failure, we only made a tiny money.

It's one of the most popular tech conferences in the world. Huge people will be there.

有時候我們會在提到「數量」時，使用描述「大小」的形容詞。

例如，如果用 tiny money 表示「小錢」，會讓人以為是錢的尺寸小；如果用 huge people 表示「很多人」，會讓人誤會是體型龐大的人。

在描述某物的「數」或「量」時，如果想使用 small、big、huge、tiny 等大小的形容詞，必須使用以下句型。

> 描述可數名詞時，用形容詞 + number of 名詞
> 描述不可數名詞時，用形容詞 + amount of 名詞

讓我們根據上述內容，重新檢視下面的句子。money 是不可數名詞，所以要用 amount 改成 a tiny amount of money。

✕　The product premiere was a total failure, we only made a tiny money.

○　The product premiere was a total failure, we only made a tiny amount of money.

產品展示會完全失敗，導致我們的收益微乎其微。

在下面的句子裡，用 huge people 來表示「很多人」是錯誤的表達方式。由於 huge 後面的 people 是可數名詞，所以應該用 number 將它改成 a huge number of people。

✕　It's one of the most popular tech conferences in the world. Huge people will be there.

○　It's one of the most popular tech conferences in the world. A huge number of people will be there.

這是全球最受歡迎的科技會議之一。一定會有很多人來。

應用

Even though I earned a higher salary at my old job, my hours are much more flexible now. I finally had the time to start investing in real estate and I'm actually earning a lot of money through my investments.

雖然我之前的工作領的薪水比較多，但現在的工作時間更有彈性。現在我終於有時間投資房地產，並且透過投資賺了很多錢。

下面是針對前面介紹過的 **with Error** 部分，修正錯誤用法後的內容，你可以在劃底線的部分確認正確的表達方式。

（智媛敲了 Michelle 辦公室的門）

Michelle
Hey, Jiwon! Come on in.
嗨，智媛！請進。
（智媛走進辦公室坐下）

Michelle
Alright, so first of all, I'd love to hear your perspective on how this month has been.
好，首先，我想聽聽你這個月過得怎麼樣。

智媛
Yeah, I'm really enjoying things so far! <u>The sales presentations were kind of difficult for me at first</u> because I don't have a lot of B2B sales experience, but I'm already more confident in my sales skills and am working hard to get better. I think I'm improving with <u>every presentation.</u>
是的，到目前為止我很享受這一切。一開始，做銷售簡報對我來說有點難，因為我並沒有太多 B2B 銷售經驗，但現在我對自己的銷售技巧有了自信，並且正在努力變得更好。我認為自己正隨著每次的簡報進步。

Also, everyone's been really friendly and helpful. I knew the office environment was good here, but it's even <u>better</u> than I expected.
另外，這裡的每個人都非常友善及樂於助人。雖然我本來就知道這裡的工作環境很好，但它比我想像得還要好。

Michelle   Great! Do you have any questions or anything you aren't sure about?

太好了！你有什麼不了解的地方或問題嗎？

智媛   Yeah, last sales meeting they asked a lot of really technical programming questions. I did my best, but I wasn't totally sure how I should answer. Should I just connect them with one of our engineers in those cases?

有。在上次的銷售會議上，我被問到許多有關程式設計的技術性問題。雖然我已經盡力了，但我不確定該如何回答。在那種情況下，我應該直接協助他們去聯繫我們的工程師嗎？

Michelle   Yeah, that happens pretty often. Jaemin handles a lot of the more technical questions from prospects and customers. Just say you'll connect them with him. After the meeting, send a group email connecting them and briefly explain the questions so Jaemin can understand.

是的，那種情況經常發生。在民負責處理來自潛在顧客和現有顧客的各種技術性問題。你只要說你會協助他們聯絡負責人。然後在會議結束後，寄一封群組電子郵件給他們和在民，讓他們互相聯絡，並在信中簡要說明好讓在民能理解問題。

智媛   Okay, got it. I've also noticed that some people seem a little hesitant to sign up for our 1 year subscription plan. Do we ever offer a 3-month plan or 6-month plan?

好，我明白了。另外，我還注意到有些人對於訂閱一年的方案感到猶豫。我們有提供 3 個月或 6 個月的訂閱方案嗎？

Michelle　Most of the time no, simply because the 1-year plan is by far the best value for them and us. What made people seem hesitant about the 1-year plan?

大多時候沒有。因為無論對客戶或我們來說，一年訂閱方案都是最有利的。是什麼原因讓他們看起來對一年訂閱方案感到猶豫？

智媛　I met with Daylight Nutrition last week. They're a health supplement startup and want to start marketing their vitamins online. They were interested in using Synthesis, but they just spent a huge amount of money opening their second offline store. They said they really want to balance their budget and cut costs right now.

上週我和 Daylight Nutrition 的人見面。那是一家保健食品新創公司，他們打算在網路上行銷維他命產品。他們對 Synthesis 感興趣，但是他們開設的第二家實體商店的支出龐大，所以現在希望能削減成本並平衡預算。

Michelle　Ahhhhh okay, that makes sense. We'd had a few different situations like that in the past. Usually in those situations we offer a delayed billing plan. We break the price up into multiple installments and allow them to start using the product before we start billing them. We can put a clause into the contract that they have to cover our installment costs if they terminate the contract early. If they are really interested in using Synthesis but don't have the cash up front, the delayed billing plan works almost every time.

喔……這樣就說得通了。我們以前也有過類似的情形。通常在那種情況下，我們會提供延遲計費方案。由我們將費用分期後，允許客戶在我們開始收費之前先使用產品。我們可以在合約中加入一項條款，要求對方於合約提前終止時支付分期付款金額。如果他們真的對 Synthesis 感興趣卻無法準備足夠的現金，大多數時候延遲計費方案都是行得通的。

智媛
Great. I'll offer that next time. Is there a standard delayed payment option or would it be case by case?
太好了。下次我會試著提供客戶這個方案。延遲付款是固定方案，還是要視情況而定呢？

Michelle
Talk to Sanghyeon about that and follow his suggestions. He does a lot of custom contracts and contract negotiations.
這個問題你可以跟尚賢討論之後，再照他的建議去做。尚賢在擬定合約和合約協商這方面的經驗很豐富。

智媛
Okay! I'll do that later today.
我明白了！我今天就會去做這件事。

Michelle
Great. Alright, let's get started with your evaluation ...
好。那麼，讓我們開始智媛你的考核……

Chapter 7

文法錯誤PART 2

Grammar Mistakes Part 2

1	explaining frequency
2	using 'mean'
3	your saying
4	all / every not, not all / every
5	I am late for 5 minutes.
6	one of (something)
7	-ed / -ing for adjectives
8	ages / quantities / lengths of time
9	using two words with the same function
10	using intensifiers
11	forgetting determiners when using many adjectives / adverbs
12	talking 'in general'

以下的敘述中包含錯誤的用法。請閱讀一遍，並試著找出不自然的表達方式。在各章節的最後會提供修正後的正確表達。

智媛拿下了與 Green Light Electronics 的合約，並做過多次業績發表。現在智媛正在與 Michelle 進行她第一個月的績效考核面談。Michelle 正針對智媛的表現提供回饋意見。

Michelle	Alright Jiwon, first let's look at your sales numbers. So far, you've met with eighteen different businesses. You've closed seven new deals and have three more pending, so that's a closing rate of about forty percent, which is actually a kind of really impressed rate. Most people start out in the twenties to low thirties. I know you said B2B sales pitches are difficult pitches, but Sanghyeon and I are both really exciting with your performance so far.
Jiwon	Thank you. Most of the potential customers that haven't signed up yet said they'd contact me later. In your experience, do potential customers ever sign up later?
Michelle	They always don't sign up later, but we can occasionally convert some of them. Usually we contact any potential leads again after we have an update or new product. This happens once per every four to six months, so keep a list of all your leads and hopefully you'll get some of them to sign up when you contact them again later this year.
Jiwon	Yeah, I've been putting all their information into the sales

team files in the portal. I also created my own spreadsheet too.

Michelle Good! Most people have their own system like that. It's more easier to keep track of everything.
A few things I've noticed. It seems like you're booking your sales meetings a bit too close together. If one meeting goes longer than expected and traffic is bad it'll be pretty hard to get to your next meeting on time.
If you're late for a few minutes or even on time but obviously in a rush, that can make a pretty bad first impression.

Jiwon Yeah, that's true.

Michelle Ideally, get there 20 minutes early so you have plenty of time to set up and check in. Also, be friendly and chat with everyone: security, receptionists, everyone. You never know who the managers will talk to after you meet. One of our old salesman was really good at giving pitches, but actually lost a few potential sales because he was rude to a company receptionist one day. We got some negative feedbacks from that company's manager after that.

Jiwon I totally understand your mean. I'll remember all of that.

Michelle Great! One other thing. Normally I would never comment on this, but I do think it would help if you improved your business English, especially your pronunciation. Sometimes it's difficult to understand your saying. I know Korean have a hard time with R and L and a few other sounds. I know a great English pronunciation coach. If you'd like, I'd be happy to connect you with him. As you know, our company covers 50% of the cost for business English lessons.

Jiwon   Yeah, that would be great! I've been looking for a good English instructor since I started working here.

Michelle   Perfect. I'll send a short email after this meeting to introduce you. Keep up the good work, Jiwon. I think you're gonna be really successful, valuable member of our sales team.

Jiwon   Thank you for your time!

1 explaining frequency

> We usually have team meetings 1 times every weeks.
>
> We try to update our applications 1 times for three months.
>
> **在表達頻率時，經常會使用生硬和不自然的句子結構。**

使用以下句子結構，可以讓你明確自然地表達頻率。

(thing happening) X time(s) every Y (length of time)

數字   數字 hour, day, week,
month, year 等

1. 要表達某件事發生的頻率時，句子裡面一定要使用動詞。

✗   We company workshops 1 time every six months.

○   We have company workshops 1 time every six months.
我們公司每六個月舉辦一次研討會。

2. 1 time、2 times 可以用 once、twice 代替。（once、twice 是更常用的說法。）

○　　I usually take the subway to work, but I drive my own car 1 or 2 times every week.

○　　I usually take the subway to work, but I drive my own car once or twice every week.

我通常搭地鐵上班，但每週有一到兩次會自己開車。

3. 如果表示時間的名詞為單數（如 just one week、month、year 等），可以用 per / a 取代 every。

　　　I attend teleconferences twice every week.
　　　I attend teleconferences twice a week.
　　　I attend teleconferences twice per week.
　　　我每週參加兩次遠距會議。

在下面的句子裡，表示時間的名詞應該用單數，卻寫成了複數（weeks），因此可以修改成下列三種說法。

✕　　We usually have team meetings 1 times every weeks.

○　　We usually have team meetings once a week.

○　　We usually have team meetings once per week.

○　　We usually have team meetings 1 time every week.

　　　（也可以寫成 once every week，但較沒有固定時間概念，可能表示本週週一開一次會，下週是週三開一次會。）

在下面的句子裡，提及時間長度時應該使用 every，卻誤用了介系詞 for。

✗ We try to update our applications 1 time for three months.

（for three months 是三個月內）

○ We try to update our applications 1 time every three months.

（every three months 是每三個月）

我們努力每三個月更新一次應用程式。

應用

In order to stay connected while working remotely, each team at my office has a virtual meeting once a week, and we have an office-wide Zoom call once a month to discuss major company issues.

為了在遠距工作期間保持聯繫，我們公司的各組每週會舉行一次遠距會議，並通過每月一次的公司全體 Zoom 通話來討論重大議題。

2 using 'mean'

What is mean? / What is this word's mean?

This mean is we need to slightly lower our prices.

→ **mean 這個動詞經常被用錯。**

首先，可以將用於一般動詞疑問句的助動詞 do 放在主詞前面。

× **What is this word's mean?**

○ **What does this word mean?**
　這個單字是什麼意思？

另外，也可以用名詞 meaning 代替動詞 mean。

× **What is this word's mean?**

○ **What is this word's meaning?**
　這個單字的意思是什麼？

此時，可以用下列表達方式來回答。

This means (that) _____.

According to the consumer survey, most people don't buy our products because they believe our prices are too high. This means we need to slightly lower our prices.

根據消費者調查顯示，大多數人不購買我們的產品是因為他們認為價格太高了。這意味著我們需要稍微調降價格。

應用

A lot of people clicked on our online advertisement, but only a small percentage actually entered their email information on the landing page. This means our ad is effective, but we need to make our landing page more appealing to our target customers.

很多人點擊我們的網路廣告，但實際上只有少數人於一頁式網站輸入他們的電子郵件資訊。這意味著廣告雖然有效，但我們必須設法讓一頁式網站更能吸引目標客群。

3 your saying

> My boss's saying was that the meeting was cancelled.
>
> I agree with his saying.
>
> I didn't fully understand her say.
>
> → **有時候會出現 saying 和 say 被當作名詞使用的情況。**

問題在於 say 明明是動詞，卻被誤認為名詞。當你要表達某人所說的話、意見或資訊時，不該用 person's say 或 person's saying，應該要用 (person) said / says / will say 才對。

(person) said / says / will say (words / opinion / information).

讓我們重新檢視下面的句子。

✕　　My boss's saying was that the meeting was cancelled.

○　　My boss said that the meeting was cancelled.
　　老闆說會議取消了。

提及別人所說的意見或資訊時，可以用 what (person) said 來表示，這通常會出現在受詞的位置。

讓我們再來看看下面幾個句子。

×　　　**I agree with his saying.**

○　　　**I agree with** what he said.

　　　我同意他所說的。

×　　　**I didn't fully understand her say.**

○　　　**I didn't fully understand** what she said.

　　　我不太明白她所說的。

應用

（製藥公司會議結束時）

A: **Alright, before we're done, does anyone have any questions?**

B: **Yeah, I didn't quite understand** what you said **about our vaccination development timeline. When exactly should we begin phase two testing?**

A：好，在結束之前，有人有任何問題嗎？

B：有，我不太明白你所說的疫苗開發時間表。準確地說，第二期臨床試驗應該什麼時候開始呢？

4 all / every not, not all / every

All not members were on time.

Every sales team didn't reach the monthly goal.

很多人分不清楚 all not 和 not all 兩者的差異。

all 和 every 是用來表示某事物 100% 存在的詞。因此當 all 和 every 後面出現 not 時，實際上就是 0% 的意思。

> **All our customers live in Seoul.**
> 我們的顧客全都住在首爾。
> **All our customers do not live in Seoul.**
> 我們的顧客都不住在首爾。

與此不同，當 not 加在 all 和 every 前面時，就變成了部分否定，也就是 not all → not 100% → 未滿 100%的意思。指的是大於 0%，小於 100%，可以解釋為「並非全部都～」。

> **Not all of our customers live in Seoul.**
> 我們的顧客並非全都住在首爾。

讓我們重新檢視下面的句子。這裡要表達的是有一部分的人開會遲到，其餘的人準時抵達，因此應該使用部分否定。

×　　　**All not members** were on time.

○　　　Not all members **were on time.**
　　　並非所有的成員都準時抵達。

即使要表達 0% 的意思，使用 all ~ not、every ~ not 的結構也可能會顯得很生硬。在這種情況下，改用代表 0% 的 none 或 no 來表達會更好。讓我們記住這一點，再來看下面的句子。

×　　　**Every sales team didn't reach** the monthly goal.

○　　　None of the sales teams reached **the monthly goal.**

○　　　No sales team reached **the monthly goal.**
　　　沒有一個銷售團隊達成當月目標。

always ~ not 和 everything ~ not 也是一樣，可改用 never、nothing 來表達會更好。

×　　　He **always doesn't contribute** to team projects.

○　　　He never contributes **to team projects.**
　　　他從來沒有對小組專案做出貢獻。

×　　　**Everything didn't go** as planned at the conference.

○　　　Nothing went **as planned at the conference.**
　　　會議上沒有一件事是按照計劃進行的。

My work hours are from 10 a.m. to 7 p.m., but I <u>don't always</u> get to leave right at seven. Sometimes I have to work a little bit of overtime, but I can almost always leave by eight.

我的工作時間是上午 10 點到下午 7 點，但我並非總是在 7 點準時下班。雖然有時候必須加班，不過我幾乎都能在 8 點前下班。

5 I am late for 5 minutes.

The meeting started early a couple of minutes.

I'm really sorry, but I am late for 5-10 minutes for the appointment later today.

→ 在使用 late 和 early 來表示遲到或提早時，有時會出現詞序排列錯誤的情況。

通常在說「我早到了 10 分鐘」、「我遲到了 1 小時」等包含時間在內的句子時，只要在 10 分鐘、1 小時等數字後面加 early / late 即可。

✗　　He will probably be late a few minutes.
○　　He will probably be a few minutes late.
　　　他可能會遲到幾分鐘。

讓我們重新檢視下面的句子。這裡應該先寫出表示時間長度的 a couple of minutes，再於其後加上 early 才對。

✗　　The meeting started early a couple of minutes.
○　　The meeting started a couple of minutes early.
　　　會議提早幾分鐘開始了。

使用 late 和 early 時，用錯句子時態也是常見的失誤，必須根據情況使用不同的時態。

1. 如果特定情況尚未開始，請使用未來式。

I will be about 30 minutes late to the team dinner tomorrow night.

明晚的小組聚餐，我可能會遲到 30 分鐘左右。

在上面的例句中，有 tomorrow night 這個明確的未來時間，所以使用了未來式。

下面的句子也一樣，後面出現了 later today 這個未來時間，所以必須使用表示未來時態的 will be late。

✕　I'm really sorry, but I am late for 5-10 minutes for the appointment later today.

○　I'm really sorry, but I will be 5-10 minutes late for the appointment later today.

很抱歉，今天的會面我可能會遲到 5 到 10 分鐘左右。

2. 如果特定情況已經開始，但目前無法抵達時，請用 (be) running late 來表達。

Let's start the meeting. Tom just messaged me that he's running about 10 minutes late, he can catch up when he gets here.

我們開始開會吧。Tom 剛才傳簡訊給我，說他會遲到 10 分鐘左右。Tom 可以抵達後再跟上我們的進度。

3. 如果是剛剛抵達的情況，請使用現在式。

I have a 3:00 p.m. appointment, but I'm about 15 minutes early.

我約了 3 點，但我提早 15 分鐘到了。

I'm so sorry I'm 10 minutes late!

對不起，我遲到了 10 分鐘。

4. 如果是某件事情已經開始，並且已於之前抵達的情況，請使用過去式。

Sorry, I was 5 minutes late to the meeting earlier this morning.

對不起，今天早上的會議我遲到了 5 分鐘。

應用

David: Hey John, I know we were supposed to have our Zoom call at 8 p.m., but I'm running about 10 minutes late. Would it be okay if we start at 8:10? Sorry for the inconvenience!

John:　No problem! Message me when you're ready to start.

David： John，我知道我們約好晚上 8 點用 Zoom 通話，但我可能會晚 10 分鐘左右。可以 8 點 10 分再開始嗎？很抱歉造成你的不便！

John：　沒問題！等你準備好再傳訊息給我。

6 one of (something)

> One of colleague will transfer departments this week.
>
> One of problems with the new application is it takes too long to load.
>
> 在名詞前面加 one of 時，有時會出現錯誤的用法。

在句子裡使用 one of 時，一定要遵循以下結構。

one of 限定詞 + 複數名詞
（＊限定詞：冠詞、所有格、數詞、指示形容詞、數量形容詞、否定形容詞）

雖然限定詞會根據情況改變，但一般最常用的是 the、my、our。因為 one of ~ 的意思是「幾位、幾個當中的一個」，所以後面出現的名詞必須是複數。另外，由於主詞是 one，因此句子裡的動詞必須用單數動詞。

Most of my clients live in Seoul, but one of my clients lives in Daejeon.

限定詞 複數名詞

單數動詞

我的客戶大多住在首爾，但其中有一位住在大田。

最常見的錯誤是沒有用限定詞，或是在必須使用複數名詞時用了單數名詞。

讓我們根據上述內容，重新檢視下面的幾個句子。

✕　**One of colleague** will transfer departments this week.

○　One of my colleagues **will transfer departments this week.**
　　我的一位同事這週要調到其他部門。

✕　**One of problems** with the new application is it takes too long to load.

○　One of the problems **with the new application is it takes too long to load.**
　　新應用程式的問題之一是加載時間過長。

Ⓓetails

1. 雖然 one of ~ 是最常見的用法，但也可以用其他數字來代替 one。

Three of my team members are Korean. The rest are American.
我們組內有三名成員是韓國人，其餘都是美國人。

2. 如果想用 0（zero）取代 one 的話，可以用 none of ~ 來表示。

None of my team members speak Korean, so I have to speak English at work all day.
我的組員當中沒有人會說韓文，所以工作時我必須整天用英文。

3. 即使名詞前面出現副詞和形容詞，也一定要加上限定詞並使用複數名詞。

One of the really pleasantly surprising things about this
week was how well our new app sold.

本週真正令人驚喜的消息之一，是我們新推出的應用程式非常熱銷。

應用

One of the biggest problems in the manufacturing
industry is supply chain efficiency. If you can't deliver
your products to your customers efficiently, you won't
be able to survive.

製造業最大的問題之一是供應鏈的效率。如果你不能有效率地將產品交
付給顧客，你便無法生存。

7   -ed / -ing for adjectives

I had so much work to do last week, so it was very tired.

I am very exciting about my new promotion.

雖然是相對簡單的文法，但有時我們仍會對於該使用以 -ed 結尾的形容詞，還是以 -ing 結尾的形容詞感到混淆。

只要記住以下兩種方法，就能正確地區分並使用以 -ed 結尾的形容詞和以 -ing 結尾的形容詞。

1. -ed 形容詞用於描述人的感受。

I gave my team the day off because they were all so tired.
組員們全都很累，所以我讓他們放了一天假。

2. 相反的，-ing 形容詞是用於描述使人產生 -ed 形容詞所對應之情緒的事物。也就是說，使人感到 tired 的物品、人或情況是 tiring 的。

I gave my team the day off because our most recent project was so tiring.
最近的專案太累人了，所以我給組員們放了一天假。

最近的專案讓組員們變得 tired，所以應該用 tiring 來形容它。

My colleague is kind of annoying.
我的同事有點煩人。

因為 My colleague 讓我變得 annoyed，所以應該用 annoying 來形容他。

We're almost finished developing our newest, most interesting product.
我們快要開發出最有趣的最新產品了。

the product 讓我們感到 interested，所以應該用 interesting 來形容它。

I had an exhausting week.
我度過了令人精疲力盡的一週。

the week 讓我感到 exhausted，所以應該用 exhausting 來形容它。

讓我們重新檢視下面的句子。由於是上週工作太多的情況導致我很累，所以這裡應該要用 tiring。

✗   **I had so much work to do last week, so it was very tired.**

○   **I had so much to do last week, so it was very tiring.**
上週我要做的工作太多了，真的很累人。

如果將主詞換成 I，那就是我累了，只要像下面的句子一樣使用 tired，就能表達相同的意義。

○   I had so much to do last week, so I was very tired.

下面這句話是主詞 I 的感受，所以應該用 excited 才對。

✕   I am very ~~exciting~~ about my new promotion.
○   I am very excited about my new promotion.
我對於這次的升遷感到很興奮。

Ⓓetails

有些形容詞的 -ed 形式不變，但會用其他形態取代 -ing 形式。

scared / scary
stressed / stressful
impressed / impressive

I don't like my boss. Being around him is so stressful.
我不喜歡我的老闆。跟他在一起壓力很大。

跟老闆在一起的情況（Being around your boss）讓我感到有壓力，所以這裡用 stressful 是對的。

很多人會用「I'm stressful.」來表達「受到壓力」的意思，但這裡要表達的是「我」這個人的感受，所以應該說「I'm stressed.」或「I get stressed.」才對。

I had to walk home really late last night. It was kind of scary.
昨天很晚的時候我不得不走路回家。感覺有點可怕。

晚上很晚走路回家的情況（walking home late at night）讓我感到害怕，所以這裡應該用 scary。

His presentation was really impressive.
他的簡報真的很出色。

他的簡報（his presentation）讓我印象深刻，所以這裡用 impressive 是對的。

應用

I never thought I would end up being an AI researcher. When I was younger, I thought science and technology were really boring. However, I had a really good business professor in college who first got me interested in the tech industry. Now, I think AI is a very exciting field and I'm really satisfied with what I do.

我從沒想過我會成為一名 AI 研究人員。小時候，我認為科學技術非常無聊。然而，我在大學時遇到一位非常棒的經營學教授，他讓我第一次對科技產業產生興趣。現在，我認為 AI 是個令人振奮的領域，並且對自己的工作感到非常滿意。

8 ages / quantities / lengths of time

The people are 15 on the finance team.

I am 29 years.

Getting a job is difficult for mid 20's people in Korea.

➔ **在說明年齡、數量、時間長短時，有時候會不知道正確的表達方式。**

首先，讓我們來看看年齡（age）和數量（quantity）的區別。一般來說，在提到年齡時，會將數字放在名詞的後面；在提到數或量時，會將數字放在名詞前面。

> **My daughter is two (years old).**
> **I have two daughters.**

大家最常犯的錯誤，就是在提到「量」的時候，把數字放在名詞後面，而不是放在名詞前面。

× **The people are 15 on the finance team.**
○ There are 15 people **on the finance team.**
  財務組有 15 名員工。

讓我們重新檢視前面的句子。乍看之下，這句話似乎是對的，但實際上如果這樣寫，意思是財務組（finance team）裡的每個人都是 15 歲。想要表達組內成員的人數，必須將數字移到名詞（people）前面，改成 15 people 才對。

通常在表示時間長度時，可以使用 for，以「for 數字 weeks / months / years」的句型來表達。

I have worked here for three years.
我在這裡工作了 3 年。

當提及人或動物的年齡時，「數字」或「數字 years old」兩種說法都可以使用。但除此之外的其他物品、公司、建築物等，請用「數字 years old」來表示。

My dog is 12 (years old).
我的狗今年 12 歲。

✕   **This building is over 400.**
○   **This building is over 400 years old.**
這棟建築物有 400 年以上的歷史。

讓我們再來看看下面的句子。由於是在談論年齡，所以可以單獨用數字表示，也可以在數字後面加 years old。

✕   **I am 29 years.**
○   **I am 29. / I am 29 years old.** 我今年 29 歲。

最後，在提到年齡時，「20 幾歲」是 in my 20s，「30 幾歲」是 in my 30s，可以根據情況修改所有格與數字並自行應用。舉例來說，20 歲

出頭、中段、後半只要將 early、mid、late 加在數字前面，說成 in my early 20s、in my mid 20s、in my late 20s 即可。

A lot of Koreans in their early and mid 20s struggle to find good jobs.
許多 20 多歲的韓國年輕人都拚命地要找到一份好工作。

讓我們根據上述說明，重新檢視下面的句子。

✕　　**Getting a job is difficult for mid 20s people in Korea.**

○　　**Getting a job is difficult for** people in their mid 20s in Korea.

○　　**Getting a job is difficult for** Koreans in their mid 20s.
　　　25 歲左右的韓國人在就業方面遭遇困難。

應用

I first started working at Sonia in 2003. I was in my early 20s and had just graduated university. I worked hard for years, slowly climbing the company ladder, until I became the youngest senior manager in 2012 when I was only 32 years old.
我於 2003 年開始在 Sonia 工作。當時我 20 歲出頭，剛從大學畢業。我多年來努力工作，穩步升遷，直到 2012 年以 32 歲的年紀成為最年輕的資深經理。

9 using two words with the same function

Our team will going to have a meeting tomorrow afternoon about finding new clients.

I heard that the prospect decided to work with our competitor instead of us. There isn't nothing we can do about it now, just learn from the situation and focus on finding new possible clients.

It should be much more easier to find high paying clients once our website looks more professional.

We could also update our ads with more professional images too.

在一個句子裡反覆使用重複的單字或片語，從文法上來看可能是不正確或不自然的。

比起寫作，在口說上更容易犯這種錯誤。

首先，讓我們來看下面的句子。在這個句子裡，重複使用了表示未來的 will 和 be going to。will 和 be going to 這兩種說法可以說意思幾乎一樣，不過請各位記住，will 是比 be going to 更正式的說法。

✕	Our team will going to have a meeting tomorrow afternoon about finding new clients.
○	Our team will have a meeting tomorrow afternoon about finding new clients.
○	Our team is going to have a meeting tomorrow afternoon about finding new clients.

我們團隊將在明天下午舉行有關開發新客戶的會議。

讓我們再來看看下面的這個句子。這個句子同時使用了 isn't 和 nothing 的雙重否定。從前後文來看，它要表達的意思是「現在沒有任何我們能做的事」，所以只需要使用一個否定説法即可。

✕	There isn't nothing we can do about it now, just learn from the situation and focus on finding new possible clients.
○	There's nothing we can do about it now, just learn from the situation and focus on finding new possible clients.
○	There isn't anything we can do about it now, just learn from the situation and focus on finding new possible clients.

現在沒有任何我們能做的事，只能從狀況中學習並專注在開發新客戶。

下面的句子也是一樣，沒有必要在比較級的 easier 前面再加 more。我們通常會在發音短的形容詞（單音節、雙音節）末尾加 -er（如 faster、better、harder 等），在發音長的形容詞（3 音節以上）前面加 more（如 more difficult、more exciting、more intelligent 等）來形成比較級。

✗　　It should be much more easier to find high paying clients once our website looks more professional.

○　　It should be much easier to find high paying clients once our website looks more professional.

如果能讓我們的網站看起來更專業，應該更容易找到高端客戶。

最後，我們來看下面的這個句子，句中用了 also（也），句尾又用了 too（～也）。由於兩者的意義重複，所以必須去掉其中一個。作為參考，also 是比 too 更正式的說法。

✗　　We could also update our ads with more professional images too.

○　　We could also update our ads with more professional images.

○　　We could update our ads with more professional images too.

我們也可以用更專業的形象來更新廣告。

[應用]

The stock's value should continue to increase.

＝　　The stock's value should increase over time.

股價將持續上漲。

10 using intensifiers

The project was kind of very difficult.

Thankfully, our team is pretty finished with this project.

Our next project will be quite same.

重複使用 very、so、really、extremely、totally、absolutely 等強調的說法，有時候會顯得不自然。

intensifier（加強副詞）指的是用來說明另一個詞的程度或強度，並強化其意義的形容詞與副詞。讓我們透過下表來確認 intensifier 與其強度的差異。

mild	moderate	intense	very intense
kind of	fairly	quite	very
slightly	somewhat		really
	pretty		extremely

1) intensifier 只能使用一次。

舉例來說，當我們說 kind of pretty difficult，由於重複使用了 kind of 和 pretty 這兩種 intensifier，所以是錯誤的句子。

✕	**The project was ~~kind of very~~ difficult.**
○	**The project was kind of difficult.**
	那個項目有點困難。
○	**The project was very difficult.**
	那個項目非常困難。

2) 在無法表示程度的情況下，不可以使用 intensifier。

舉例來說，「My grandfather is kind of dead.」這個句子，由於人只會有兩種狀態，不是活著（alive），就是死了（dead），所以不可能有「kind of dead」這種説法。

在商務英文中，使用 finished / done 的時候要特別留意。pretty finished / done 這種説法在邏輯上是不成立的。如果你想表達「快完成了」的意思，你應該使用 partially 或 almost 等副詞，你可以説 partially finished / done 或 almost finished / done。

下面的句子是指專案還未完全結束的情況，所以用 almost 取代 pretty 會比較自然。

✕	**Thankfully, our team is ~~pretty finished~~ with this project.**
○	**Thankfully, our team is almost finished with this project.**
	謝天謝地，我們小組快要完成這個專案了。

我們再來看下面的這個句子。只要有一點不同就是不同，所以對 same 這個詞使用 intensifier 是不恰當的。在這種情況下，只要將 same 改成 similar，就可以使用 intensifier 了。

✗   Our next project will be **quite same**.

○   Our next project will be quite similar.

我們的下一個專案會跟這一個非常相似。

應用

Unfortunately, I will be quite busy this week, but I'm pretty sure Mike's schedule is open. I know he's very interested in attending more seminars, so you should ask him to go instead.

可惜這週我會很忙,但我肯定 Mike 沒有安排其他行程。我知道 Mike 很想多參加一些研討會,你應該請他去。

11 forgetting determiners

> I had really interesting conversation with one of my colleagues today.
>
> Our new application is highest-reviewed, best-selling application we've ever made.
>
> 當可數名詞前面的修飾語太長時，會發生漏掉限定詞的情況。

指示形容詞 demonstrative	所有格 possessive	數量形容詞 quantifiers
this, that, these, those	my, your, his, her, its, our, your, their	some, any, every, more, much, few, little
冠詞 articles	序數 ordinals	基數 numbers
a, an, the	first, second, third, last, next	one, two, three, four, twenty, fifty, hundred

✗ We experienced **problem** at the office today.

○ We experienced a problem at the office today.

今天公司裡發生了一個問題。

在上面的句子裡，problem 是可數名詞，所以前面必須要加限定詞。

✕   We experienced pretty big, unexpected problem at the office today.

○   We experienced a pretty big, unexpected problem at the office today.
今天公司裡發生了一個意想不到的嚴重問題。

即使 problem 前面加了 pretty、big、unexpected 等形容詞和副詞，讓修飾語變得很長，但 problem 仍是可數名詞，所以一定要加限定詞。

至於要使用哪種限定詞，則取決於情況與名詞。下句所用的 conversation 並非指稱特定對話，因此前面只要加不定冠詞 a / an 即可。

✕   I had really interesting conversation with one of my colleagues today.

○   I had a really interesting conversation with one of my colleagues today.
今天我和一位同事的對話非常有趣。

在下面的句子裡，用形容詞和關係子句確切說明了 application，所以只要加上定冠詞 the 或所有格即可。

✕   Our new application is highest-reviewed, best-selling application we've ever made.

○   Our new application is the highest-reviewed, best-selling application we've ever made.

○   Our new application is our highest-reviewed, best-selling application we've ever made.
我們新開發的應用程式，是我們開發過的應用程式中最受好評和最暢銷的。

This was longest, most difficult project of my career.

→ This was the longest, most difficult project of my career.

這是我職業生涯中最長，也最困難的項目。

12   talking 'in general'

> As a customer service rep, I spend most of my day talking to customer on the phone.
>
> Korean university are pretty competitive.
>
> ➔ 在泛指一般事物的情況下，犯下使用單數名詞的錯誤。

在泛指一般事物時，一定要使用複數名詞。例如，在「I just bought a smartphone.」這個句子裡，a smartphone 不是指特定的某支智慧型手機，而是一支一般的智慧型手機。但是像「I just bought the newest Samsung Galaxy smartphone.」這句，指稱特定品牌的智慧型手機時，就必須加上定冠詞 the 才行。

讓我們根據上述內容重新檢視下面的句子。我的工作是和顧客通話，這裡的顧客是通稱，所以應該要改成 customers。

✕   As a customer service rep, I spend most of my day talking to customer on the phone.

○   As a customer service rep, I spend most of my day talking to customers on the phone.
身為客服人員，我一天大部分的時間都在與顧客通電話。

下面的句子指的是一般的韓國大學，並非指某一所特定的大學，所以比起用 Korean university，改用 Korean universities 會更恰當。

✗ **Korean university are pretty competitive.**

◯ **Korean** universities **are pretty competitive.**

  韓國的大學競爭非常激烈。

應用

Good English skills are important for employees in international companies.

對跨國公司的員工而言，擁有出色的英文實力很重要。

下面是針對前面介紹過的 with Error 部分，修正錯誤用法後的內容，你可以在劃底線的部分確認正確的表達方式。

Michelle

Alright Jiwon, first let's look at your sales numbers. So far, you've met with eighteen different businesses. You've closed seven new deals and have three more pending, so that's a closing rate of about forty percent, which is actually a really impressive rate. Most people start out in the twenties to low thirties. I know you said B2B sales pitches are difficult, but Sanghyeon and I are both really excited with your performance so far.

好，智媛，讓我們先來看看你的銷售數據。到目前為止，你跟 18 家公司接洽過。你已經完成 7 筆新交易，還有 3 筆以上正在進行中，成交率約為 40%，這是非常了不起的數據。大多數員工是從 20% ～ 30% 開始。雖然你說 B2B 的銷售話術很難，但你至今的表現讓尚賢和我都感到非常興奮。

智媛

Thank you. Most of the potential customers that haven't signed up yet said they'd contact me later. In your experience, do potential customers ever sign up later?

謝謝。大部分未簽約的潛在顧客也表示他們日後會再與我聯繫。之前有過潛在顧客後來才簽約的案例嗎？

Michelle

They don't always sign up later, but we can occasionally convert some of them. Usually we contact any potential leads again after we have an update or new product. This happens once every four to six months, so keep a list of all your leads and hopefully you'll get some of them to

sign up when you contact them again later this year.
雖然並非所有客戶都會在日後簽約，不過偶爾會讓一些客戶改變心意。一般當有產品升級或新品時，我們會再次聯繫潛在客戶。這些事情通常每 4～6 個月會發生一次。所以保留那些潛在客戶的名單，也許今年再次與他們聯繫時，你有望可以再拿下幾筆合約。

智媛   Yeah, I've been putting all their information into the sales team files in the portal. I also created my own spreadsheet.
是，我已經將潛在客戶的所有資訊儲存在入口網站的銷售組檔案裡了。我還建立了自己的試算表。

Michelle   Good! Most people have their own system like that. It's easier to keep track of everything.
太好了！大多數人都會像那樣建立自己的系統。這樣比較容易掌握每一件事。

A few things I've noticed. It seems like you're booking your sales meetings a bit too close together. If one meeting goes longer than expected, and traffic is bad, it'll be pretty hard to get to your next meeting on time. If you're a few minutes late or even on time but obviously in a rush, that can make a pretty bad first impression.
我注意到一些問題。智媛你似乎將銷售會議安排得太緊湊了。如果會議時間超出預期，或是遇到交通堵塞等問題，可能會導致你難以準時出席下一場會議。如果你開會遲到，或是準時抵達卻很匆忙，就很難給人留下良好的第一印象。

智媛   Yeah, that's true.
是這樣沒錯。

Michelle	Ideally, get there 20 minutes early so you have plenty of time to set up and check in. Also, be friendly and chat with everyone: security, receptionists, everyone. You never know who the managers will talk to after you meet. One of our old salesmen was really good at giving pitches, but actually lost a few potential sales because he was rude to a company receptionist one day. We got some negative feedback from that company's manager after that.

提早 20 分鐘抵達是較為理想的。這樣子你才有充分的時間準備和報到。另外,請友善並與所有人交談,包括警衛和接待人員。因為你永遠不會知道,對方的經理在和你開完會之後會跟誰交談。以前我們公司的一位銷售人員非常擅長推銷話術,但他某天對一家公司的接待人員無禮,並因此錯失了一些銷售機會。在那之後,我們收到來自該公司經理的負面評價。

智媛	I totally understand what your mean. I'll remember all of that.

我完全明白你的意思。我會將這些銘記在心。

Michelle	Great! One other thing. Normally I would never comment on this, but I do think it would help if you improved your business English, especially your pronunciation. Sometimes it's difficult to understand what you're saying. I know Korean have a hard time with R and L and a few other sounds. I know a great English pronunciation coach. If you'd like, I'd be happy to connect you with him. As you know, our company covers 50% of the cost for business English lessons.

好！還有一件事。我通常不會說這樣的話，但我認為提升商務英文實力，尤其是改善發音是對你有益的。有時候，我很難理解你在說什麼。我知道韓國人在 R 和 L，以及其他部分發音上有困難。我認識一位很優秀的英文發音老師。如果你願意的話，我想介紹你們認識。你應該知道，我們公司會補助商務英文進修 50% 的費用。

智媛　　Yeah, that would be great! I've been looking for a good English instructor since I started working here.
那真是太好了！自從開始在這裡工作之後，我就一直在尋找好的英文老師。

Michelle　Perfect. I'll send a short email after this meeting to introduce you. Keep up the good work, Jiwon. I think you're gonna be a really successful, valuable member of our sales team.
很好。這次面談結束後，我會寄一封簡短的電子郵件引薦你們認識。智媛，請繼續努力。我認為你會成為我們銷售團隊中一位成功且可貴的人才。

智媛　　Thank you for your time!
謝謝你抽出寶貴的時間！

Chapter 8

詞彙選擇錯誤
Word Choice Mistakes

1	question
2	menu
3	schedule
4	shocked
5	cheer up
6	expect
7	almost
8	organize
9	cheap
10	appointment
11	fresh
12	satisfied
13	matter
14	moment
15	overwork
16	promotion
17	retire
18	bear
19	point out

以下的敘述中包含錯誤的用法。請閱讀一遍，並試著找出不自然的表達方式。在各章節的最後會提供修正後的正確表達。

週五下午，尚賢和智媛在銷售組的 Google Hangouts 上進行一對一即時通訊。

Sanghyeon　Happy Friday, team! Quick favor, would anyone be able to a little overwork this weekend? We would need someone to lead a Zoom meeting with a US customer Saturday morning.

Mike　Sorry, I have an appointment with my family Saturday. We have tickets to the Doosan Bears vs Lotte Giants KBO game.

Charlie　I've had so many schedules lately, I was really hoping to just relax and be fresh this weekend. I can do it if no one else can, though.

Jiwon　No worries Charlie, I can do it. Would I need to come to the office or can I do the call from home?

Charlie　Thanks, Jiwon!

Sanghyeon　Great! It's not a matter. As long as your Internet's good you can do it wherever. Thanks Jiwon, hope it's not inconvenient for you.

Jiwon	It's no problem! I didn't have any schedule for this weekend anyway.
Sanghyeon	Perfect. I'll send you a PM with more info.

(personal chat between Sanghyeon and Jiwon)

Sanghyeon	Thanks again, Jiwon. I attached a document with background on this customer and the meeting agenda. This customer is a Korean-US fashion brand called Allure. We've been working with them for a really long moment, so it shouldn't be too much work. They just want to question you about some upcoming product updates. Everything's already planned, so you would just need to answer questions and organize the meeting.
Jiwon	Great, I'll take a look and let you know if I have any questions. Hey Sanghyeon, I don't understand the part of the meeting agenda that mentions data upgrades.
Sanghyeon	Ah yeah … They've used almost their data storage on their current plan. I was going to suggest they upgrade to the Enterprise package so they'll have more data. That would be cheaper than buying extra data near the end of each month after they run out.
Jiwon	Got it, I'll suggest that. I'm curious though, you usually do all of the Saturday morning calls. Are you busy this weekend?

Sanghyeon   This stays between us, but I actually have an interview with the US branch Saturday. I'm applying for an overseas director position.

Jiwon   Wow, I'm so shocked! Congratulations!

Sanghyeon   Thank you! I've been wanting to promote for a while now. This is a huge opportunity for me and my family. I can't bear the thought of just staying at this role for the rest of my career.

Jiwon   That sounds great. I hope the interview is successful!

Sanghyeon   Thank you. I expect this opportunity. I'll be really satisfied if I get this position. You know Jiwon, if I do promote, they'll be looking for someone to fill my position here. You've been doing a great job and I think you'd be a prime candidate.

Jiwon   Wow, that's really satisfying to hear, thank you for the compliment. Do you think I'm ready?

Sanghyeon   Cheer up! You're a fantastic sales rep with a lot of experience. They also want someone who is bilingual in this role. I think you'd be very successful. Plus, having that leadership experience will look great if you ever decide to retire.

Jiwon   It's really an honor to hear that. I hope your interview goes well and we'll see what happens!

1 question

Hi Mike,

Sorry to bother you, but can I question you about the new Dropbox system?

將 question 視為動詞並錯誤使用的情形經常出現。

question 通常作為意指「問題」的名詞使用。有時候 question 也會作動詞使用,但此時它具有其他含義,並非指單純的「提問」,這點必須特別留意。動詞 question 大多作下列兩種意義使用。

question 1. to ask someone a series of questions in a formal situation usually because you think they did something wrong (正式的)質問、詢問、詰問

當 question 作此意義時,通常是用於與法律相關情況(legal situations)。

> The police <u>questioned</u> the criminal for hours. Finally, the criminal admitted to committing the crime.
> 警察詢問犯人好幾個小時,犯人終於承認了犯行。

question　2. to express doubt, hesitance, or an objection to something 懷疑或提出異議

> **At first, I really questioned transferring to a new department. However, now I know I made the correct choice. (I doubted and was hesitant about transferring to a new department)**
> 起初，我對於轉調新部門這件事抱持懷疑。但現在我知道我做了正確的選擇。（我對轉調新部門的事抱持懷疑並猶豫不決）

因此，最前面第一個句子說 question Mike about the Dropbox system，意味著質問或質疑 Mike，從前後文來看是不恰當的。

在這裡不該將 question 作動詞使用，應該改為名詞，以 ask a question 的說法來表達。請參考下列句型。

> I questioned [sb] → I asked [sb] a question
> I questioned [sb] → I asked a question to [sb]
>
> I asked my teacher a question.
> = I asked a question to my teacher.
> 我問了老師一個問題。
>
> I asked my boss a question.
> = I asked a question to my boss.
> 我問了老闆一個問題。

如果不止一個問題的話，你可以說 a few questions 或 some questions。讓我們重新檢視下面的句子。

✗ Hi Mike,

Sorry to bother you, but can I question you about the new Dropbox system?

○ Hi Mike,

Sorry to bother you, but can I ask you a few questions about the new Dropbox system?

你好，Mike：

很抱歉打擾你，我能問你一些關於新的 Dropbox 系統的問題嗎？

應用

I really dislike the way Jayden constantly questions my ideas just because he's older than me.

我真的很討厭 Jayden 只因為自己比我年長，就一直對我的看法提出質疑。

At the end of the presentation, there will be plenty of time to ask questions.

在簡報的最後，會有充分的時間可以提問。

2 menu

- You can order many menus at this restaurant.

  The menus at this restaurant taste great.

→ 在餐廳裡，經常會誤用 menu 一詞來指稱餐點或飲料。

menu n. the list of all the food and drinks available at a restaurant
餐廳提供的所有餐點和飲料的清單

menu 指的並非是餐點或飲料，而是我們常說的菜單。我們去餐廳會看著 menu 點餐。而印在 menu 上供人選擇的餐點則叫作 dish。

現在讓我們重新檢視下面這幾個句子。我們可以根據情況，以實際點餐的餐點名稱來取代 menu。

×　**You can order ~~many menus~~ at this restaurant.**
○　**You can order** many different types of food **at this restaurant.**
　　在這間餐廳，你可以點各式各樣的餐點。

○ **You can order** many types of sushi / wine / kimchi etc. **at this restaurant.**

在這間餐廳，你可以點各種壽司 / 紅酒 / 辛奇等。

✕ **The menus at this restaurant taste great.**

○ The food **at this restaurant tastes great.**

這家餐廳的餐點非常美味。

○ The appetizers / main dishes / desserts etc. **at this restaurant taste great.**

這家餐廳的開胃菜 / 主菜 / 甜點非常好吃。

應用

The catering service has a few possible menu **options for our event. Look at these and let me know which** menu **looks best!**

餐飲供應服務為我們舉辦的活動提供了幾種可能的方案。看看這些，然後告訴我哪種菜單看起來最好！

3 schedule

I have many schedules this week.

Sorry, I can't meet you then. I have another schedule at that time.

很多人不知道 schedule 的正確用法。

schedule　n. a timetable that lists all of your duties / obligations / events and when they happen 所有待辦事項的行程表

由於 schedule 指的是所有的待辦事項，所以 many schedules 這種說法在邏輯上不成立。因此，如果要表達有很多行程，你可以說 many things / tasks / events / obligations on my schedule。也可以用 have a very busy / tight schedule 或 have a full schedule 的說法來表達。讓我們根據這些內容來重新檢視下面的句子。

×　　**I have ~~many schedules~~ this week.**

○　　**I have a very busy schedule this week.**
　　　我這週的行程非常緊湊。

增加待辦事項時，不能用 more schedules，要表示自己有其他行程時，也不能用 another schedule。但是，你可以說「I have another obligation. I'm busy.」，或是「I have other plans.」。讓我們再來看看下面的句子。

✕	Sorry, I can't meet you then. I have ~~another schedule~~ at that time.
○	Sorry, I can't meet you then. I have another obligation at that time.

抱歉,那個時間我無法與你會面。因為我有其他事情要做。

○	Sorry, I can't meet you then. I will be busy at that time.

抱歉,那個時間我很忙,可能無法與你會面。

Ｑetails

不過,如果是分別管理的不同行程表,就可以用 schedules 或 another schedule 來表示。舉例來說,一個人可能會同時 有與工作相關的 work schedule、安排運動行程的 workout schedule,還有單獨管理家族活動的 family schedule。然而, 在大多數的情況下,說自己有 many schedules 這種說法是不 正確的。

應用

I would love to attend the fintech Zoom conference next week, but unfortunately my schedule is completely full. If your team hosts another virtual event, please let me know!

我很想參加下週舉辦的金融科技 Zoom 會議,可惜我的行程已經排滿了。如 果您的團隊有舉辦其他線上活動,請通知我!

4 shocked

在應該用 surprised 來表達的情況下，使用 shocked 是常見的失誤，其實這兩個用詞的語感截然不同。

首先，shocked 是比 surprised 更加強烈的表達方式。當你說「I'm shocked」，意思是你被嚇到連話都說不出來。所以 shocked 是用於極度震驚的情況。另外，shocked 大多用於負面的情形，不會用在幸福快樂的時候。最好只在非常煩憂（very upsetting）、驚慌（disturbing surprises），以及因意外情況（unexpected situations）而受到打擊的時候使用。

讓我們來假設一種可以用 shocked 來表達的情況。例如，警察來到家裡，說他們以殺人嫌疑逮捕了你的鄰居。認識很久的鄰居竟然是殺人犯，這種事情是你做夢也想不到的。在這種情況下，你就可以說「When the police came to my apartment and explained why they arrested my neighbor, I was shocked.」。

現在讓我們重新檢視下面的句子。

✗ **Wow, I'm so shocked that you noticed! Thank you!**

○ **Wow, I'm surprised that you noticed! Thank you!**

哇，我很驚訝你竟然看出來（我換髮型）了！謝謝你！

Ⓓetails

請記住，除了 shocked 之外，shocking 也一樣只能用於非常震驚、令人慌張的負面情況。

I heard some sad, shocking news today at work. My colleague Christina's husband suddenly passed away from a heart attack. He was only 38.

我今天在公司聽到令人傷心又震驚的消息。我同事 Cristina 的丈夫因心臟麻痺猝死了。他才 38 歲而已。

應用

Our CEO suddenly quit without telling anyone. Everyone at the company is shocked and confused by his decision.

我們執行長沒有告訴任何人就突然辭職了。公司裡的每個人都對執行長的決定感到震驚與困惑。

5 cheer up

> • It's very important for parents to cheer up their children.
>
> （對明天有重要面試的朋友說）
> Cheer up! You can do it!
>
> → 有些人會錯誤地使用 cheer up 這個片語。

cheer up to make or become less sad or upset and start to feel happy again 激勵

cheer up 是在對方傷心（sad）或沮喪（upset）時，為了讓對方打起精神而使用的表達方式。如果僅僅只是要幫助、支持、鼓勵或激勵對方，用 cheer up 會顯得很尷尬。在這種情況下，可以用 help、support、encourage、motivate / inspire 等說法來代替 cheer up。

讓我們重新檢視下面的句子。

× It's very important for parents to ~~cheer up~~ their children.

○ It's very important for parents to support / encourage / help / motivate their children.
父母支持 / 激勵 / 幫助 / 鼓勵孩子是很重要的。

如果你想對面臨重要面試的朋友說「加油！」，你不該用 cheer up，
應該要使用下列說法。

×　　Cheer up! You can do it!

○　　Good luck! You can do it! 祝你好運！你一定可以的！

○　　I believe in you! You can do it! 我相信你！你一定可以的！

○　　You'll do great! You can do it! 你會做得很好！你一定可以的！

應用

I really appreciate how supportive and encouraging the
team leaders are here at Google.
我非常感謝 Google 的各位組長對我的支持與鼓勵。

One of my best friends just lost his job due to a company
layoff. I feel really bad for him, so we're going to meet up
this weekend to cheer him up.
我的一位好朋友因為公司裁員而失業了。我真的很為他感到難過，所以我
們打算這個週末跟他見面，讓他打起精神來。

6 expect

（約親近的同事在工作結束後一起去喝酒）

It's been a long week. I expect to get drinks with you all later.

（招聘人員與應徵者的對話）

recruiter: Okay, we scheduled your in-person interview for 9 a.m. next Friday here at our Seoul office.

candidate: Thank you very much. I really expect that.

有些人會在必須使用 excited 或 look forward to 的情況下，使用 expect。

expect v. to think something is likely to happen 預期

expect 只是考慮某事發生的可能性，並沒有表達個人對這種可能性的好惡。

I recently invested in Bitcoin because I expect that its value will go up soon.
我最近投資了比特幣，因為我預期它會升值。

I can't believe our new smartphone app reached 100,000 downloads! We expected it would be popular, but we didn't expect 100,000 downloads within the first month!

我真不敢相信，我們新推出的手機應用程式下載數竟然高達 10 萬！雖然我們預想到它會受歡迎，但沒料到第一個月的下載數就能達到 10 萬！

人們經常在希望某事發生時，用 expect 來表達，但此時應該改用 excited 或 look forward to。作為參考，excited 是一種友好、輕鬆的表達方式，所以最好是與對方有一定認識且關係親近才能使用。相比之下，look forward to 給人較為鄭重且專業的感覺，通常可用在較為正式的場合。

I am excited to watch the Lotte Giants this weekend!
這週末可以看到樂天巨人隊的比賽讓我很興奮！
I really look forward to the chance to speak at the tech conference this weekend.
我很期待這週末在科技會議上發表演說的機會。

現在讓我們重新檢視下面這幾個句子。

✕　It's been a long week. I expect to get drinks with you all later.
○　It's been a long week. I'm excited to get drinks with you all later.
真是漫長的一週。期待等一下能跟你們一起喝一杯。

A: Okay, we scheduled your in-person interview for 9 a.m. next Friday here at our Seoul office.
A：好的。我們已經安排你於下週五上午 9 點，在首爾辦公室進行面試。

✗　B: Thank you very much. I really ~~expect~~ that.

○　B: Thank you very much. I really look forward to that.

B：非常謝謝你。期待能盡快見面。

應用

The product premiere actually went even better than expected! We were hoping to sell 500 units but we ended up selling almost 700.

事實上，產品展示會進行得比預期的更加順利！我們原本以為能賣出 500 台就很好了，沒想到賣了將近 700 台。

（收到正式的工作錄取通知後）

Thank you so much. I really look forward to joining your team and helping the company grow.

非常感謝你。我真心期待加入貴公司的團隊，並為公司的發展助一臂之力。

7 almost

> English is very important for my team, but almost team members have trouble speaking English naturally.
>
> I almost have meetings Monday morning, but this week we don't have any urgent issues, so there's no meeting.

→ 有些人會在應該使用 almost all、almost every、almost always 的情況下,卻單獨使用 almost 來表達。

almost adv. very nearly, but not quite 幾乎

almost 是用來指某事可能發生或接近事實,但最終沒有實現的情況。此外,由於它是副詞,所以其作用是用來修飾形容詞、動詞或其他副詞。因此,如果把它當作修飾名詞的形容詞使用,會顯得很尷尬。

> The movie was so sad that I almost cried. → 修飾動詞
> 那部電影太悲傷,我差點就哭出來了。
> Finding affordable housing in Gangnam is almost impossible. → 修飾形容詞
> 要在首爾江南區找到價格合宜的住宅幾乎是不可能的。

He is very good about checking his emails, and responds almost immediately. → 修飾副詞

他經常確認電子郵件，而且幾乎是立刻回覆。

副詞 almost 不能用來修飾名詞片語 team members。在這種情況下，只要將 almost 改成 almost all、almost every，不僅能表達相同的含義，也能用以修飾名詞。另外，需要特別留意的一點是，與 all 結合時，必須使用複數名詞，與 every 結合時，必須使用單數名詞。

✗　　**Almost the workers at my company are Korean.**

○　　Almost all the workers **at my company are Korean.**
　　　（all + 複數名詞）

○　　Almost every worker **at my company is Korean.**
　　　（every + 單數名詞）
　　　我們公司的員工大部分都是韓國人。

讓我們重新檢視下面的句子。

✗　　**English is very important for my team, but almost team members have trouble speaking English naturally.**

○　　**English is very important for my team, but** almost all my team members **have trouble speaking English naturally.**

○　　**English is very important for my team, but** almost every team member **has trouble speaking English naturally.**
　　　英文對我們這組來說非常重要，但幾乎所有組員都無法說出道地的英文。

要表達幾乎 100% 會重複的行為時，應該使用 almost always。

I almost always go to Pilates after work.

我通常下班後都會去做皮拉提斯。

讓我們根據上述內容，重新檢視下面的句子。

✗　I ~~almost~~ have meetings Monday morning, but this week we don't have any urgent issues, so there's no meeting.

○　I almost always have meetings Monday morning, but this week we don't have any urgent issues, so there's no meeting.

我週一上午通常都有安排會議，但本週因為沒有緊急事項要商議，所以就沒有安排會議。

┌─ 應用 ───┐

Okay, so we're almost finished with our meeting, but before we end let's briefly review what we covered today.

好，會議已接近尾聲。在結束之前，讓我們快速地回顧一下今天討論的內容。

Our weekly meetings are pretty small, usually only 5 or 6 people, but almost every employee attends the quarterly meetings.

每週例會的規模較小，通常只有五到六個人參加，但幾乎所有員工都會出席季度會議。

I'm technically supposed to finish work at 5:30 p.m., but I almost always have to stay an extra 30-40 minutes to finish all my work.

嚴格來說，我應該在下午 5 點 30 分下班，但我幾乎都要多花 30 ～ 40 分鐘才能完成所有工作。

8 organize

（上司召開 Zoom 群組會議）

I just emailed all of you the agenda for today. Let's try to follow it so we can organize this conference.

很少有人能準確區分 organize 和 organized 兩者含義上的不同。

organize　v. to arrange or put things into a structured order 整理

當事情雜亂無章（messy）或不明確（unclear），而你想要整理或糾正它的時候，你可以用 organize 這個動詞來表達。如果是已經整理好（organized）的情況，當主詞為人時，可以用 keep (something) organized，當主詞為情況（event / situation）時，可以用 stay organized 來表達。

The moderator kept the meeting organized.
主持人讓會議井然有序地進行。
The meeting stayed very organized because everyone closely followed the agenda.
由於每個人都嚴格遵守議程，所以會議進行得有條不紊。

讓我們重新檢視下面的句子。上司希望所有人都能確實遵守議程，讓已經安排好的會議順利進行到最後。在這種情況下，用 keep this conference organized 才是對的。

✗ I just emailed all of you the agenda for today. Let's try to follow it so we can organize this conference.

○ I just emailed all of you the agenda for today. Let's try to follow it so we can keep this conference organized.
我已經將今天的議程用電子郵件寄給各位了。讓我們遵照議程，確保這次會議能井然有序地進行。

┌─ 應用 ────────────────────────────────────┐

It's very important that we keep all our Slack conversations organized. So, please make sure you only send relevant information, and check that it's the correct group before sending any files.
讓我們所有的 Slack 對話有條有理是很重要的。因此，請你確認只傳送相關資訊，並在傳送檔案前確定是否傳送到正確的群組。

9 cheap

（電腦銷售人員在介紹產品）

Our laptop has all the basic features you're looking for, and is also very cheap.

由於 cheap 一詞的語感，有時會傳達不同於說話者意圖的負面意義。

cheap 的意思是「便宜」，但在語感上略帶有負面意義。當我們說「Something is cheap.」時，意思是某樣東西的價格低廉，但同時也意味著它的品質（quality）不怎麼樣。

Most of the products at Daiso are cheap.
大創的商品大部分都很便宜。

若想避免帶有貶義的語感，可以使用下列兩個詞彙來取代 cheap。

1) inexpensive

inexpensive 意味著低成本（low cost），卻沒有低品質（low quality）的含義。

2) affordable

affordable 指的是產品價格與其品質相比並不貴，會給人一種產品價值超越其價格的正面印象。

讓我們根據上述說明，重新檢視下面的句子。在介紹公司產品時，最好使用給人正面印象的 affordable。

✕　Our laptop has all the basic features you're looking for, and is also very cheap.

○　Our laptop has all the basic features you're looking for, and is also very affordable.

我們的筆記型電腦不僅具備各位想要的所有基本功能，而且價格也相當實惠。

應用

If you want cheap products, you can always go to Daiso, but if you want real quality products at very affordable prices, you should check out our website.

如果你想要的是便宜的東西，隨時都可以去大創買；但如果你想要的是物美價廉的商品，你應該查看我們的網站。

10   appointment

（已經跟同事約好一起吃晚餐，卻因孩子生病而不能去。）

I'm really sorry, but I can't attend our appointment tonight because my son is sick at home.

許多人連在隨意的對話中，也會使用 appointment 這個正式用詞。

---

appointment   n. an arrangement to meet someone at a particular time and place 在特定時間和地點與某人見面的約定

appointment 比較適合用於接待或交易等特定情況，不適合用於以友誼為目的，輕鬆見面的關係。

> **doctor's appointment**
> **dentist / dental appointment**
> **massage appointment**

如果是與某人輕鬆地見面，可以直接說出見面後要做的事（如 have coffee、have dinner 等），或是使用 hang out、meet up 等表達方式。

讓我們根據以上說明，重新檢視下面的句子。

×   I'm really sorry, but I can't attend our appointment tonight because my son is sick at home.

○   I'm really sorry, but I can't have dinner with you all tonight because my son is sick at home.

真的很抱歉，我兒子生病在家，所以我今天沒辦法跟大家一起吃晚餐了。

○   I'm really sorry, but I can't meet up with you all tonight because my son is sick at home.

真的很抱歉，我兒子生病在家，所以我今天晚上沒辦法跟大家見面了。

應用

Sorry I can't go to lunch with you. I have a physiotherapy appointment during my lunch break. If you want though, we can meet up for drinks after work.

對不起，我沒辦法跟你一起去吃午餐。因為我午休時間預約了物理治療。
如果你願意，我們可以下班後再見面喝一杯。

11 fresh

（度過一個輕鬆的週末之後，週一早上與同事聊天。）

Last week was really busy. I was super stressed, but after this weekend I feel fresh again.

在描述人的感受時，誤用 fresh 的情況很常見。

fresh　1. adj. new and different, not previously known or done 新的

After working in the engineering industry for 10 years, I decided I needed a fresh start so I became a programmer.
在工程領域工作了 10 年後，我認為自己需要一個新的開始，所以我轉而去當一名程式設計師。

fresh　2. adj. (about food) recently made, picked, or cooked so it is not spoiled and safe to eat. (this is especially common for fruits and vegetables) （與食品相關）新鮮的

My grandmother's fresh kimchi is the best kimchi I've ever eaten.
我奶奶做的新鮮辛奇，是我吃過最好吃的辛奇。

雖然在某些情況下也會用 fresh 來形容人的感受，但是大部分都不太自然。當有人使用 feel fresh 這種説法，通常是處於以下兩種情況。

1. 經歷身體不適後，重新恢復正常時。

然而，即使在這種情況下，使用「I feel (much) better.」、「I feel recovered.」 或「I feel rejuvenated.」 來表達，還是比用「I feel fresh.」更加自然。

2. 單純心情好的時候

在這種情況下，也可以使用「I feel good.」和「I feel great.」來取代「I feel fresh.」。

讓我們重新檢視下面的句子。

✗　　Last week was really busy. I was super stressed, but after this weekend I feel fresh again.

○　　Last week was really busy. I was super stressed, but after this weekend I feel much better.
上週真的很忙。雖然壓力很大，但過了這一個週末之後，我感覺好多了。

> 應用
>
> After meeting with all the sales teams, we've decided we need a fresh approach to our sales strategies.
> 在與所有銷售團隊開完會後，我們決定我們需要一種全新的銷售策略。

12　satisfied

（親近的同事問我對於居家上班的看法）

Overall, I'm very satisfied with this situation. It's really convenient being able to avoid the 90-minute commute to the office every day.

（上司展示新辦公室並問我是否喜歡）
Wow, this looks great! I am very satisfied, thank you.

由於 satisfied 是一種正式的說法，所以在親近的人，尤其是在朋友之間使用會顯得很尷尬。

很多人只知道 satisfied 是「滿意（content and pleased）」的意思，但在商務情境中，satisfied 作為一種正式的說法，通常會在與客戶或上司交談，以及進行面試或發表的情況下使用。

（汽車業務員對來看車的客戶說）
I think you'll be very satisfied if you choose to buy this car.
您若是購買這輛車，一定會很滿意。

（在面試中談到自己的優點時）

My biggest strength is my outstanding customer service.
I always make sure every customer is <u>satisfied</u> with their
experience, and have fantastic customer reviews.

我最大的優點就是優良的客戶服務。我一直致力於讓所有顧客擁有滿意的消費經驗，也因此獲得優良的評價。

讓我們根據上述說明，重新檢視下面的句子。跟親近的同事說話，用 satisfied 聽起來多少有些生硬。在這種情況下，使用 like 或 love，可以更自然地表達喜歡的意思。

✕　　Overall, I'm very satisfied with this situation. It's really convenient being able to avoid the 90-minute commute to the office every day.

○　　Overall, I like working from home a lot. It's really convenient being able to avoid the 90-minute commute to the office every day.

整體來說，我挺喜歡居家上班的。因為可以省下每天花 90 分鐘通勤的時間。

另外，satisfied 是一種較為克制的情緒表達。當然，它表達了對某事物的滿足程度，但並非是直接地表達喜悅或快樂的用詞。因此，如果你想確切地表達如 happiness、excitement 等情緒，最好使用 love 或 hate。

✕　　Wow, this looks great! I am very satisfied, thank you.

○　　Wow, this looks great! I love it, thank you so much!

哇，這看起來真棒！我很喜歡，太謝謝你了！

13 matter

For the new sales position, we're looking for someone with experience, confidence, and communication skills. Those qualities are really matter when it comes to sales.

We really need to get our financial report done by the end of this week. It is not a matter who does it, we just need to finish it by Friday.

在 matter 必須作動詞使用時，有時會被誤作名詞使用，或是被加上 be 動詞。

matter v. to be of importance / have significance 重要

由於 matter 是動詞，所以不需要另外加 be 動詞。

✗   It is a really matter that we stay within our budget for this project.

○   It really matters that we stay within our budget for this project.
不要超出這個企畫的預算是非常重要的。

讓我們根據這一點來重新檢視下面幾個句子。

✕　　For the new sales position, we're looking for someone with experience, confidence, and communication skills. Those qualities ~~are really matter~~ when it comes to sales.

○　　For the new sales position, we're looking for someone with experience, confidence, and communication skills. Those qualities really matter when it comes to sales.

我們正在尋找有經驗、有自信、溝通能力強的人來擔任新的銷售職位。那些素質對於銷售工作非常重要。

如果是否定句，可以用 does not matter 來表達。

✕　　We really need to get our financial report done by the end of this week. It ~~is not a matter~~ who does it, we just need to finish it by Friday.

○　　We really need to get our financial report done by the end of this week. It doesn't matter who does it, we just need to finish it by Friday.

我們必須在這週之內完成財務報告。不管由誰來做都可以，只要在週五之前完成就行了。

> **應用**
>
> In my opinion, education and academic credentials don't really matter when it comes to career success. What matters is your job performance, professional experience, and continued personal development.
>
> 在我看來，教育和學歷對於職涯上的成功並非如此重要。真正重要的是你的工作表現、專業經驗和持續的個人發展。

14　moment

> The past few months have been a pretty difficult moment for our business. Sales are down and expenses are up.
>
> 在提及很長的時間單位時，有時候會誤用 moment 來表達。

moment　n. a very brief, specific period of time 瞬間

moment 是一種時間概念，指的是非常短暫的瞬間，用於確切的情況。

> **The moment the customer smiled and said 'that's reasonable' after hearing our prices, I knew I could close the sale.**
> 當顧客在聽到價格後，笑著說「這個價格很合理」的那一刻，我就知道可以成交了。

顧客笑著說價格很合理，是一個非常短暫的瞬間。也許根本不超過幾秒鐘。在這種情況下，就應該使用 moment 來表達。

如果是持續時間較長的情況，使用 time 來表達會較為自然。moment 可以用於很短的時間，從幾秒到幾分鐘；而 time 則不受時間長度限制，無論是以幾分鐘為單位，甚至是以幾年為單位都可以使用。

I had a great time at the team building workshop last weekend.

上週末我在團體協作工作坊度過了愉快的時光。

讓我們重新檢視下面的句子。

✗ The past few months have been a pretty difficult **moment** for our business. Sales are down and expenses are up.

○ The past few months have been a pretty difficult time for our business. Sales are down and expenses are up.

過去幾個月是我們公司事業上相當艱難的一段時間。銷售額減少，支出增加。

[應用]

My time spent traveling in Europe had a big impact on my career. I knew I wanted to become an architect the moment I first saw the Eiffel Tower in person.

在歐洲旅行的那段時間，對我的職涯產生了深遠的影響。當我第一次親眼看到艾菲爾鐵塔的那一刻，我就知道我想成為一名建築師。

15 overwork

This was a really busy week for me. I overworked every day for 2 or 3 hours.

overtime 和 **overwork** 具有細微的語感差異。

overwork	1. v. to work too much / too hard 過勞
	2. v. to force someone else to work too much / too hard 讓別人過度工作
overtime	n. (business) extra work time in addition to your normal working hours 正常工作時間以外的加班時間

如果經常 overtime（加班）就是 overwork，看起來似乎兩種說法都可以使用，但實際上我們幾乎不會使用 overwork。

這是因為 overwork 更常作第二種詞義使用，也就是讓別人過度工作的意思。當你說「My company is overworking me.」，意思是公司使喚你做太多的工作。因此，如果要表達「加班」的意思，應該要用 work overtime、work late、stay late 等說法。

✗   I had to ~~overwork~~ yesterday.
○   I had to work overtime yesterday.
       我咋天不得不加班。

讓我們重新檢視下面的句子。

✗   This was a really busy week for me. I **overworked** every day for 2 or 3 hours.

○   This was a really busy week for me. I worked overtime every day for 2 or 3 hours.

本週對我來說真是非常忙碌的一週。我每天都加班兩到三個小時。

應用

I'm so glad I found a new job. At my previous company I was <u>overworked</u> and undervalued. I often had to <u>work overtime</u>, was underpaid, and was almost always stressed out about something.

我很開心找到一份新工作。我在之前的公司工作繁重，又沒有獲得重視。經常需要加班，薪水又低，總是一直承受著某種壓力。

16   promotion

> I will plan my promotion this weekend.
>
> I promoted to senior director two years ago.
>
> 很多人不知道 promotion 的正確用法。

promotion 1. n. effort and activity done to increase awareness or sales revenue 促銷活動

> **Our promotion for our newest product bundle starts next week.**
>
> 我們最新產品搭售的促銷活動將於下週開始。

promotion 2. n. the action or raising someone to a higher level / rank 晉升、升職

> **I really hope I get a promotion before the end of the year.**
>
> 我很希望能在今年內升職。

promotion 有「宣傳」和「晉升」兩種意思。問題在於,有時候我們不確定它指的是兩者中的哪一種,因此明確地指出這一點是非常重要的。

在下面的句子裡，並未明確指出 promotion 指的是「宣傳」或「晉升」的意思。建議可以在 promotion 前面加上 sales / product，確切地指出它在這裡作「宣傳」之意會比較好。

✗   I will plan ~~my promotion~~ this weekend.
○   I will plan our summer sales promotion this weekend.
     我計劃在這個週末進行夏季促銷活動。

promotion 的動詞型 promote，兩種詞義皆可作主動語態和被動語態使用。當 promote 代表「宣傳」的意思時，必須使用以下的結構表達。

主動   company + promote + product

        Samsung is promoting its new smart TV.
        三星正在宣傳新的智慧型電視。

被動   product + be promoted

        The smart TV is promoted on Naver and YouTube.
        智慧型電視在 Naver 和 YouTube 上宣傳。

當 promote 代表「晉升」的意思時，必須使用以下的結構表達。

主動   company / boss + promoted + person (receiving
        promotion) to + new job position

        The senior managers promoted me to lead product
        designer.
        資深經理們提拔我擔任首席產品設計師。

被動　person (receiving promotion) + be promoted to + new job position

I was promoted to lead product designer.
我被晉升為首席產品設計師了。

讓我們再來看看下面的句子。由於是被晉升為 senior director，所以必須使用 be promoted，而且這裡是過去式（ago），因此應該修改為 I was promoted 才對。作為參考，be promoted 中的 be 動詞也可以用 get 取代，使用 get 來表達時，會讓人感覺重點在升職的「人」身上。

✕　I ~~promoted~~ to senior director two years ago.
○　I was promoted to senior director two years ago.
○　I got promoted to senior director two years ago.
我在兩年前被升為資深總監。

應用

I was promoted to sales team leader last year. I manage the sales teams and plan all our in-store promotions.
去年我被升為銷售組長。我管理所有銷售團隊，並規劃所有店內宣傳活動。

347

17 retire

I'm planning on retiring in my late 40s and opening a restaurant.

意指「退休」的 retire 一詞，也有需要特別注意的語感。

retire v. to leave one's job and completely stop working, usually when one reaches a usual age to quit working 退休

retire 的重點在於「完全停止工作」，也就是不再工作賺錢的意思。

最容易犯的錯誤，是在換工作時使用 retire。如果你辭掉現在的工作之後，未來還打算從事其他工作，你可以用 quit (my) job 來取代 retire。

讓我們根據這些內容，重新檢視下面的句子。

× I'm planning on ~~retiring~~ in my late 40s and opening a restaurant.

○ I'm planning on quitting my job in my late 40s and opening a restaurant.
我計劃在快 50 歲的時候辭掉公司的工作，自己開餐廳。

My career goals are to continue getting work experience here, then in a few years move to the US and work in an international company. I want to raise my kids in the US and hopefully <u>retire</u> in my late 60s.

我的職涯目標是在這裡持續累積工作經驗，過幾年再搬到美國並在跨國企業工作。我希望能在美國撫養孩子們長大，並在快 70 歲的時候退休。

18 bear

I had to bear my demanding former boss for almost a year.

I can't bear working overtime.

→ bear 是現在不常用的表達方式。

bear   v. to endure a difficulty or negative situation 忍受、承擔

用 bear 來表示忍受某件事，從文法上來看並沒有錯，但由於是現在不常用的說法，所以會顯得不自然。具有相同的意義，而且更自然、最近更常使用的說法是 put up with。

讓我們試著用 put up with 來修改下列句子。

✕   I had to bear my demanding former boss for almost a year.
○   I had to put up with my demanding former boss for almost a year.
我不得不忍受我那挑剔的前老闆，忍了將近一年的時間。

此外，如果要表示「無法再忍受」的意思，我們不常用 can't bear，大多會用 can't stand 來表達。這種表達方式更加自然，意思是非常討厭某事，以至於再也無法接受或容忍它了。

✗   I can't bear working overtime.

○   I can't stand working overtime.

我無法再接受加班了。

應用

I seriously can't stand one of my colleagues, Jake. He is the most annoying person I've ever worked with.

我真的很受不了一個叫 Jake 的同事。他是我至今共事過的人之中,最令人討厭的人。

19　point out

If there are any errors in my writing, please point me out.

He pointed me out that the discount ends this week so I should make my purchase as soon as possible.

→ 有些人會用錯 point out 的受詞。

point out (phrasal verb)　to bring attention to something or make people aware of something（為了引起注意）指出

關於 point out，最常犯的錯誤是用「人」作為 point out 的受詞，而非「資訊」或「被指出的問題」。point out 的受詞必須是大家應該注意的資訊。

讓我們重新檢視下面的句子。這裡應該是要請對方指出自己的錯誤（errors），而不是指出自己（me）。因此，可以看作是 point out the errors，並改用 them 來代替重複出現的 errors。

×　　If there are any errors in my writing, please point me out.

○ **If there are any errors in my writing, please** point them out.
如果我寫的文章有任何錯誤，敬請指教。

在下面的句子裡，point out 的對象是 that the discount ends next week，所以只要簡單地刪去 me，就能變成文法正確的句子了。

✕ **He** ~~pointed me out~~ **that the discount ends this week so I should make my purchase as soon as possible.**

○ **He** pointed out **that the discount ends this week so I should make my purchase as soon as possible.**
他指出折扣將於本週結束，因此我應該盡快購買。

應用

Mike pointed out **that our team productivity has definitely gone up since we ended mandatory morning meetings. Maybe just letting people work uninterrupted is more efficient after all.**
Mike 指出，自從我們停止強制性的早會之後，團隊的生產力明顯提升了。
也許讓人不受干擾地工作，才是更有效率的方式。

下面是針對前面介紹過的 with Error 部分，修正錯誤用法後的內容，你可以在劃底線的部分確認正確的表達方式。

尚賢   Happy Friday, team! Quick favor, would anyone be able to work a little overtime this weekend? We would need someone to lead a Zoom meeting with a US customer Saturday morning.

祝大家週五愉快！我有一件急事要拜託大家，這個週末有人可以加班嗎？我們需要有人在週六早上，主持一個與美國客戶的 Zoom 會議。

Mike   Sorry, I have plans with my family Saturday. We have tickets to the Doosan Bears vs Lotte Giants KBO game.

很抱歉，我週六跟家人有其他安排了。我們有斗山熊隊和樂天巨人隊＊的棒球比賽門票。（＊兩隊皆為南韓的職業棒球隊）

Charlie   I've had such a busy schedule lately, I was really hoping to just relax this weekend. I can do it if no one else can, though.

我最近的事情非常多，所以這個週末我很想好好休息。但如果沒有其他人可以幫忙，就由我來吧。

智媛   No worries Charlie, I can do it. Would I need to come to the office or can I do the call from home?

別擔心，Charlie。我可以幫忙。我需要去公司，還是可以在家進行通話？

Charlie	Thanks, Jiwon! 謝謝你，智媛！
尚賢	Great! It doesn't matter. As long as your Internet's good you can do it wherever. Thanks, Jiwon, hope it's not inconvenient for you. 太好了！地點無所謂。只要網路順暢，在哪裡進行都可以。謝謝你，智媛。希望沒有造成你的不便。
智媛	It's no problem! I didn't have any plans for this weekend anyway. 沒關係！反正我這個週末本來就沒有計劃。
尚賢	Perfect. I'll send you a PM with more info. 太好了。詳細資訊我再私訊給你。

（尚賢和智媛的私下對話）

尚賢	Thanks again, Jiwon. I attached a document with background on this customer and the meeting agenda. This customer is a Korean-US fashion brand called Allure. We've been working with them for a really long time, so it shouldn't be too much work. They just want to ask you questions about some upcoming product updates. Everything's already planned, so you would just need to answer questions and keep the meeting organized. 再次謝謝你，智媛。我已經附上客戶的背景與會議議程。這次的客戶是一個叫 Allure 的韓美時尚品牌。我們已經跟他們合作很久了，所以應該不會有太多事情要做。他們只是想向你詢問一些關於產品更新的問題。所有事情都已經安排好了，你只需要回答問題和讓會議順利進行即可。

智媛	Great, I'll take a look and let you know if I have any questions.

太好了，我會先把資料看過一遍，如果有疑問再告訴你。

Hey Sanghyeon, I don't understand the part of the meeting agenda that mentions data upgrades.

尚賢，我不太懂會議議程中提到有關數據升級的那個部分。

尚賢	Ah yeah ... They've used almost all their data storage on their current plan. I was going to suggest they upgrade to the Enterprise package so they'll have more data. That would be more affordable than buying extra data near the end of each month after they run out.

喔，是的……他們在目前的方案中，幾乎用完了所有的數據儲存空間。所以我打算建議他們升級成企業方案來增加數據使用量。這樣會比每個月月底在數據耗盡後購買額外數據更划算。

智媛	Got it, I'll suggest that. I'm curious though, you usually do all of the Saturday morning calls. Are you busy this weekend?

我懂了，我會提出這個建議。不過我有點好奇，通常你會負責所有週六早上的通話。這個週末你特別忙嗎？

尚賢	This stays between us, but I actually have an interview with the US branch Saturday. I'm applying for an overseas director position.

這件事我們兩個人私底下講就好了，其實我週六有一場美國分公司的面試。我正在申請一個海外協理的職位。

智媛	Wow, that's great! Congratulations!

哇，真是太棒了！恭喜你！

尚賢

Thank you! I've been wanting to get promoted for a while now. This is a huge opportunity for me and my family. I can't stand the thought of just staying at this role for the rest of my career.

謝謝！我一直很想升職。這對我和我的家人來說是一次很好的機會。一想到日後只能一直停留於現在的職位，我就覺得無法忍受。

智媛

That sounds great. I hope the interview is successful!

這聽起來很棒。我預祝你面試成功！

尚賢

Thank you. I am really excited for this opportunity. I would love to get this position. You know Jiwon, if I do get promoted, they'll be looking for someone to fill my position here. You've been doing a great job and I think you'd be a prime candidate.

謝謝。我真的很期待這次的機會，也很想得到這個職位。智媛你應該知道吧，如果我升職了，就要找人來接替我的位置。你一直表現得很好，我認為智媛你會是最佳的人選。

智媛

Wow, that's really nice to hear, thank you for the compliment. Do you think I'm ready?

哇，很高興聽到你這麼說。謝謝你的誇獎。你認為我準備好了嗎？

尚賢

I do. You're a fantastic sales rep with a lot of experience. They also want someone who is bilingual in this role. I think you'd be very successful. Plus, having that leadership experience will look great if you ever decide to switch jobs / companies.

當然。你是一位經驗豐富的優秀銷售員，而且公司也希望由能說兩種語言的人來擔任這個職位。我認為你一定會非常成功。另外，有領導經驗在你要調換職務或離職時也是有益的。

| 智媛 | It's really an honor to hear that. I hope your interview goes well and we'll see what happens!
很榮幸聽到你這麼說。希望你面試順利,然後就讓我們拭目以待吧! |

Chapter 9

與數字相關的錯誤
Number Related Mistakes

1   large numbers

2   decimals and rounding

3   percentages

4   saying dates

5   saying years

6   saying fractions

以下的敘述中包含錯誤的用法。請閱讀一遍，並試著找出不自然的表達方式。在各章節的最後會提供修正後的正確表達。

在尚賢到海外任職後，智媛晉升為銷售組長。現在她在公司裡扮演更多角色，也承擔了更多責任。在季度會議上，智媛要向各位資深經理說明銷售組的業績。

Sales By Team			
Amounts in Thousands USD			
Team	2021 Q1 Goals	2021 Q1 Actual	2020 Q1
Sales Team A	650.0	619.71	571.20
Sales Team B	600.0	669.82	520.03
Sales Team C	650.0	651.75	597.94
TOTAL	1,900	1,941.28	1,689.17

Income Statement Q1			
In Thousands USD			
Revenue	2021 Q1	2020 Q1	2019 Q1
Total Sales	1,941.2	1,689.1	1,468.3
Cost of Goods Sold	469.8	453.2	420.0
Gross Profit	1,471.4	1,235.9	1,048.3
Gross Profit	75.8%	73.2%	71.4%

Income Statement Q1 In Thousands USD			
Expenses	2021 Q1	2020 Q1	2019 Q1
Salaries and benefits	680.1	634.2	598.0
Rent / Energy	150.2	137.1	135.4
Travel	25.5	28.5	25.5
Other Expenses	89.1	77.9	81.0
Total Expenses	944.9	877.7	839.9
Operating Profit	526.5	358.2	208.4
Operating Profit %	27.1%	21.2%	14.2%
Interest Expenses	220.5	74.5	57.6
Taxes	115.8	78.8	45.8
Net Profit	190.2	204.9	105
Net Profit %	9.8%	12.1%	7.2%

2021 Q1		% change YOY
Sales Revenue	1,941.2	14.9%
Gross Income	1,471.4	19.05%
Operating Income	526.5	47%
Net Income	190.2	7.2%

| Michelle | Alright everyone, to start things off I just want to look through our quarterly financial statement and compare it to last year. Then, Jiwon will break down our revenue by sales team. After that, we're going to review our strategies for the upcoming quarter. |

To start, we generated one thousand and nine hundred forty one thousand in sales revenue for Q1. This is an increase of one hundred fifteen percent compared to Q1 last year, which we're really satisfied with. Congrats to everyone. Also did really well keeping our expenses under control. Our total expenses were nine hundred thousand forty four dot nine, which is only slightly higher than last year. Our operating income is way up because of that, we increased our operating income percent by twenty seven dot one, which is the highest in company history.

You might notice our net income is slightly down. Total net income decreased about negative seven percent compared to last year, but that was mostly because we're trying to pay off our debts as soon as possible. We started this quarter with two large loans. We completely paid off our first loan June thirty, which is great.

Our remaining loan is with Korea National Bank. We've paid off two third of it and will hopefully be able to completely pay it off by twenty twenty two January or February.

As you all know, we're planning on downsizing our office next quarter. Since more of you are working from home it would be great to reduce our rent and energy expenses. I'm meeting with the building owners next September third Friday to discuss downsizing our office. We'll have a team meeting the week after that to review our plans.

Alright, Jiwon, why don't you go ahead and start?

Jiwon   Great. So the good news is that every sales team increased revenue compared to last year. Sales Team B really shined this quarter, they exceeded their sales goal by over sixty nine. Mike led that team in sales with two hundred thirty in revenue. Awesome job, Mike.

Team A struggled a bit and didn't quite reach their revenue goal. However, there are several deals still being negotiated, so Team A should have a pretty big Q2. We're hoping if all goes well Team B should make at least seven hundred thousand in revenue next quarter.

Team C was able to reach their goal just barely. They ended the quarter with six hundred fifty one dot seventy five thousand. Overall, we exceeded our total revenue goal for the quarter. We're currently finalizing our forecasts for Q2. We'll share the exact numbers next week, but we're hoping for over two million point two hundred thousand in revenue.

Michelle   Sounds great, thanks Jiwon. Okay, let's move on to our strategies for next quarter ...

1 large numbers

在英文中，要表達單位大的數字時，必須知道以下幾點。

digit　n. a single 0-9 that is part of a number

所有數字都至少具有一個以上的 digit（位數）。我們來舉例以便區分它與數字（number）概念的區別。

> 7 → **one digit:** 7
> 540 → **three digits:** 5 4 0
> 35,999 → **five digits:** 3 5 9 9 9
> 1,000,000,000 → **ten digits:** 1 0 0 0 0 0 0 0 0 0
> 010-2345-9876 → **eleven digits :** 0 1 0 2 3 4 5 9 8 7 6

在英文中，大的數字每三位會被分開並加上逗號（,），讀的時候要分別加上 trillion、billion、million、thousand。

000,000,000,000,000

| trillion | billion | million | thousand | hundred ten one |

用英文讀數字時，以三位為一組，並且用一樣的方式表達其所對應的數字。例如，235 的讀法是 two hundred thirty-five。那麼，下面的數字應該要怎麼唸呢？

235,000,000

在唸出 235（two hundred thirty five）之後，必須說出逗號所對應的單位，正如我們前面學過的，235 後面的逗號代表的是 million。

$$000,000,\mathbf{000},000,000$$

trillion　　billion　　**million**　　thousand

因此，235,000,000 的讀法是 two hundred thirty-five million。

讓我們再舉一個例子。37,900,500 應該要怎麼唸呢？首先，要從前面開始以逗號（,）為基準，分開來看。

> 37 → thirty-seven
> 000,000,**000**,000,000 → million
>
> 900 → nine hundred
> 000,000,000,**000**,000 → thousand
>
> 500 → five hundred

因此，37,900,500 的讀法是 thirty-seven million nine hundred thousand five hundred。

簡而言之，大的數字可以藉由插入逗號來分隔成 3 digits，在唸完數字之後加上逗號所對應的單位即可，接著再繼續讀下一個三位數字的單位。在此提供大家一個訣竅，讀的時候請於逗號處稍微停頓（pause）一下！

那麼，在提到錢的時候又該怎麼說呢？此時，可以套用上述方法先讀出數字，最後再加上貨幣單位即可。

以前面提到的數字為例，$37,900,500 USD 可讀作 thirty-seven million nine hundred thousand five hundred USD，或是 thirty-seven million nine hundred thousand five hundred dollars。

韓國貨幣（won）也可以套用同樣的原理，如果是 37,900,500 KRW，可以讀作 thirty-seven million nine hundred thousand five hundred Korean won，或是 thirty-seven million nine hundred thousand five hundred won。讓我們再來看看其他例子。

> 1,550,475,000 KRW
>
> 1 → one
> 000,000,000,000,000 → billion
>
> 550 → five hundred fifty
> 000,000,000,000,000 → million
>
> 475 → four hundred seventy-five
> 000,000,000,000,000 → thousand

從前面開始依序唸下來，就是 one billion five hundred fifty million four hundred seventy-five thousand。

如果中間有三位為 000，只要省略不讀那個部分即可。

> 10,000,500,700
>
> 10 → ten
> 000,000,000,000,000 → billion
>
> 000 → million（省略）

500 → five hundred

000,000,000,**000**,000 → thousand

700 → seven hundred

也就是説，10,000,500,700 只要讀作 ten billion five hundred thousand seven hundred 即可。

PRACTICE 1

請試著將下列數字寫成英文。

1. $85,769,092

85 =

000,000,**000**,000,000 =

769 =

000,000,000,**000**,000 =

092 =

$85,769,092 =

2. 1,475,090

1 =

000,000,**000**,000,000 =

475 =

000,000,000,**000**,000 =

090 =

1,475,090 =

3. 50,055,500,005 KRW

    50 =
    000,000,000,000,000 =

    055 =
    000,000,000,000,000 =

    500 =
    000,000,000,000,000 =

    005 =

    50,055,500,005 KRW =

4.   592,000,019

    592 =
    000,000,000,000,000 =

    019 =

    592,000,019 =

5. $101,000,000,111

    101 =

000,000,000,000,000 =

111 =

$101,000,000,111 =

6. $582,175,019 =

7. 6,000,575,039 =

8. 400,000,000 KRW =

9. 65,340,285 =

10. 7,513,203 KRW =

PRACTICE 2

這次反過來，請試著寫出下列英文所對應的實際數字。

1. three hundred eighty-seven million four hundred Korean won
    three hundred eighty-seven million =
    000,000,000,000,000

    four hundred =

    three hundred eighty-seven million four hundred Korean won =

2. one million eighty-one thousand two hundred
   twenty five
   one million =
   000,000,000,000,000

   eighty one thousand =
   000,000,000,000,000

   two hundred twenty-five =

   one million eighty-one thousand two hundred twenty-five =

3. **nine billion nine hundred million ninety thousand nine =**

4. **one hundred fifty-seven million five hundred thirty thousand
   dollars =**

5. **one trillion three hundred ten billion two hundred million
   Korean won =**

PRACTICE 1
ANSWERS

1. $85,769,092
85 = eighty-five
000,000,<u>000</u>,000,000 = million
769 = seven hundred sixty-nine
000,000,000,<u>000</u>,000 = thousand
092 = ninety-two
$85,769,092 = eighty-five million
seven hundred sixty-nine thousand
ninety-two dollars

2. 1,475,090
1 = one
000,000,<u>000</u>,000,000 = million
475 = four hundred seventy-five
000,000,000,<u>000</u>,000 = thousand
090= ninety
1,475,090 = one million four hundred
seventy-five thousand ninety

3. 50,055,500,005
50 = fifty
000,<u>000</u>,000,000,000 = billion
055 = fifty-five
000,000,<u>000</u>,000,000 = million
500 = five hundred
000,000,000,<u>000</u>,000 = thousand
005 = five
50,055,500,005 KRW = fifty billion
fifty-five million five hundred
thousand five Korean won

4. 592,000,019
592 = five hundred ninety-two
000,000,<u>000</u>,000,000 = million

019 = nineteen
592,000,019 = five hundred ninety-
two million nineteen

5. $101,000,000,111
101 = one hundred one
000,<u>000</u>,000,000,000 = billion
111 = one hundred eleven
$101,000,000,111 = one hundred one
billion one hundred eleven dollars

6. $582,175,019
five hundred eighty-two million one
hundred seventy-five thousand,
nineteen dollars

7. 6,000,575,039
six billion five hundred seventy-five
thousand thirty-nine

8. 400,000,000 KRW
four hundred million Korean won

9. 65,340,285
sixty-five million three hundred forty
thousand two hundred eighty-five

10. 7,513,203 KRW
seven million five hundred thirteen
thousand two hundred three Korean
won

1.

three hundred eighty-seven million
= 387,000,000
four hundred = 400
three hundred eighty-seven million
four hundred Korean won =
387,000,400 KRW

2.

one million = 1,000,000
eighty-one thousand = 81,000
two hundred twenty-five = 225
one million eighty-one thousand two
hundred twenty-five = 1,081,225

3.

nine billion nine hundred
million ninety thousand nine =
9,900,090,009

4.

one hundred fifty-seven million five
hundred thirty thousand dollars =
$157,530,000

5.

one trillion three hundred ten billion
two hundred million Korean won =
1,310,200,000,000 KRW

2 decimals and rounding

由於準確地說出大單位的數字會需要花很長的時間，所以為了方便起見，我們通常會用相對簡單的四捨五入或小數等方式來表達。

舉例來說，在進行商務會議時，我們很少使用下面的說法。

> Last month, we generated ten million four hundred ninety-seven thousand two hundred thirty-two dollars in sales revenue.
> 上個月，我們創造了 10,497,232 美元的銷售收入。

但是，可以將其簡化如下。

> Last month, we generated around ten point five million dollars in sales revenue.
> 上個月，我們創造了近 1,050 萬美元的銷售收入。

為了能正確地讀出包含小數點的數字，我們必須知道以下幾點。

第一點，有些人會將小數點唸作 dot 或 period，但 point 才是正確的說法。

3.5 thousand

= **three point five thousand**

✗ **three dot five thousand**

10.4 million

= **ten point four million**

✗ **ten period four million**

第二點，小數點後面的數字要分開讀出各個位置的 digit。

1.54 million

= **one point five four million**

7.641 billion

= **seven point six four one billion**

第三點的內容比較複雜。如前所述，我們在說明三位數字為一組（sets of three digits）的單位時，所使用的詞彙如下。

trillion（兆）→ **billion**（十億）→ **million**（百萬）→ **thousand**（千）

在提到數字時，一定要按照這個順序。如果打亂順序說成 thousand million，可能會造成混亂。由於每三位數就會斷開來讀，所以在 trillion、billion、million 前面不可能會出現 thousand。

下面是一份假設的損益表（income statement），讓我們一起來看看吧！

由於單位是 millions，所以 2018 年的銷售額 $785.5，應該讀成 seven hundred eighty-five point five million dollars。2019 年的銷售額應該

讀作 nine hundred twenty point eight million dollars。但是，2020 年的銷售額 $920.8 可以讀成 one thousand seven million 嗎？完整的數字寫出來是 1,007,500,000 dollars，所以應該要讀成 one billion seven point five million dollars 才對。

NextGen A.I. 年度收入	
年度	總收入（單位：millions USD）
2018	$785.5
2019	$920.8
2020	$1,007.5

下面是另一個例子。

Instagram 的廣告曝光次數是 715,800 次，四捨五入後就是 716,000 次，因此我們可以說「Our Instagram ads generated about seven hundred sixteen thousand impressions.」。

YouTube 的曝光次數是 841,900 次，如果要說成約 842,000 次，我們可以說「Our YouTube ads generated about eight hundred forty-two thousand impressions.」。

Naver 的曝光次數是 1,189,400 次，四捨五入後就是 1,200,000 次，因此我們可以說「Our Naver ads generated about one point two million impressions.」。（impression：廣告曝光次數）

NextGen A.I. 廣告數據	
平臺	曝光（單位：千次）
Instagram	715.8
YouTube	841.9
Naver	1,189.4

第四點，當我們使用小數點時，表示它並非 100% 準確的數字，所以最好在數字前面加上 around、about、approximately、roughly 等詞，用以表示它是一個近似值。

例如，雖然我們可以將 8,297,104 說成 eight point three million，但它們並不是相同的數字。因此，如果我們在數字前面加上 around，說成 around eight point three million，對方就會知道這是一個大概的說法。以下是提到四捨五入後的數字時，幾種可用的表達方式。

Word	When To Use It	Example
just over	實際數字略高於我提的數字時	actual number: $1,412,058 We generated just over $1.4 million in revenue last month. 我們上個月的銷售額是 140多萬美元。
almost	實際數字略低於我提的數字時	actual number: 36,942 We had almost 37 thousand visitors to our website. 有近 37,000人訪問了我們的網站。
around about approximately	實際數字接近我提的數字，有可能低於或高於此數字。	actual number: 37.2 My temperature is around 37 degrees. 我的體溫約為 37度。

3 percentages

如下所示，用英文表達百分比本身並不困難。

70% = seventy percent

10.5% = ten point five percent

但是，有些人會在表達百分比的增減時出錯。讓我們先來看下面的圖表。

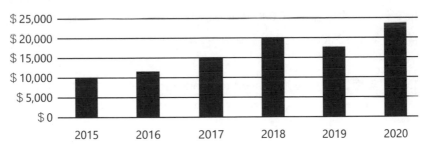

Revenue vs. Year

請查看下表中各年度的銷售數據，並找出各年度之間銷售額的百分比變化。

首先，2015 年的銷售額由 $10,000 增加至 $12,000。要表達這樣的比率增減，可以計算並表示如下。

年收入 2015-2020	
年度	收入（單位：thousands）
2015	$10,000
2016	$12,000
2017	$15,000
2018	$20,000
2019	$18,000
2020	$24,000

% 增長率 = ((數值 2 − 數值 1) / 數值 1) × 100%

2015 → 2016 % change
= ($2,000 / $10,000) × 100% = 20%

要小心別計算錯誤，把增加 20% 算成增加 120%。增加 100% 意味著變成 2 倍。如果收益從 10,000 美元增加了 120%，那應該會增加 12,000 美元，變成 22,000 美元。以下是可用來表示這種變化的幾種表達方式。

1. In + 年度 , revenue increased to + amount
In 2016, revenue increased to $12 million.

2. In + 年度 , revenue increased by + amount of change
In 2016, revenue increased by $2 million.

3. In + 年度 , revenue increased by + amount of change
In 2016, revenue increased by 20%.

4. ... which is a + amount or change OR percent of change + increase compared to + previous year

... which is a 20% increase compared to 2015.

只要搭配使用以上四種表達方式，便可準確地說明大部分的情況。

> **In 2016, revenue increased to $12 million, which is a 20% increase compared to 2015.**
> 2016 年的銷售收入增至 1,200 萬美元，比 2015 年增加了 20%。

與 2018 年相比，2019 年的銷售額減少了。銷售額從 2018 年的 20,000 減少至 18,000，因此可以計算如下。

> 2019 → 2018 % change
> = (-$2,000/$20,000) × 100% = -10%

要說明這種情況，可以利用前面學過的句型，只要將其中的 increase 改成 decrease 即可。

> **In 2019, revenue decreased to $18 million.**
> 在 2019 年，銷售收入減少至 1,800 萬美元。

> **In 2019, revenue decreased to $18 million, which is a 10% decrease compared to 2018.**
> 2019 年的銷售額為 1,800 萬美元，比 2018 年減少了 10%。

也就是說，當百分比的變化為 +（positive）時要使用 increase，百分比變化為 -（negative）時要使用 decrease 來表達。

請參考前面的柱狀圖,計算自 2017 年到 2019 年的變化率(%),並從 increase 和 decrease 之中選一個表達。

1. 2016 → 2017 % change
= ($3,000/$12,000) × 100% = _____ %
2016 to 2017 : a _____ % (increase / decrease)

2. 2017 → 2018 % change
=
2017 to 2018 : about _____ % (increase / decrease)

3. 2018 → 2019 % change
=
2018 to 2019 : a _____ % (increase / decrease)

PRACTICE ANSWERS

1. 2016 → 2017 % change
= ($3,000/$12,000) × 100% = 25%
2016 to 2017 : a 25% (increase / decrease)

2. 2017 → 2018 % change
= ($5,000/$15,000) × 100% = 33.33%
2017 to 2018 : about 33.33% (increase / decrease)

3. 2018 → 2019 % change
= (-$2,000/$20,000) × 100% = -10%
2018 to 2019 : a -10% (increase / decrease)

4 saying dates

這一次，我們要學習如何用英文準確自然地說出日期與年份。當你要說一個完整的日期時，請遵循以下順序。

Day of the week, Month, Day, Year（小概念 → 大概念）

> Thursday, November 26th, 2020
> (Thursday November twenty-sixth two thousand twenty)

寫日期時，可以寫成「26」，也可以寫成「26th」，但是在讀日期時，只能說「26th」。

另外，也可以用以下方式來表達。

> Thursday, the 26th of November, 2020

不過，還是建議大家使用一開始提到的依序說出 Day of the week, Month, Day, Year 的方式，因為按照這個順序是最安全，也最自然的，而且不需要另外加 of 或 the 等介系詞和冠詞，所以也是最簡單的。

Ⓓetails

1. 正如前面所說（Thursday, November 26th, 2020），口語中提到特定日期時，一定要用序數，不可使用基數。

基數（cardinal numbers）

1, 2, 3, 4, 5, 6, 7, 8 ...

one, two, three, four, five, six, seven, eight ...

序數（ordinal numbers）

1st, 2nd, 3rd, 4th, 5th, 6th, 7th, 8th ...

first, second, third, fourth, fifth, sixth, seventh, eighth ...

所以 12 月 1 日可以寫作 December 1，但讀的時候必須讀作 December first。

2. 我們不見得每次都會將四種資訊（day of the week, month, day, year）全部列出。在這種情況下，只要省略未提及的部分並保留其他順序即可。

October 23rd, 2020（省略了星期）
Monday the 5th（省略了年份和當月月份）
the first Friday in September（省略了年份和日期）
May 2021（省略了星期和日期）

3. 在星期前面要用 on，如 on Monday；在月份或年份前面要用 in，如 in January / in 2021。

on October 23rd, 2020
on Monday, June 29th
in October
in 2020

5 saying years

在説到年份的時候，必須先記住三件事情。

第一，在 2000 年之前的年份要兩位數、兩位數分開來説。

> 1930 = nineteen thirty
> 1987 = nineteen eighty-seven
> 1845 = eighteen forty-five

其中有幾種例外的情況。

1. 假如第三個數字為 0（如 1904），此時的 0 要讀成「oh」的發音。

> 1904 = nineteen oh four (nineteen four)
> 1809 = eighteen oh nine (eighteen nine)

這一點主要是用於口語交談的時候，書寫時最好直接使用數字。

2. 假如第三和第四個數字皆為 0（如 1900 年），要在說完前兩位數字後，再加上 hundred。

> 1900 = nineteen hundred (nineteen oh oh)
> 1800 = eighteen hundred (eighteen oh oh)

第二，從 2000 年到 2009 年，要先說 two thousand，再說後面的兩位數字。

2000 = two thousand (**twenty hundred**)
2002 = two thousand two (**twenty two**)
2007 = two thousand seven (**twenty seven**)

第三，從 2010 年到現在，上面提到的兩種說法都可以使用。

2010 = two thousand ten / twenty ten
2015 = two thousand fifteen / twenty fifteen
2020 = two thousand twenty / twenty twenty
2022 = two thousand twenty-two / twenty twenty-two

6 saying fractions

現在讓我們來談談分數。分數永遠是由兩個數字組成，而分子與分母的讀法各自不同。分子採用基數的讀法，分母採用序數的讀法。另外，當分母為 2 時，要讀作 half。

> 1/2 = one half

除此之外，當分母大於 3，就要讀作序數，如 third、fourth、fifth、sixth 等。

> 1/3 = one third
> 1/6 = one sixth

此外，當分子大於 1 時，必須在分母後面加上 -s 作複數型。

> 1/3 = one third   2/3 = two thirds
> 1/6 = one sixth   5/6 = five sixths

最後，當分數與整數混在一起時，只要採用以下讀法即可。

> **整數 and 分數**
> 2 1/3 = two and one third
> 1 3/5 = one and three fifths

下面是針對前面介紹過的 with Error 部分，修正錯誤用法後的內容，你可以在劃底線的部分確認正確的表達方式。

Sales By Team（各組銷售額） Amounts in Thousands USD（美金，單位 $1,000）			
Team	2021 Q1 Goals（2021 年第一季度目標）	2021 Q1 Actual（2021 年第一季度實績）	2020 Q1（2020 年第一季度）
Sales Team A（銷售 A 組）	650.0	619.71	571.20
Sales Team B（銷售 B 組）	600.0	669.82	520.03
Sales Team C（銷售 C 組）	650.0	651.75	597.94
TOTAL（總計）	1,900	1,941.28	1,689.17

Income Statement Q1（各年度第一季度損益表） In Thousands USD（美金，單位 $1,000）			
Revenue（收入）	2021 Q1（2021 年第一季度）	2020 Q1（2020 年第一季度）	2019 Q1（2019 年第一季度）
Total Sales（總銷售額）	1,941.2	1,689.1	1,468.3
Cost of Goods Sold（銷貨成本）	469.8	453.2	420.0
Gross Profit（毛利）	1,471.4	1,235.9	1,048.3
Gross Margin（毛利率）	75.8%	73.2%	71.4%

Income Statement Q1（各年度第一季度損益表） In Thousands USD（美金，單位 $1,000）			
Expenses（費用）	2021 Q1 （2021 年第 一季度）	2020 Q1 （2020 年第 一季度）	2019 Q1 （2019 年第 一季度）
Salaries and benefits （薪資獎金）	680.1	634.2	598.0
Rent / Energy （租金／電費）	150.2	137.1	135.4
Travel（交通費）	25.5	28.5	25.5
Other Expenses（其他費 用）	89.1	77.9	81.0
Total Expenses （總開銷）	944.9	877.7	839.9
Operating Profit （營業利益）	526.5	358.2	208.4
Operating Margin % （營業利益率）	27.1%	21.2%	14.2%
Interest Expenses （利息費用）	220.5	74.5	57.6
Taxes（稅金）	115.8	78.8	45.8
Net Profit（淨利）	190.2	204.9	105
Profit Margin %（淨利 率）	9.8%	12.1%	7.2%

	2021 Q1 %	change YOY
Sales Revenue （銷售收入）	1,941.2	14.9%
Gross Income（毛利）	1,471.4	19.05%
Operating Income （營業利益）	526.5	47%
Net Income（淨收入）	190.2	7.2%

| Michelle | Alright everyone, to start things off I just want to look through our quarterly financial statement and compare it to last year. Then, Jiwon will break down our revenue by sales team. After that, we're going to review our strategies for the upcoming quarter. |

好的，各位，我們會先看季度財務報表，再與去年比較。接下來智媛會劃分各組別的銷售額。之後，我們再來檢討下一季度的銷售策略。

To start, we generated one million nine hundred forty-one thousand(1,941.2) in sales revenue for Q1. This is an increase of fifteen percent compared to Q1 last year, which we're really satisfied with. Congrats to everyone. Also did really well keeping our expenses under control. Our total expenses were nine hundred forty four point nine thousand(944.9), which is only slightly higher than last year. Our operating income is way up because of that, we increased our operating income percent to twenty seven point one(27.1%), which is the highest in company history.

首先，我們第一季度的銷售收入達到 194 萬 1 千美元。這比去年第一季度增長了 15%，令人非常滿意。恭喜各位。另外，我們在支出管理的部分也做得很好。公司的總開銷為 94 萬 4 千 9 百美元，比去年略高一點。因此我們的營業利益大幅增加，營業利益率提升至27.1%。創下公司史上最高的記錄。

You might notice our net income is slightly down. Total net income decreased by about seven percent(7.2%) compared to last year, but that was mostly because we're trying to pay off our debts as soon as possible. We started this quarter with two large loans. We completely paid off our first loan <u>June thirtieth</u>(June 30th), which is great.

你可能會注意到我們的淨收入略為下降。總淨收入比去年減少了 7% 左右，但這是因為我們正努力盡快還清債務。公司在本季度開始時，借了兩筆巨額貸款，第一筆貸款已於 6 月 30 日全部還清。這是很棒的一件事。

Our remaining loan is with Korea National Bank. We've paid off <u>two thirds</u> of it and will hopefully be able to completely pay it off by <u>January or February twenty twenty-two</u>(Jan or Feb 2022).

剩下的一筆是韓國銀行的貸款。我們目前已償還了三分之二，希望能在 2022 年 1 月或 2 月之前全額還清。

As you all know, we're planning on downsizing our office next quarter. Since more of you are working from home it would be great to reduce our rent and energy expenses. I'm meeting with the building owners next <u>Friday, September third</u>(Sep 3rd) to discuss downsizing our office. We'll have a team meeting the week after that to review our plans.

正如各位所知，我們計劃於下一季度縮小辦公室規模。由於越來越多人開始居家上班，這樣做應該有益於節省租金和電費。我將於 9 月 3 日下週五與房東見面討論縮小辦公室規模。然後我們會在下下週召開團隊會議來檢討這個方案。

Alright, Jiwon, why don't you go ahead and start?

好，接下來就請智媛先開始吧。

智媛 Great. So the good news is that every sales team increased revenue compared to last year. Sales Team B really shined this quarter, they exceeded their sales goal by over sixty-nine thousand dollars(69.8). Mike led that team in sales with two hundred thirty thousand dollars in revenue. Awesome job, Mike.

好的。好消息是與去年相比，所有銷售團隊的銷售收入都增加了。銷售 B 組本季度的表現非常出色，他們達成的銷售收入比目標超出了 6 萬 9 千美元。Mike 帶領團隊創造出 23 萬美元的銷售收入。做得好，Mike。

Team A struggled a bit and didn't quite reach their revenue goal. However, there are several deals still being negotiated, so Team A should have a pretty big Q2. We're hoping if all goes well Team B should make at least seven hundred thousand in revenue.

A 組遭遇了一些困難，未能達成銷售目標。不過，他們還有幾筆交易正在協商中，所以 A 組第二季度的收益是值得期待的。我們期待如果一切進行順利，B 組應該能在下個季度創造至少 70 萬美元以上的收益。

Team C was able to reach their goal just barely. They ended the quarter with six hundred fifty-one point seven five thousand(651.75). Overall, we exceeded our total revenue goal for the quarter. We're currently finalizing our forecasts for Q2. We'll share the exact numbers next week, but we're hoping for over two point two million(2,200) in revenue.

C 組也勉強達成了銷售目標。本季度最終銷售收入為 65 萬 1 千 7 百 50 美元。總體而言，我們已超過本季度的銷售目標總額。我們目前

正在設定第二季度的預期目標。確切的數字大約在下週可以公開，我們目前預期的收入是 2 百 20 萬美元以上。

Michelle   Sounds great, thanks Jiwon. Okay, let's move on to our strategies for next quarter ...

聽起來很不錯，謝謝你，智媛。好，接下來讓我們繼續討論下一季度的銷售策略……

Chapter **10**

實用的商務英文詞彙
Useful Business English Words

1	significantly / significant
2	positively / negatively impact
3	objective / subjective
4	indefinitely
5	commute
6	innovation
7	unfortunately
8	pros and cons
9	commit
10	hesitant
11	clarify
12	mandatory
13	assertive
14	proactive
15	stand out
16	micromanage
17	delegate
18	maximize / minimize
19	elaborate
20	opportunity
21	scale up
22	insight

以下的敘述中包含錯誤的用法。請閱讀一遍，並試著找出不自然的表達方式。在各章節的最後會提供修正後的正確表達。

智媛獲得能在新加坡舉辦的大型商務會議上介紹 Onward Tech 的機會。以下對話是智媛在會議上發表的開幕演說。

Jiwon   Okay, who here wants to know their customers better?

(audience members raise their hands)

Who wants to be able to scale up their businesses in the most efficient way possible?

(more audience members raise their hands)

As today's business world becomes increasingly competitive, it's more important than ever to stand out, be proactive, and innovate. This is especially important when we consider just how overexposed we all are to advertising. Research shows that on average, a person sees over 5,000 advertisements a day. We're constantly having products and services pushed in our faces whether that's on TV, online, or simply walking down the street.

This situation has its pros and cons for both companies and consumers. On one hand, it's never been easier for companies to connect with their target customers. On the other hand, if your ads don't communicate the right message, then it will turn customers off, hurt your brand reputation, and ultimately have you wasting money on ads that actually negatively impact your business. Unfortunately, a vast majority of companies today aren't getting the best possible ROIs on their marketing campaigns. This is often because they aren't using objective analytics to maximize their ad effectiveness and learn what their customers really want. Understanding your customers and speaking to them in a way that makes your business stand out is mandatory.

At Onward Tech, we are committed to two things. First, we're committed to helping startups scale and expand their business. Second, we're committed to improving the communication and relationships between consumer and company. We do this by providing the most cutting-edge marketing analytic and automation services in the world.

We have a number of different AI and marketing automation tools that can take a lot of the guesswork out of advertising and help companies like you significantly improve their advertising ROIs. Not only are our products effective, they're also affordable, practical, and easy to use. We've helped hundreds of startups expand their businesses, reach new customers, and improve their marketing ROIs. So, when you're ready to not only scale up, but also gain new insight into your customers in the most efficient way possible, you can set up a free consultation with one of our sales reps today. Thank you for your time, and I'll now open the floor to questions.

Audience 1   Can you clarify how your products work?

Jiwon   That really depends on which product you use, but in general our marketing analytics AIs analyze every

possible performance metric for your online advertisements
to maximize your advertising ROI. Our programs also develop customized ad strategies that are easy to implement.

Audience 2   What sets your products apart from other marketing analytics services?

Jiwon   Great question. First, how easy our products are to use. All the data analysis and recommendations are presented in an easy-to-understand format. The communication and organization is all very straightforward. It's very easy to delegate tasks and communicate with your teammates within our software. Because our programs are accessible on any smart device, your team can stay connected whenever and wherever they are. A lot of people are a bit hesitant towards the idea of AI because they think it will be incredibly complex. A vast majority of our clients are not in the tech / programming industry, but still have no problem using our products.
Second, would be how our products can not only analyze your ad performances, but also share recommendations based on your target customers and budget. It's like having an analytics team and a marketing consultant in one. I'm a bit biased, but I truly believe there's no other single product on the market right now that does what our products do.

Audience 3   How does your pricing system work?

Jiwon   Our pricing system is very flexible. After meeting with one of our sales reps you can set up a low-cost trial period. After seeing how much our products help your online marketing, we're positive you'll want to sign up for one of our full subscription models. We offer one, two, and three-year plans which can be further extended indefinitely. Any more questions?...

Alright, well thank you all for your time. Like I said, Onward Tech is committed to your success by bringing you and your customers closer together. If you like what you've heard today and want to learn more about how we can help your business grow, please visit our booth in the main convention center later today. Have a great rest of your day, and best of luck with your business endeavors.

1 significantly / significant

significantly adv. by a large amount, in a huge / notable way worthy of attention 非常、顯著地

significant adj. in a great / sufficient way worthy of attention 相當的、顯著的

在描述「變化」時，經常會使用 big、a lot、huge 等詞，但我們還可以用更專業的方式來表達。尤其是想強調與增加（increase）、減少（decrease）、改善（improvement）相關的變化時，可使用 significant / significantly 來有效表達。

> **Our market share significantly increased this year.**
> 今年我們的市占率顯著上升。

> **After the new HR manager took over, there was a significant increase in worker satisfaction.**
> 自從新的人資經理上任後，員工滿意度便大幅提升了。

> **Our old boss wasn't great, but unfortunately the new team manager the company hired is significantly worse.**
> 雖然前上司也不好，但不幸地公司新聘的經理明顯比他更糟。

significant / significantly 通常會與 improve、better、decrease
等表示變化的詞彙一起使用。
significant 是形容詞（adjective），所以主要用來修飾名詞，或用
於 be 動詞之後。

a significant increase
顯著增加（最常的用法）
The increase is significant.
增加很顯著。

significantly 是副詞（adverb），所以會放在形容詞之前或動詞
前後，用來表示強調之意。

significantly larger 明顯更大（形容詞之前）
It significantly decreased. 顯著減少。（動詞之前）
It grew significantly. 顯著增加。（動詞之後）

2 positively / negatively impact

positively impact　adv + v. to change something in a good / beneficial way 產生正面影響（cf. positive impact 正面影響）

negatively impact　adv + v. to change something in a bad way 產生負面影響（cf. negative impact 負面影響）

有時候我們會說 in a good way（正面地）、in a bad way（負面地），雖然這並非錯誤的表達方式，但在商務英文中有更專業的說法。

你可以試著用 positive / positively impact 來表示積極的變化，用 negative / negatively impact 來表示消極的變化。

> **Finally getting rid of our old, demanding bosses had a huge positive impact on our office environment. People are happier, more relaxed, and enjoying work much more.**
> 終於趕走又老又刻薄的上司，為辦公環境帶來非常正面的影響。大家變得更開心、更自在，也更樂在工作了。

> **Despite COVID-19 negatively impacting our total revenue, we saved so much money by working from home that our profit is actually higher than last year.**
> 儘管 COVID-19 影響了總銷售收入，但居家上班讓我們節省了很多費用，所以利潤反而比去年更高了。

(D)etails

如 have an positive impact on ~（對～產生正面影響）、have a negative impact on ~（對～產生負面影響），在產生影響的對象前面要加介系詞 on。但如果用的是 positively impact、negatively impact 等，則不需要在受詞前面加介系詞。

Our newest advertising campaign had a positive impact on sales.
我們最新的廣告活動對銷售產生了正面影響。
Working from home may negatively impact salespeople.
居家上班可能會對銷售人員造成負面影響。

3 objective / subjective

objective　adj. totally related to facts and logic, not based on emotion or feelings 客觀的（adv. objectively 客觀地）
subjective　adj. based on emotion and feelings rather than facts and logic 主觀的（adv. subjectively 主觀地）

在對話過程中，有時候會表達主觀意見，有時候會說到客觀事實。在這種情況下，可以分別用 objective / objectively（客觀的 / 客觀地）和 subjective / subjectively（主觀的 / 主觀地）來表示。不過，在商務情境中通常更重視客觀事實或指標，因此較常使用 objective / objectively 來強調客觀事實。

During interviews, it's important to give objective evidence of your strengths. Anyone can say 'I'm a good programmer.' However, saying 'I developed 15 best-selling applications and won developer of the year at my previous company.' is much more convincing.
在面試中，能夠客觀地證明自己的長處是很重要的。任何人都可以說「我是一名優秀的程式設計師」。但是，說出「我開發了 15 個最暢銷的應用程式，並在之前的公司得到年度最佳開發人員獎」會顯得更有說服力。

Our cloud software has an <u>objectively</u> better value than other products in the market. We give users more data and more customer support at a lower price.

比起市面上的其他產品，我們的雲端軟體客觀上來說價格更優。我們以較低的價格提供使用者更多的數據與客戶支援。

ⓓetails

我們也可以用 objective / objectively 來強調某件事確實是錯誤或不好的。舉例來說，如果某個資訊不是事實，或者是不好的，我們就可以說 objectively false / objectively worse。

I really <u>admire</u> my current boss. She's always fair, rational, and <u>objective</u>.

我非常尊敬現在的上司。她總是公平、講理又客觀。

4 indefinitely

indefinitely　adv. for an unspecified amount of time 無限期地

當不確定某事何時會結束時，我們可以用 indefinitely 一詞來表達。

> My office just shut down indefinitely due to COVID-19.
> Everyone is working from home. When the pandemic is
> finally over, the office will reopen.
>
> 辦公室因 COVID-19 而無限期關閉。所有員工目前都居家上班。待疫情結束
> 後，辦公室將重新開放。

> A: How long are you going to work abroad in Singapore?
> B: I plan on staying here indefinitely. I really like my job and
> 　　living in a foreign country. I'll probably move back to
> 　　Korea eventually, but I don't know when.
>
> A：你預定在新加坡工作多久？
> B：我打算長期留在這裡。我很喜歡我的工作，也很喜歡在國外生活。也許我
> 　　以後會回韓國，但我不確定是什麼時候。

5 commute

commute   n. the time / distance a person travels to and from work each workday 通勤、上下學

commute   v. to travel / complete the journey from your home to work and then back to your home 通勤、上下學

commute 一詞可用來表示從居住地移動到工作地點所需的時間或距離，無論是單程或往返都可以使用。但是，如果要表示單程移動，另外加上 each way 能讓語意變得更加明確。

> **My commute is 45 minutes each way, so my total commute time is about 90 minutes.**
> 我的通勤時間單程就要花 45 分鐘，往返總共需要 90 分鐘左右。

> ⒟etails
> commute 可作名詞與動詞使用。

> **I commute almost two hours per day.**
> 我每天要花近兩小時的時間通勤。
> **My commute is almost two hours per day.**
> 我一天的通勤時間差不多是兩小時。

6 innovation

innovative   adj. (about a product) creative, new, and unique（產品）創新的

innovative   adj. (about a person / company) having many new, original, creative ideas 獨創的

innovation   n. the overall concept of creating innovative products and ideas 創新

innovate   v. to create innovative products and ideas 創造、創新

在談論有創意的（creative）、新穎的（new）、獨創的（original）事物時，innovative 是一個很好用的詞彙。因為它是一個專業的高級詞彙，所以只要用對了，便能給對方留下良好的印象。

We're looking for a passionate, hardworking, innovative graphic designer to join our design team. As a startup company, we constantly need to innovate to stand out from our competition. We're hoping to find someone that shares our vision and can make beautiful designs that make a great impression on our customers.

我們正在尋找有熱忱、勤勉並具有創新精神的平面設計師加入我們的設計團隊。作為新創公司，我們必須不斷創新才能在業界脫穎而出。我們希望能找到與我們有共同願景，並且能以出色的設計讓顧客留下良好印象的設計師。

7 unfortunately

unfortunately adv. used to say that you wish something was not true or that something had not happened 遺憾地、可惜地

在處理業務時也會發生很多不好的情況，例如專案延遲或產品銷售低迷等。如果這種情況是由其中一方的失誤造成的，當事者可以使用 I'm sorry 或 I apologize 等說法，但如果是無法歸因於公司或個人的情況，此時就可以用 unfortunately 來表達。

Unfortunately, we'll have to redesign our product prototype. It didn't get very good reception when it was beta tested by our customers.
很遺憾，我們必須重新設計產品原型。我們的顧客對它進行了 Beta 測試，但反應不太好。

Unfortunately, the winter programming workshop has been cancelled due to a severe snowstorm.
很遺憾，冬季程式設計研討會因為強烈暴風雪而取消了。

Ｄetails
如上述例句所示，unfortunately 一般都放在句子的最前面，後面會加逗號（,）。

8 pros and cons

pro n. an advantage, good result, or argument in favor of something 贊成、優點

con n. a disadvantage, negative result, or argument against something 反對、缺點

pros and cons 是對某種情況表示支持或反對，以及談論其利弊時所使用的說法。另外，在掌握某個選項的優缺點並做出相關決定時，pros and cons 也能派上用場。

（必須決定是否要調到海外辦公室）

Transferring to the Tokyo office has its pros and cons. Some of the pros are that the international work experience would really help me move up in my career, and I've heard that the Tokyo office has a great work environment. However, the biggest con is that moving would be really expensive and I couldn't save money by living with my parents any more.

調到東京辦公室有利有弊。優點是海外工作經驗有助於我的職涯發展，而且我聽說東京辦公室的工作環境很棒。然而，最大的缺點是搬遷費用非常貴，而且那樣我沒辦法再跟父母住在一起省錢了。

如果要說「～的優點」、「～的缺點」，可以用 the pros of ~, the cons of ~ 來表示；如果要說「～的優缺點」，可以用 The pros and cons of ~ 的方式來表達。

The pros of working from home are you don't have to commute and you can take breaks when you want to.
居家上班的優點是不需要通勤，而且可以在想休息的時候休息。

Running a business has its pros and cons.
經營事業有利有弊。

作為參考，與 pros and cons 相似的詞彙有 benefits and drawbacks。

The benefits of working from home are you don't have to commute and you can take breaks when you want to.
居家上班的優點是不需要通勤，而且可以在想休息的時候休息。

The drawbacks of working from home are it's easier to get distracted and you can't speak with your colleagues directly.
居家上班的缺點是容易分心，而且無法和同事直接交流。

9 commit

commit　v. to promise or be very dedicated to something 承諾、致力於

committed　adj. be very dedicated to something 致力於

在描述個人或公司為了實現某種目標而全力以赴的情況時，commit 非常有用。如果你 commit 某件事，就代表你將竭盡全力執行或完成特定行為以實現那件事。

> **My company is committed to providing the best smartphone component on the market for a very reasonable price.**
> 我們公司致力於以合理的價格提供最好的智慧型手機零件。

> **I emailed the quarterly sales goals to each sales team. Can you all commit to achieving these?**
> 我已經用電子郵件將各季度的銷售目標寄給各個銷售團隊了。大家都能全力達成這些目標嗎？

10 hesitant

hesitant adj. unsure or cautious about something. not ready to act / make a decision 猶豫的、遲疑的

有時候我們會使用 hesitate 這個動詞來表示不確定的意思，但事實上，用 (be) hesitant 來表達會更加自然。此外，當一個人或組織對某事感到不確定並謹慎以對時，也可以用 hesitant 來形容。

> **At the beginning of the sales consultation, the customer was quite hesitant. She really wasn't sure if she wanted to work with us. However, by the end of the meeting she was ready to sign up.**
> 剛開始進行銷售諮詢時，那位顧客相當猶豫不決。她不確定自己是否想與我們合作。但是在會議結束時，她已經準備好要跟我們簽約了。

11　clarify

clarify　v. to make information / a statement more clear and easy to understand (usually by explaining it again in a simpler, easier-to-understand way) 闡明、使清晰易懂

clarify 是在重述或確認某資訊時很好用的詞彙。此外，當你想請對方重新說明某事時，也可以用 clarify 來提問。

（你剛才向顧客介紹即將推出的新產品。顧客對你的說明有所誤解，以為可以馬上買到該產品。）
To clarify, this won't be available until February. However, you can preorder one today and we'll ship it to you as soon as we can.
我要澄清一下，這項產品要到 2 月才會上市。但是您可以今天預訂，我們會盡快出貨。

Could you clarify what you just said about the new machine learning algorithms? I didn't quite understand.
你能詳細解釋一下剛才提到的，有關新的機器學習演算法的內容嗎？我不太明白。

12 mandatory

mandatory adj. required (usually due to laws, rules, or policies), not optional （根據法律或規則）規定的、強制性的

mandatory 是很適合放在必須做的事情、行為，或必須遵守的規則、政策前面的詞彙。

> We'll have a company dinner next Thursday night after work. I hope you all can attend, but it isn't mandatory.
> 我們下週四晚上下班後要聚餐。我希望大家都能參加，但這並非強制性的。

> Button-up shirts and ties for men are now part of the new mandatory dress code.
> 男性著襯衫和領帶是新的服裝規定之一。

> It's mandatory that you get approval from a manager before using any of your vacation days.
> 在排假之前，你必須先獲得經理的批准。

13　assertive

assertive　adj. having a strong, confident, forceful personality 有主見的、自信的

有時候我們會用 aggressive 一詞來形容很有主見且非常積極的人，但 aggressive 在語感上多少帶有負面意義。如果想以肯定的意義來形容很有主見的個性，建議使用 assertive 來表達會比較好。assertive 和 aggressive 的意思相近，但語感上具有褒義，因此可以用來形容立場堅定且有自信的人。

If you want to move up in the business world, you have to be assertive. No one will hand you opportunities. You have to make them happen for yourself.
想在商界取得成功，你就必須積極進取。沒有人會給你機會。你必須自己創造機會。

Ⓓetails
assertive 的反義詞是 passive。當我們用 passive 來形容一個人，代表他是一個缺乏自信且被動的人。

14 proactive

proactive adj. causing or initiating something instead of just responding / reacting 積極的、主導的、主動的

當我們用 proactive 來形容個人或組織時，意思是其積極執行某件事的能力很強。proactive 的人不會等著別人幫他做事，也不會被外在因素所左右。

proactive 的人通常會主導情勢並主動創造機會。另外，proactive 的企業／組織會勇於嘗試新事物，開展新事業，並在業界中創造新的趨勢。

proactive 的反義詞是 reactive，大多作貶義使用。在人或企業 reactive 的情況下，他們通常會落後於最新的業界趨勢，因為比起創造新的機會，他們只會應付已經發生的情況。

> I used to wait for potential clients to contact me, but I realized my business could grow much faster if I was proactive. Now, I research possible clients and contact them directly.
> 以往我只會等待潛在客戶與我聯繫。但我意識到如果我主動採取行動，我的業績會成長得更快。現在我會研究潛在客戶，並直接與他們聯繫。

15 stand out

stand out   to be easily noticeable because you're clearly better or more significant 突出、顯眼

stand out 是一個動詞片語，用於描述因具備正向特質或成果卓越而特別顯眼的人或公司。

All the UX designers made great UIs for this project, but Jin's really stood out. This is one of the most beautiful UI designs I've ever seen. Fantastic work, Jin.
所有的 UX 設計師都為這個專案製作了很出色的 UI，不過珍的 UI 特別突出。
這是我目前為止見過最漂亮的 UI 設計之一。做得很好，珍。

There are tons of e-commerce platforms in Korea, but Coupang stands out as one of the best.
雖然韓國有許多電子商務平台，但 Coupang 脫穎而出，是最好的平台之一。

Ⓓetails
另外也可以使用 outstanding 一詞來表達，它是與 stand out 意義相近的形容詞。

Jin's design work is outstanding. 珍的設計很出色。

16 micromanage

micromanage　v. to manage and control every aspect of someone / something, even tiny, unimportant details 連私人事物也過度干涉和控制

micromanager　n. a person who often micromanages 連微不足道的小事也要干涉的人

在職場生活中，有時候會發生上司或同事連瑣碎的小事也想控制的情形，你可以用 micromanage 來表達這種情況。另外，由於它指的是過度干涉並惹惱對方的意思，所以語感上帶有貶義。

My old boss was a complete micromanager. He would seriously check on each employee 10 to 15 times a day to make sure they were working. It was really annoying and not very efficient.

我的前任老闆是連微不足道的小事也要干涉的人。他為了確認員工有沒有在工作，一天會監督每位員工 10 到 15 次。真的很煩人，而且非常沒有效率。

17 delegate

delegate　v. to assign authority or a task to another person / people
委託

delegate 是很適合用於分配和指派（assign）任務（task）的詞彙。通常在組長分配工作給組員的情況下，就可以用 delegate 來表達。使用的句型為「person + delegate (work) to + person / people」，或是「work + was delegated to + person / people」。

> **I delegated the task to Jayden.**
> 我把那項工作委託給 Jayden 了。
> **The task was delegated to Jayden.**
> 那項工作已經交由 Jayden 負責了。
>
> **A good manager knows when to do the work oneself and when to delegate it to another employee.**
> 一名優秀的主管知道什麼時候該自己親力親為，什麼時候該將工作委派給其他員工。
> **We're going to be really busy the next few weeks, so let's delegate each project step to a specific team member.**
> 接下來的幾週將會非常忙碌，所以我們把專案的每個步驟分別派給特定的組員負責吧。

18 maximize / minimize

maximize　v. to make something as large or as great as possible 最大化

minimize　v. to reduce something to the smallest amount or level possible 最小化

maximize 主要用於正向特質（positive qualities or features），而 minimize 通常會與負面或不可取的特質（negative or undesirable qualities）一起使用。在句子結構上，直接受詞的位置，就會出現對應於 maximize / minimize 的特質。

> **Our new hard drive is incredibly efficient. It maximizes performance while minimizing battery usage, so your computer can work properly for nearly 10 hours without needing to recharge.**
> 我們的新硬碟效能非常好。它將性能最大化，同時最大限度地減少電池使用量，所以你的電腦無需充電就能以最佳狀態運轉近 10 小時。

19 elaborate

elaborate v. to explain something (usually a theory, system, or complex information) in more detail 詳盡說明

elaborate 是一個轉折詞（transition word），用於要開始詳細說明某事的時候。它可用於進行簡報或產品演示的情況，或者用來要求對方提供更詳細的資訊，此時也能在 elaborate 後面加介系詞 on，針對特定主題說明。

Can you please elaborate more on what makes your products unique?
能否請你針對貴公司的產品差異化做更詳盡的說明？

I just sent an email that elaborates on how the new computer system works. Let me know if you have any questions!
我剛才寄了一封電子郵件，裡面詳細說明了新電腦系統的運作模式。如果你有任何疑問，請告訴我！

20 opportunity

opportunity n. a chance or possibility to do something positive or for something positive to happen 做積極之事的機會

提到「機會」時，我們經常會混用 chance 和 opportunity，但相比之下，chance 的語氣是中立的，用來指正面或負面的情況都可以，而 opportunity 則是正面意義較為強烈。

另外，chance 一般會用在偶然發生、無法控制結果的事情上。

> **When you flip a coin, there is a 50% chance that it lands on heads.**
> 當你丟銅板時，出現正面的機率是 50%。

丟銅板的結果是隨機（random）出現、無法控制的，自然應該用 chance。

相反的，opportunity 意味著人的行為會影響其結果。

> **Now that our main competitor left the market, we have the opportunity to significantly increase our market share.**
> 現在我們的主要競爭對手退出市場，讓我們有機會大幅提升市場占有率。

在上面的句子裡，大幅提升市場占有率（significantly increase our market share）不是隨機（random）出現的結果，而是需要敏捷行動並做出良好決策才有可能實現的結果。也就是說，在強調積極的結果或特定行動會影響結果的情況下，我們應該要使用 opportunity，而非 chance。

下面的句子也一樣，由於是在感謝某人給你機會，所以自然應該用 opportunity 來表達。

Thank you so much for the opportunity to speak at this conference. I'm really looking forward to talking with you all today.
真心感謝你們給我在這場會議上發言的機會。我很期待今天與各位的對話。

Working from home presented a lot of challenges as well as some exciting new opportunities for our business.
居家上班為我們的事業提供了一些令人興奮的新機會，同時也帶來了許多挑戰。

21 scale up

scale up   to increase the size, amount of scope of something in a carefully-planned way 擴大規模

在提到擴展事業、增加生產，或是以經過規劃的系統化方式擴大行銷時，scale up 是相當有用的表達方式。

> **One of the main reasons I'm writing this English book is so I can scale up my business and help more Korean adults improve their English.**
> 我寫這本英文書的主要原因之一，是可以拓展我的事業並幫助更多韓國成年人提升英語實力。

> **The factory scaled up its production by buying a lot more machinery.**
> 那間工廠藉由購買更多機器來擴大生產規模。

22 insight

insight n. clear, deep understanding knowledge or wisdom about something, sometimes discovered in a very sudden way 洞察力

insight 指的是對特定主題的深刻理解或知識。通常會與介系詞 into 一起使用，後接所討論的主題或資訊。一般作不可數名詞使用，但在具體說明對多個主題的不同 insight 的情況下，也可以作可數名詞使用。

> **If you'd like to gain more insight into the mechanical engineering industry, please sign up for our webinar next Tuesday.**
> 如果你想更深入了解機械工程產業，請報名參加下週二舉辦的網路研討會。

> **Does anyone have any insight into how we can better reach our customers?**
> 對於如何改善顧客觸及策略，有人有什麼好見解嗎？

我們也經常會用 gain insight 來表示「獲得洞察力」的意思。

> **I study marketing analytics to gain insight into what our customers really want.**
> 我正在研究行銷分析，希望能洞察顧客真正的需求。

你可以在對話中畫底線的部分，確認正確的表達方式。

智媛　　　Okay, who here wants to know their customers better?
好，在座的各位有誰想要更了解您的顧客？
（有觀眾舉手）

Who wants to be able to scale up their businesses in the most efficient way possible?
有誰想要以最有效率的方式擴展業務？
（有更多觀眾舉手）

As today's business world becomes increasingly competitive, it's more important than ever to stand out, be proactive, and innovate. This is especially important when we consider just how overexposed we all are to advertising. Research shows that on average, a person sees over 5,000 advertisements a day. We're constantly having products and services pushed in our faces whether that's on TV, online, or simply walking down the street.
隨著現今業界的競爭日趨激烈，提升能見度、積極行動和實現創新比以往任何時候都更加重要。尤其是考量到我們每個人暴露在多少廣告之中，這些就顯得更加重要。根據一項調查顯示，一個人平均每天會看到超過 5,000 則廣告。無論是在電視上、網路上，或者僅僅只是走在路上，我們都會不斷地接觸到商品與服務。

This situation has its pros and cons for both companies and consumers. On one hand, it's never been easier for companies to connect with their target customers. On the other hand, if your ads don't communicate the right message, then it will turn customers off, hurt your brand reputation, and ultimately have you wasting money on ads that actually negatively impact your business.

無論是對公司或消費者來說,這種情況都各有利弊。一方面,與目標客群之間的接觸變得比以往更為容易。但是,如果廣告沒有正確地傳達訊息,就會導致顧客流失、品牌聲譽受損,最終害您浪費廣告費用,還會對您的事業造成負面影響。

Unfortunately, a vast majority of companies today aren't getting the best possible ROIs on their marketing campaigns. This is often because they aren't using objective analytics to maximize their ad effectiveness and learn what their customers really want. Understanding your customers and speaking to them in a way that makes your business stand out is mandatory.

令人遺憾的是,現今大多數企業並未從他們的行銷活動中,獲得最佳的投資報酬率(ROI)。這是因為他們沒有進行客觀的分析,以使廣告效果最大化並了解顧客的真正需求。了解您的顧客,並且透過與顧客對話來突顯您的商品或服務是非常重要的。

At Onward Tech, we are committed to two things. First, we're committed to helping startups scale and expand their business. Second, we're committed to improving the communication and relationships between consumers and the company. We do this by providing the most cutting-edge marketing analytics and automation services in the world.

Onward Tech 致力於兩件事情。第一,我們致力於幫助新創公司拓展業務。第二,我們致力於改善顧客和企業之間的溝通與關係。我

們藉由提供最尖端的市場行銷分析及自動化服務來實現這兩點。

We have a number of different AI and marketing automation tools that can take a lot of the guesswork out of advertising and help companies like yours significantly improve their advertising ROIs. Not only are our products effective, they're also affordable, practical, and easy to use. We've helped hundreds of startups expand their businesses, reach new customers, and improve their marketing ROIs. So, when you're ready to not only scale up, but also gain new insight into your customers in the most efficient way possible, you can set up a free consultation with one of our sales reps today. Thank you for your time, and I'll now open the floor to questions.

我們擁有各種 AI 和行銷自動化工具，可以排除廣告行為的大量盲目推測，並使像是各位的公司大幅提升廣告投資報酬率。我們的產品不僅有效，而且價格實惠、實用又容易操作。我們已經幫助數百家新創公司拓展業務、觸及新顧客，並改善他們的行銷 ROI。因此，如果您不僅想要擴展規模，還希望能以最有效的方式取得對顧客的新見解，今天您可以與我們的銷售人員進行免費諮詢。感謝各位抽出寶貴的時間。現在開始接受提問。

觀眾 1　　Can you clarify how your products work?
關於你們產品的運作方式，你可以再說清楚一點嗎？

智媛　　That really depends on which product you use, but in general our marketing analytics AIs analyze every possible performance metric for your online advertisements to maximize your advertising ROI. Our programs also develop customized ad strategies that are easy to implement.

這取決於您使用哪種產品，但一般來說，市場分析 AI 會盡可能分析線上廣告的所有性能指標，以使廣告 ROI 最大化。此外，我們的程式也會開發容易執行的客制化廣告策略。

觀眾 2　What sets your products apart from other marketing analytics services?

你們的產品跟其他市場分析服務有何不同呢？

智媛　Great question. First, how easy our products are to use. All the data analysis and recommendations are presented in an easy-to-understand format. The communication and organization are all very straightforward. It's very easy to delegate tasks and communicate with your teammates within our software. Because our programs are accessible on any smart device, your team can stay connected whenever and wherever they are. A lot of people are a bit hesitant towards the idea of AI because they think it will be incredibly complex. A vast majority of our clients are not in the tech / programming industry, but still have no problem using our products.

這是個好問題。首先，是我們產品非常易於使用。所有數據分析及建議事項都會以容易理解的形式呈現。交流方式與架構都非常簡單。用我們的軟體，您可以很輕鬆地分配工作並與組員交流。所有的智慧型設備都可以連結我們的程式，因此您的團隊可以隨時隨地保持聯繫。許多人認為 AI 相當複雜，因此感到猶豫不決。儘管我們大部分的客戶並非從事科技 / 程式設計相關產業，但截至目前為止，他們在產品使用上並沒有問題。

Second, would be how our products can not only analyze your ad performances, but also share recommendations based on your target customers and budget. It's like having an analytics team and a marketing consultant in one. I'm a bit biased, but I truly believe there's no other single product on the market right now that does what our products do.

其次，我們的產品不僅能分析顧客的廣告成效，還能根據您的目標客群及預算提供建議。就像將分析團隊與行銷顧問合而為一。我可能有點偏頗，但我真心認為目前市面上沒有一款產品像我們的產品這麼令人滿意。

觀眾 3 　　How does your pricing system work?
　　　　你們怎麼計價？

智媛 　　Our pricing system is very flexible. After meeting with one of our sales reps you can set up a low-cost trial period. After seeing how much our products help your online marketing, we're positive you'll want to sign up for one of our full subscription models. We offer one, two, and three-year plans which can be further extended indefinitely.

我們的價格制度非常有彈性。與我們的銷售人員面談後，您可以設定一個低成本的試用期。在確認該產品對貴公司網路行銷產生的效益後，我相信您一定會想要加入我們的訂閱方案。我們提供 1 年、2 年和 3 年的方案，並且可無限期延長。

Any more questions?
還有其他問題嗎？

Alright, well thank you all for your time. Like I said, Onward Tech is committed to your success by bringing you and your customers closer together. If you like what you've heard today and want to learn more about how we can help your business grow, please visit our booth in the main convention center later today. Have a great rest of your day, and best of luck with your business endeavors.

好的,謝謝各位抽出寶貴的時間。正如我前面所說,Onward Tech 致力於拉近您與顧客之間的距離,並藉此幫助您取得成功。如果您喜歡今天聽到的內容,並想進一步了解我們可以如何幫助您的業務成長,歡迎您在今天下午參觀我們位於主會議中心的展位。祝您有個愉快的一天,也祝福各位的公司。

What Now?!

Alright, so now we've covered over 140 common Korean English mistakes and you've learned some great new business English vocabulary. You've corrected all of the example narratives as well as some mistakes you were making with your own English communication. In this final chapter, I want to lay out five important strategies you should follow to improve your professional English communication as quickly and efficiently as possible. As I said in the very first chapter, I truly want to see you succeed, so let's talk a little bit more about how you can make your English goals a reality! If you're serious about improving your English as efficiently as possible, you need to ...

到目前為止，我們已經看過了 140 多個韓國人使用英文時常犯的錯誤，也學習了一些實用且新的商務英文詞彙。現在大家不僅能修正範例中錯誤的敘述，也能糾正自己平時用英文溝通時曾犯過的錯誤。接下來，我想提出五個重要的方法，幫助各位盡可能迅速有效地提升職場英文溝通的能力。如同我在第一章所說的，我真的很想看見各位成功，所以讓我們再多談談該用哪些方法才能達成各位的英文目標！如果你是認真地想有效的提升英文實力，你需要⋯⋯

1. Get Personalized feedback on your speaking

1. 取得對於個人口說（speaking）的意見回饋

Because traditional Korean English education limits speaking time, many Koreans believe that if they just speak more and spend more time talking with native speakers, their English will improve. This is only partially true. Yes, you need to speak English often if you want to become a highly skilled English communicator. However, to truly reach your potential and unlock the communication abilities needed to progress in your career, you need to be doing more than just 'speaking English'. It's incredibly important to also get detailed feedback on your speaking and the mistakes that you make.

由於韓國的傳統英文教育較少涉及口說部分,所以很多人認為多開口說英文、多與母語人士交談就能提升英文實力,這種說法只有部分是正確的。沒錯,想要說好英文,就必須時常說。但是,如果想要激發潛力並培養自己職涯發展所需的溝通能力,你需要做的不僅僅是「說英文」而已。取得對於各位的口說表現,以及常犯錯誤的詳細意見回饋也是非常重要的。

We covered a lot of common mistakes in this book, but it would be impossible to cover everything. Every English learner is unique and has unique communication issues. These can be related to grammar, pronunciation, speaking rhythm, the way you form sentences, vocabulary, or just your mindset / emotions while speaking English. It's important to find a method, course, or person capable of pointing out your communication issues / weaknesses and fixing them.

雖然本書已經探討了許多常見錯誤，但不可能涵蓋所有的錯誤。這是因為每位英文學習者都有各自不同的溝通問題。這些問題可能與文法、發音、說話節奏、句型結構、詞彙有關，也可能只是與你說英文時的心態或情緒有關。這就是為什麼找到可以指出並糾正各位溝通問題與弱點的方法、課程或專家如此重要的原因。

A vast majority of Korean English learners know that their English isn't perfect, but they might not know the specific mistakes they're making. Even if they know some of the mistakes, they likely don't know how to fix them. So, whether it's through an application, language exchange program, or professional 1:1 tutor, get feedback on your English so you can fix your mistakes and improve your communication.

大多數學習英文的韓國人都知道自己的英文並不完美，但可能不知道自己具體犯了哪些錯誤。即使知道，也大多不知該如何改正。因此，我建議大家最好能藉由下載英文學習應用程式、參加語言交換活動，或是接受專業的一對一輔導等方式，來取得對於你英文實力的意見回饋，你才可以糾正錯誤並提升溝通技巧。

2. Practice the actual communication you do at work.

2. 練習職場中的實際對話

If you use English at work now or are planning to do so in the future, then it's very important to make your practice as close as possible to the English you use in your professional life. Sitting in a lecture class without any chance to speak and unstructured 'free talking' classes where you discuss what you did on the weekends aren't going to help you improve your sales pitches, presentations, meetings with clients, and other work-specific English situations.

如果你目前需要在工作時使用英文，或是未來有這樣的計劃，那麼在練習時盡可能貼近各位於職場生活中實際使用的英文是非常重要的。沒有給予口說機會的課堂，或是隨意地談論週末做了什麼事的「自由對話」課程，無法培養各位進行推銷、簡報、與客戶會面及執行其他業務時所需的英文表達能力。

For this reason, it is quite important that you roleplay and practice the specific conversations and presentations you have at work. A majority of my clients work in international companies, and we spend about 40% of our class time practicing and reviewing the conversations, emails, presentations, and speeches they need to perform at their jobs. This extra practice and feedback will help you communicate your ideas more effectively and make a big difference in your work performance. You'll feel much more comfortable when you actually attend that meeting or give that presentation because it won't be the first time you've done it. So, if you don't feel confident in your presentations, emails, interviews, and other work-specific English communication, find an expert that can help you. They're out there!

基於這個理由，透過角色扮演等方式，練習職場上特定場合的對話與簡報是非常重要的。我的學生大多數都在跨國企業工作，我會將 40% 的課堂時間用於練習並檢討他們在工作時需要用到的對話、電子郵件、簡報，以及演講等內容上。如果各位也能像這樣多加練習並取得意見

回饋，你將能夠更有效地表達自己的想法，並為你的工作表現帶來巨大改變。即使是在實際開會或進行簡報的時候，你也不會覺得這是第一次，因此心理上會感到更加安定。所以若是你對自己的簡報、電子郵件、面試及其他工作上的英文交流沒有信心，你應該尋求專家的幫助。他們就在那裡！

3. Focus on improving the structure / organization of your communication.

3. 集中在改善溝通的結構

About a year ago, I started to notice that many of my more advanced English clients rarely made obvious speaking and grammar mistakes, but their communication still seemed inefficient and unorganized. When we practiced presentations, I often had a hard time following everything they said. I would have to read their example business emails slowly multiple times to understand everything. When we practiced speaking in our classes, they would often give overly lengthy answers that included a lot of unnecessary information.

大約一年前，我發現很多英文高級班的學生很少出現明顯的口語和文法錯誤，但他們的溝通仍然沒有效率和條理。每當練習發表的時候，我常在聽完他們說的話之後仍難以理解他們想表達的意思。他們練習寫的商務電子郵件，我必須慢慢地閱讀好幾遍，才能理解全部的內容。在課堂上練習口說時，他們經常回答太多不必要的冗長內容。

Many of these clients were well aware of the fact that their English was unclear and inefficient, but they didn't know why and didn't know how to fix it. It was also hard for me to help them because their problem was much more complex than pointing out a simple grammar mistake. Eventually I figured out a solution, and it has significantly changed the way that I teach.

很多學生很清楚自己的英文表達並不明確且毫無效率,卻找不到原因,也不知道該如何改善。我也很難提供幫助,因為他們的問題比起單純地指出文法錯誤更加複雜。但最終我還是找到了解決辦法,而我的教學方式也起了很大變化。

The reason for this problem is that as an English learner, you've likely spent a lot of time learning grammar, vocabulary, and pronunciation but not very much time at all learning how to actually structure your communication in the most effective way possible. This is an essential skill that unfortunately a lot of English learners lack simply because they were never taught it and have never practiced it.

之所以會出現這樣的問題,是因為作為英文學習者,各位花了很長的時間學習文法、詞彙和發音,卻根本沒學過用最有效率的方式去組織你的溝通對話。這是一項必備的基本技能,遺憾的是,許多英文學習者缺乏這項技能,僅僅是因為他們從未學過,也從未練習過。

The reason that my clients' presentations were hard to follow was that they would rarely have a clear introduction and conclusion. They also weren't using any transition statements, so it seemed like they were jumping from topic to topic in unexpected ways. Their emails were hard to follow not because they contained tons of errors, but because they often contained extremely long run-on sentences and lacked structure. Their in-class speaking would stray off topic and include unrelated background information instead of directly answering the question being asked.

我的學生們的報告之所以難以理解，是因為引言（introduction）與結論（conclusion）不夠明確。另外，由於沒有使用轉折語句（transition statements），所以當主題從這個主題接到另一個主題時，會令人措手不及。他們的電子郵件也不是因為錯誤太多，而是因為句子太冗長、文章缺乏架構，所以才難以閱讀。在課堂上的發表則是偏離主題，且沒有直接回答問題，只傳達了無關的背景資訊。

After discovering this, I started focusing on communication structures and organization strategies in my classes in addition to English errors / corrections. For example, for presentations I would help my clients improve their word choice and grammar, but we would also focus on:

在得知此事實後，我在課堂上除了糾正英文錯誤之外，還集中在溝通結構與組織方法上。以簡報為例，我除了幫助學生提升他們的詞彙選擇與文法能力之外，也將重點放在下列幾件事情上面。

1. How to have a clear introduction that not only explains the goal / topics of the presentation, but also gets the audience interested in what they're about to hear.
2. How to organize presentation topics in a logical way and use transition statements to clearly move from topic to topic.
3. How to ask for and answer audience questions in a natural way that doesn't break the flow of the presentation.

4. How to clearly conclude the presentation in a way that makes a great impression on the audience and ensures everyone understands what to do next.

1. 如何建構清楚明瞭的引言（introduction），不僅僅是說明簡報目的或主題，還要讓聽眾對接下來的內容感興趣。
2. 如何按照邏輯安排簡報主題架構，並利用轉折語句（transition statements）明確地銜接不同主題。
3. 如何在不干擾簡報流程的情況下，自然地向聽眾提問和回答問題。
4. 如何為簡報做簡潔的收尾，讓聽眾留下好印象，並讓所有人都知道接下來該做的事是什麼。

By focusing on these problems and teaching in this way, my clients were able to significantly improve the effectiveness of their workplace communication in a short amount of time. This confirmed for me that these organizational communication problems are very fixable, but will not be fixed unless they're addressed directly.

專注在這些問題上並以這種方式進行教學，使我的學生們的職場溝通效率在短時間內有了顯著的提升。這讓我確定這種結構上的溝通問題是可以改正的，但除非各位親自解決，否則是改不了的。

To fix these issues, I recommend finding and studying resources outside of the realm of traditional ESL. These can be presentation guides, email writing tips, and public speaking tips for real business professionals, not ESL resources. There are plenty of great presentation, communication, and interview books / courses /

coaches out there that are well worth investing in. So, if you struggle to communicate in a direct, professional, and organized manner, rest assured that this is a very fixable problem. However, it won't be fixed unless you do something about it. Find good professional resources and invest in your success. It will absolutely pay off in the long term.

為了解決這些問題，我建議各位可以搜尋並研究傳統 ESL（English as a second language 英文作為第二語言）領域之外的資料。它們可能是針對商務人士的簡報指南、電子郵件寫作技巧和公開演講訣竅等，而不是針對 ESL。有很多與簡報、溝通、面試相關的優良書籍／課程／專家，都非常值得你投入時間與金錢。因此，如果你發現自己很難用直接、專業、有條理的方式去溝通，請放心，這是一個可以解決的問題。然而，如果各位不親自去實踐，問題自然無法改善。請試著尋找優質、專業的資源。從長遠來看，各位一定能有所收穫。

4. Always discuss new topics and learn the culture of your audience.

4. 不斷討論新主題並學習談話對象的文化

Earlier I mentioned how important it is to focus on your work communication and avoid pointless 'free talking'. This is true, but that doesn't mean you should only practice your very serious, formal workplace communication. Another interesting trend I've noticed over the years is that a lot of my higher-level clients struggle more with unstructured, casual conversations than they do formal presentations they've spent a lot of time preparing.

我在前面強調了專注於職場溝通，以及避免無意義的「自由對話」之

重要性。這是事實，但這並不代表你只需要練習非常嚴肅和正式的職場溝通。這幾年我發現另一件有趣的事情，就是對於許多高級課程的學生而言，進行不限形式的日常對話比進行長時間準備的正式簡報還要困難。

If this sounds like you, then the best thing for you to do is to constantly discuss new topics in English. In addition to everything related to your job / industry, you should also discuss history, politics, traveling, fitness, technology, current news... the list goes on. By doing so, you'll feel much less 'limited' by your English. You'll have a richer vocabulary, be able to share your opinions on a wider variety of topics, and feel a lot more comfortable in more casual conversations with your English-speaking colleagues.

如果你覺得這正是你的寫照，那麼你最好不斷地練習用英文討論新的主題。除了職業 / 行業相關主題之外，也需要討論與歷史、政治、旅行、運動、科技、時事新聞等有關的主題。這樣做可以讓你覺得你的英文不再那麼受限。這使你的詞彙變得更豐富，可以針對更多不同的主題發表意見，並且能更自在地與說英文的同事隨意的交談。

In addition to discussing new topics, it's also great to learn more about the culture of the English speakers you communicate with. When I first moved to Korea in 2016, many of my communication difficulties / confusions were actually from a lack of cultural understanding. I didn't understand Korean culture or Korean communication style, and many of the Koreans I worked with were not very familiar with American culture.

除了討論新主題之外，你還可以進一步學習英文母語者的文化。2016年我第一次來韓國的時候，許多溝通上的困難與困惑，其實是源自缺乏文化理解。當時我並不了解韓國的文化與溝通方式，而與我共事的大部分韓國人也不熟悉美國文化。

The good news is that there are tons of useful books, articles, and resources all about the different communication styles of different cultures (several resources like this are on my website for free right now). When you know more about the culture and communication style of the English speakers you interact with, you'll not only be able to understand what they say, you'll also be able to understand why they speak and act the way that they do. This will help make communication much easier, clearer, and will build better relationships between you and your colleagues.

幸運的是，關於不同文化的不同溝通方式，有不勝枚舉的實用書籍、文章和資源可供參考（很多像這樣的資源在我的網站上免費提供）。當各位更深入地了解與你交流的英文母語者的文化與溝通方式，你不僅能理解他們所説的話，還能夠理解他們行為的理由。這種方式可以讓溝通變得更容易、更明確，也能改善各位與同事之間的關係。

5. Make your listening practice as close as possible to the real world.

5. 在盡可能接近現實的環境中進行聽力練習

The first four tips have all been about speaking and writing, but I wanted to leave you with one tip related to listening. Having good listening comprehension is important because if you can't understand what other people are saying to you, then you can't communicate effectively even if you have good speaking skills. A lot of Korean English learners struggle to communicate effectively in the real world because they can't understand 'real world' English. There's a major difference between 'classroom' English and 'real world' English. Classroom English is often slow, overly simplified, and made to be as clear as possible. In the real world, people speak much faster, use filler words such as 'umm' or 'like', and conversations often quickly switch topics. It's very important that your listening practice is as close as possible to what you'll experience in your real life.

前面所説的四種訣竅都是關於口説和寫作的,現在我想再提供一個關於聽力的訣竅。聽力理解能力很重要,因為若是你聽不懂別人在説什麼,即使你的口説能力再好,也無法有效地進行溝通。許多學習英文的韓國人因為無法理解「現實世界的」英文,因此難以在現實世界中進行有效溝通。「課堂」英文和「現實」英文之間有很大的差異。課堂英文是刻意放慢速度、過度簡化和盡可能清晰表達的英文。在現實世界裡,人們的説話速度快很多,會習慣性使用 umm 或 like 等表達方式,談話主題也會快速切換。因此,在盡可能接近現實生活的情境下練習聽力是非常重要的。

One recommendation I give to all my intermediate and advanced Korean clients is to listen to unscripted English content as often as possible. What I mean by 'unscripted' is that it's real English speakers having real conversations. TV and movies are great, but they're still actors reading lines. You want to experience all those filler words, quick topic changes, and interruptions that often happen in real English conversations. Some of the best English listening resources are live interviews, talk shows, debates, podcasts, and group discussions. If you work in a specific industry such as IT or finance, it's also great to find listening resources about your industry. There are podcasts and YouTube channels about basically everything now, so with a bit of searching you should be able to find some interesting, relevant resources that will really help your listening and communication abilities. By listening to natural, unscripted English, you'll be much more prepared to understand and respond effectively to the English you experience in the workplace.

我推薦處於中高級階段的韓國學生做的一件事，是盡可能多收聽沒有劇本的（unscripted）英文內容。「沒有劇本」意味著是真正英語圈人士實際進行的對話。雖然電視和電影也很好，但裡面出現的演員只是讀劇本上的台詞。各位需要的是體驗母語人士在實際對話中常用的填充詞、快速變換的話題和插話等情況。有一些很棒的英文聽力資料，就是直播採訪、脫口秀、辯論、播客和小組討論。如果你從事 IT、金融等特定行業，也可以尋找與該領域相關的聽力資料。基本上現在的播客和 YouTube 頻道上什麼主題都有，你只要簡單搜尋就能找到一些有趣的相關資源，這些對各位的聽力與溝通能力有很大的幫助。藉由收聽沒有劇本的自然英文，可以幫助各位做好有效理解和應對職場英文的準備。

FINAL WORDS

結語

You've made it to the end of this book, so you obviously care a lot about improving your English. I commend you for your hard work and great attitude. In addition to providing a ton of actionable English knowledge, I hope this book has left you feeling encouraged and inspired. It's been an honor sharing some of my knowledge with you, and I look forward to continuing to help you and countless other motivated Koreans become the most effective English communicators possible. I wish you the best of luck on your English journey and hope we get the chance to reconnect sometime in the future. I believe in you.

將本書讀到最後的各位，一定是對提升英文實力非常感興趣的人。我要為各位的努力以及良好的學習態度獻上掌聲。除了實用的英文知識之外，希望這本書也能帶給各位一些鼓勵與啟發。很榮幸能與各位分享我所擁有的知識，今後我將繼續幫助各位和無數積極學習的韓國人成為高效的英文溝通人士。祝各位在英文學習旅程上一切順利，希望有機會再與各位聯繫。我相信各位。

EZ TALK
職場英文精準表達：掌握140個常用字句，跨國外商溝通零失誤

作者	Grant Sundbye, LookLook English
譯者	韓蔚笙
主編	潘亭軒
責任編輯	謝有容
裝幀設計	Lady Gu Gu
版型設計	洪伊珊
內頁排版	洪伊珊
行銷企劃	張爾芸
發行人	洪祺祥
副總經理	洪偉傑
副總編輯	曹仲堯
法律顧問	建大法律事務所
財務顧問	高威會計事務所

出版	日月文化出版股份有限公司
製作	EZ叢書館
地址	臺北市信義路三段151號8樓
電話	(02) 2708-5509
傳真	(02) 2708-6157
網址	www.heliopolis.com.tw
郵撥帳號	19716071日月文化出版股份有限公司

總經銷	聯合發行股份有限公司
電話	(02) 2917-8022
傳真	(02) 2915-7212
印刷	中原造像股份有限公司
初版	2023年5月
定價	420元
ISBN	978-626-7238-63-9

職場英文精準表達：掌握140個常用字句,跨國外商溝通零失誤 /
Grant Sundbye, LookLook English著 ; 韓蔚笙譯. -- 初版. -- 臺
北市 : 日月文化出版股份有限公司, 2023.05
　　面 ；　公分. -- (EZ talk)
譯自 : 비즈니스 영어 실수 고침 사전
ISBN 978-626-7238-63-9(平裝)

1.CST: 英文 2.CST: 會話 3.CST: 商務傳播

805.188　　　　　　　　　　　　　　112003034

Original Title: 비즈니스 영어 실수 고침 사전
Business English Rebuilding Project by Grant Sundbye and LookLook English
Copyright © 2021 Grant Sundbye, LookLook English
All rights reserved.
Original Korean edition published by Gilbut Publishing Co., Ltd., Seoul, Korea
Traditional Chinese Translation Copyright © 2023 by Heliopolis Culture Group
This Traditional Chinese Language edition published by arranged with Gilbut Publishing Co., Ltd.
through Agency Liang